in Paris in 1947, Christian Jacq first visited
pt when he was seventeen, went on to study
ptology and archaeology at the Sorbonne, and
ow one of the world's leading Egyptologists.
s the author of the internationally bestselling
MSES and THE MYSTERIES OF OSIRIS
es, and several other novels on Ancient Egypt.
istian Jacq lives in Switzerland.

# Christian JACQ
## the brother of fire

### The Mozart Series

*Translated by Tamsin Black*

**SIMON &
SCHUSTER**

London · New York · Sydney · Toronto

A CBS COMPANY

First published in France by XO Editions under the title
*Le Frère du Feu*, 2006
First published in Great Britain by Simon & Schuster UK Ltd, 2011
A CBS Company

1 3 5 7 9 10 8 6 4 2

Simon & Schuster UK Ltd
1st Floor
222 Gray's Inn Road
London WC1X 8HB

www.simonandschuster.co.uk

Simon & Schuster Australia
Sydney

A CIP catalogue record for this book is available
from the British Library

HB ISBN: 978-0-74329-523-9
TPB ISBN: 978-0-74329-524-6

Typeset by Hewer Text UK Ltd, Edinburgh
Printed and bound in the UK by CPI Mackays, Chatham ME5 8TD

We have revealed the secret; there's no more to be said.

*The Marriage of Figaro*, Act I, Scene ii

He who dines on
Heavenly food
Has no need for the food of mortals!

*Don Giovanni*, Act II, Scene xv

# 1

*Vienna, 6 January 1785*

Who had denounced Thamos the Egyptian, Mozart's initiator? A neighbour? An intruder? The alchemist was used to moving his laboratory about and took nothing but a sack of gold.

Fortunately, the policemen were lackadaisical, coughing chestily, scraping their boots and barking out orders. This was conquered territory and they went about their business sure of success.

Every secret residence Thamos had occupied was fitted with a concealed exit. Here, he had removed a few bricks and stepped out into a passageway that led to a narrow street with warehouses either side. The moment the snow crunched beneath his feet, a massive blast shook the neighbourhood.

The alchemist's furnace had blown up in the officers' faces.

The Count of Thebes calmly regained his palace. The rich and good praised his generosity towards the poor and parentless. Discreet and influential, the wealthy Egyptian enjoyed an excellent reputation. No one suspected him of occult practices outlawed by the Church.

*Vienna, 7 January 1785*

Thamos the Egyptian inspected the area around the building where Mozart was to be initiated into the degree of Fellow Craft. When he was satisfied that no one was spying on True Union Lodge, he thought of his master, Abbot Hermes, who had revealed to him the secrets of the priests of Ancient Egypt before he died at the hands of fanatical Muslims.

Thamos would probably never see his homeland again. His mission now was to pass on the tradition of initiation to a handful of Freemasons, not least among whom was the Great Magician, Wolfgang Mozart, who, after long years of training, had been received as an Entered Apprentice, at the age of twenty-eight on 14 December 1784.

Since the recent inauguration of the Grand Lodge of Austria, Viennese Freemasonry was virtually an official institution and a loyal supporter of the liberal policies of Emperor Josef II.

Thamos did not share this rosy view. Although he had no evidence, he felt sure that a kind of demon was lurking in the shadows and following the moves and activities of the Freemasons, intent on destroying the Order.

But the current lull was useful for leading Mozart to the Great Mysteries and giving him all the keys to the magic masterpieces whose glory would outlive them all.

It had not been easy to arrange this Masonic meeting. Mozart ought to have been promoted from Entered Apprentice to Fellow Craft in Beneficence Lodge, where he was a member. But Ignaz von Born, Grand Secretary of the Grand Lodge of Austria and spiritual master of those Freemasons in search of genuine initiation, wanted to reveal the secrets of the Fellowship in the lodge where he presided, True Union Lodge.

With more than two hundred officially registered members, most of whom rarely attended, the lodge brought together poets, doctors, scientists, philosophers and artists.

Tonight, Ignaz von Born would treat Mozart to a ritual based on the elements of *The Book of Thoth*, passed down by Thamos.

When he entered the lodge, after a long meditation in the primeval cave known as the 'Chamber of Reflection', Wolfgang had taken off the hoodwink, just as he had done in the first ceremony, when the candidate ceased to be profane and became a Brother or Entered Apprentice.

The temple consisted of a rectangular room lit by candles and a chandelier that hung from a cord. At the eastern end, the source of light, sat the Venerable. The gaunt face, expansive brow and dark eyes of forty-three-year-old Ignaz von Born, an alchemist and mineralogist, gave him a spiritual authority that no one contested.

Of slight build, with fine blond hair, a long prominent nose and bright, slightly bulging eyes, Wolfgang might have passed unnoticed. But through his outward timidity there shone an energy and radiance, and everyone could tell that he was not like other people, seeming to move in a world apart, as though he did not fully belong on this earth.

His real place was in this temple.

'Here begins the teaching that opens hearts and minds, instructs the ignorant and reveals what is and what the Great Architect of the Universe created,' intoned the Venerable Priest, citing a passage from *The Book of Thoth*.

During the ritual, the Entered Apprentice discovered the Mysteries of the degree of Fellow Craft and the raw material of the Work and its secret architecture, as he travelled into the cubical stone, wherein lay the keys to knowledge.

The Venerable showed Mozart the way of the Holy Number of the degree, the number Five. When he had exercised the Apprentice's ternary thought, he opened his five senses and contemplated, at the heart of the stone, the compass that the Great Architect used to create the world with every passing moment.

From having been chaotic, the senses now became the site of intangible perceptions and formed a harmony centred on the heart, which apprehended the invisible. Wolfgang breathed the fragrance of the subtle being of all things, tasted their essence, heard the Word of the Orient, touched the living stone and experienced intuitive vision.

Then he saw the flashing Star of Wisdom.

At its centre were two apparently incompatible ways, yet he would have to follow both without division, reconciling the short road and the long: Fire and Water.

The Great Architect built the Universe, and the stars made up its vast body and were united by love. The primordial Water purified and passed on the Tradition of initiation, which generated infinite forms of birth; Fire united high and low, and creation occurred according to the laws inscribed in the Stone of Wisdom.

Thamos took Wolfgang on a new journey along a spiralling road. And so he crossed the borders between worlds.

'You who know the Art of Tracing,' said the Venerable, 'engrave the star on your heart.'

# 2

*Vienna, 7 January 1785*

In a second state, Wolfgang learnt the signs specific to his degree. One passage of the lesson consisted of questions and answers between the First Overseer, bearer of the level, and the new Fellow Craft, and concerned him directly.

'How were you initiated to the degree of Masonic Fellow Craft?'

'To the sound of divine music, perfect harmony and accord.'

'Why did the Fellow Crafts initiate you in this way?'

'To commemorate the rebuilding of the Temple, whose foundation stones were laid to the sound of trumpets and cymbals.'

The ceremony was over, and the Venerable initiated a servant to the degree of Entered Apprentice. Nervously, the initiate's employer, who now had to call him 'my

Brother', made a long speech on the duties of Servant Brothers.

Ignaz von Born's assistant, Count Franz-Joseph Thun, who deputized for him in his absence, warmly congratulated Wolfgang.

'The spirits are still on your side! Our good friend Mesmer would be proud of you. I knew the magic of the invisible world would bring you to this. Believe me, it will take you much further, and you will become our best member.'

Considered eccentric by the rationalists, Count Thun had studied esotericism for many years. He was joined in his studies by his wife, Maria Wilhelmina, one of Mozart's most fervent admirers, who had encouraged him when he first arrived in Vienna. Before his marriage, he had dined with her nearly every day.

'Thanks to the splendid teaching of this degree, my Brother Wolfgang, you will now have the compass always in your inner eye! Divine Proportion will guide your thoughts and you will write spontaneously, according to the Golden Number. Whatever you do, don't waste time calculating like the uninitiated. Now you know the meaning of creation, you should work tirelessly on the symbols: they will give you inspiration.'

Ignaz von Born invited Mozart and Thamos to continue the evening in his alchemy laboratory. Together, they put into practice the revelations of the ritual of the Fellow Craft, and as day broke, they marvelled at the blazing solar stone.

*Vienna, 9 January 1785*

Geytrand, a former Freemason with a grudge against the Society because his singular talents had not been recognized and rewarded with the presidency of a lodge, now set out to destroy the Order. Working as a spy for Josef Anton, Count of Pergen, he had woven a network of remarkably efficient informants. They included renegade Brothers betraying their lodge for revenge, for money, or simply for the fun of making mischief.

So, Geytrand knew nearly everything about what the various lodges were up to. His informants enabled his boss to act swiftly and, sooner or later, he would wipe out the initiates.

'I'm worried, my lord.'

Officially President of the Government of Lower Austria, a position he occupied with exemplary competence, Josef Anton had directed the secret service for many years and made it his life's work to get all the Freemasons on file and pave the way for the end of that dreadful secret society, whose real aim was to depose the king and bring down the Church in political and social revolution.

Unfortunately, Emperor Josef II relied on many powerful Freemasons who supported his reforms and his battles with the Archbishop of Vienna, a reactionary and bigoted Catholic. Josef Anton's initiatives were thwarted by this chance alliance. Still, the emperor was sensible enough to keep the lodges tightly in check and he had ordered the Count of Pergen to pursue his underground mission.

'Is something wrong, Geytrand?'

'The problem is Mozart.'

'That confounded musician again! Has he got into trouble?'

'No, but his trajectory intrigues me. He was initiated into Beneficence Lodge and should have become a Fellow Craft in it. But he appears to have enjoyed some kind of preferential treatment, because none other than Ignaz von Born raised him to that degree in the Lodge To True Union.'

'A Fellow Craft, already? That didn't take long!'

'Most Freemasons soon become Master Masons. The grandees among them are keen to attract them to the higher degrees where they can deck themselves out in collars and full regalia. That wasn't what von Born had in mind. I'd swear he's chosen Mozart as his disciple.'

'He may be a fashionable musician, but he's hardly a great celebrity. He doesn't have an important position.'

'That doesn't bother von Born,' answered Geytrand. 'The only things he's interested in are esoteric research, alchemy and deciphering the Masonic symbols. He's not interested in birth, wealth and titles.'

'You mean, he intends to train Mozart up and make him a leader of Freemasonry?'

'Too soon to say, but we shouldn't dismiss the possibility. One thing bothers me: my main informants weren't there at his initiation to the degree of Fellow Craft.'

'Does von Born suspect them?'

'A lot of Brothers were absent, either because they weren't particularly interested or because they weren't told soon enough.'

'Did the Venerable hold the ceremony just for his followers?'

'That's exactly what I think, my lord. The usual text for the degree of Fellow Craft sometimes raises a smile for its weaknesses and naivety. Von Born is an expert on Ancient Egypt and wouldn't settle for that.'

'Has he set up a secret branch within Viennese Freemasonry?'

'We've no way of knowing.'

'Your informants must find out!'

'They can only do that if they're involved in the enterprise.'

'They will just have to manage! If needs be, pay them more money. If they're not fit for the job, find some others. Do we still have nothing on von Born? No mistresses, no gambling debts or peccadilloes . . . it doesn't matter how small?'

'Nothing at all,' lamented Geytrand.

'Have him followed.'

'Extremely hazardous, my lord. Von Born is a reputable academic and Secretary of the Grand Lodge of Austria. The emperor likes and trusts him.'

'Find me a sleuth capable of total secrecy who won't put a foot wrong. I want to know everything about von Born and bring him into disrepute. Without him, Viennese Freemasonry will have lost its mastermind and stumble into blind alleys. Then we'll exploit its mistakes and divisions.'

# 3

*Vienna, 10 January 1785*

'We should like to know what you thought of the initiation,' Thamos told Wolfgang.

'How can one describe such incredible experiences?'

The Egyptian smiled. 'Aren't you a musician?'

Without more ado, Wolfgang set to work in his vast office and composed a quartet, his preferred form for personal confidences. It would be the fifth* in the series of six he intended to dedicate to Josef Haydn, who might become his Masonic Brother.

It was the first work he had composed since being received to the degree of Entered Apprentice. A changed man wielded the pen. In receiving the Light, Wolfgang had gained access to the First Mysteries and

---

*K464, in A major. K is an abbreviation for Köchel. Sir Ludwig von Köchel (1800–1877) was the first to attempt a complete catalogue of Mozart's works.

was now not just a musician but an initiate in a long tradition.

For years, he had not behaved as a good Catholic and had broken away from blind, doctrinal beliefs. The ritual had set him on a pathway to knowledge that transcended religious forms.

The lodge was not like a church and the Great Architect of the Universe did not demand devotion. It was up to every Brother to broaden his mind by helping to build the temple according to the laws of harmony. And it was up to Mozart to produce a musical language worthy of what he had received and what he wanted to pass on. This duty would now be central to his thought and work.

So, Wolfgang notated his impressions as an Entered Apprentice in a string quartet in A major, a key that was unusual for him but which allowed him to emphasize the number Three associated with the first degree because it had three sharps. The first two movements, an Allegro and a Minuet, evoked the lure of the temple and the desire to see its doors open at last.

Then an Andante with six variations recalled certain elements of the ritual: the need to limp; the requisite help of a Brother represented by the cello, and the order to bow on entering the lodge and cover one's eyes. The newcomer was then raised up and required to undertake three perilous journeys, symbolizing the ordeals of Air, Water and Fire whose creative spark he needed to understand.

At first confident and determined, the music became anxious, almost hesitant, as it progressed. Increasing obstacles sprang up, but the initiate had to put his trust in his guide and go on.

With the handle of his sword, a Brother had struck Wolfgang's lips three times, demanding silence about the work of the lodge.

When he had uttered the solemn oath, the Venerable asked his Brothers the decisive question: 'Do you allow this sufferer, the recipient, to see the Light that he has not known from the hour of his birth until this happy moment?'

Then the cloth fell, revealing a terrifying scene.

No bright light, no tranquil joy, no warm brotherhood, but threatening swords and the suggestion of a crime.

For, betrayal and death had been present since the start of the initiation and only the coherence of the community body could cast them aside.

The final Allegro of the quartet conveyed the communion of the initiates who had created a new Son of Light.

Thamos took Wolfgang to Ignaz von Born's alchemy laboratory. The young Fellow Craft described how he had poured out his impressions of initiation to the degree of Entered Apprentice in his latest quartet.

The Egyptian was satisfied. The Great Magician's mind was developing, and provided he could overcome future ordeals, he would draw on the power of the rituals to reach unprecedented heights.

'I intend to write another quartet to continue the theme of the ceremony,' Wolfgang told him, 'and I'll give Haydn a collection of six.'

'Your new Brother will like them,' von Born observed.

'My new Brother?'

'True Union Lodge has just accepted Josef Haydn's petition and informed the sister lodges. They have eight days to oppose it. When that formality has been dealt with, we can initiate him.'

Wolfgang was delighted about his favourite musician's decision. Life was showering him with happiness!

'In dedicating the magic of your art to initiation, you have reached a milestone,' declared the Venerable. 'You have huge responsibilities, my Brother, for you must evoke initiation without betraying it, unite your genius with the magic of the Tradition and rites, and master your language and craft in such a way that you remain loyal to the Great Work. You are no longer a composer like any other.'

'I still have so much to learn, Venerable Master!'

'Continue to assimilate the heritage of Johann Sebastian Bach and you will master a science that you will soon express with Wisdom, Strength and Harmony. But you need to know the last secret of our Order. That is why Thamos, the Middle Chamber and I have decided to raise you to the degree of Master Mason.'

Wolfgang was dumbfounded. Everything was happening so fast, too fast!

'Venerable Master, I don't feel ready, I . . .'

'No one ever is, my Brother.'

15

# 4

*Vienna, 13 January 1785*

'I have the feeling I am being watched and followed,'
Ignaz von Born told Thamos. 'For the past few days,
the same man has been prowling around my house. He
is clearly keen to cover his tracks, but I have spotted
him outside the lodge. It is too much of a coincidence.
Baron Van Swieten's enquiries have produced no results
but I'm convinced there really is a secret service whose
business is to observe the Freemasons.'

'Starting with the most important one: you. The
emperor may pretend he trusts you, but he is suspicious
of the Order. Worse still, with or without his agreement,
his agents may be trying to damage your reputation.'

'If I fall, others will replace me.'

'I do not share your optimism,' Thamos said bluntly.
'Flattery between Brothers is unworthy, and you know
I am not capable of it. Which is why I say with total

objectivity that you are currently irreplaceable. Who else would link official Freemasonry, which sets so much store by its decorum, with the esoteric tradition? From the most conceited Brothers to the genuine initiate, everyone respects your authority.'

'For how long, Thamos? There are only a few of us involved in this research.'

'That has been the case in every era.'

'Even in the time of the pyramids?'

'Like the other temples, they were built by a handful of initiates with the help of technicians, craftsmen, workmen and labourers. There are hundreds of good musicians but only one Mozart.'

'The Great Magician . . . Tonight, we will reveal to him our formative myth and let him experience the Great Mysteries. Whatever happens, we will have acted as links in a chain, as our duty demands.'

'There is still much to do,' Thamos commented. 'Will Mozart be able to express the powers he carries within him, and will the outside world give him the opportunities he needs?'

'He is predestined and therefore cannot stray from his path.'

'If he fails, he will be consumed on the spot.'

'Are you that worried?'

'Exceptional being, exceptional ordeals. Will he survive the blows of fate, hatred, abuse, disappointments and the mediocrity of most of his Brothers? He may be young, but we need to introduce him to the secrets of the

Master Mason, as the Ancients conceived of them. It is a huge risk, commensurate with Mozart.'

'He, and he alone, will perceive the totality of *The Book of Thoth*,' ventured von Born.

'One Brother per generation is enough to keep the spirit of initiation alive until an enlightened being of the same dimension takes up the torch. No doubt one day the human chain will be broken and wisdom will remain among the stars.'

'Are you going back to Egypt, Thamos?'

'According to the instructions of Abbot Hermes, my rightful place is with the Great Magician. Taking him to the temple was just a stage. Now, I must help him to develop himself so that he can develop his work.'

'Don't you find your exile difficult?'

'Nothing can make up for the palm grove where my monastery was hidden, the routine of daily rites, the sweetness of the evenings and my wanderings in the desert. I was lucky to live in total serenity. At the smallest problem, I needed only to ask Father Hermes. I had forgotten that we were surrounded by fanatics determined to impose their beliefs.'

'The Turks are now at the gates of Vienna,' von Born reminded him, 'and Islam has not given up trying to conquer Europe.'

'She will be its next prey,' Thamos predicted, 'and no one will notice the danger. On the contrary, most of the governors will praise the predator.'

'I should so have liked to visit Egypt,' mused von Born, 'but my health, my family and my position do not allow me to undertake so long a journey.'

'Does your wife disapprove of your Masonic allegiance?'

'She and my eldest daughter would rather not know about it. They would both like to see me scheming and progressing. That is why my alchemy laboratory is known to no one but you and Mozart. Here, I take succour and test my powers.'

'Do your official title and the emperor's protection not reassure your family?'

'My family, yes, but not me. The lodges are caught in a net from which they will not get out unscathed.'

'When I arrived in Europe,' Thamos confessed, 'I had hoped for more. Neither Strict Templar Observance nor the other Masonic trends have taken the road to initiation. They have strayed and become slaves to religion or politics.'

'Then, let us try to restore the degrees of Entered Apprentice, Fellow Craft and Master Mason by making them worthy of the Egyptian Tradition you have passed down to us! Does not the Light of the Orient shine again in our temples?'

'Of course, but it is still weak.'

'I am aware of the danger, Thamos, and I am not convinced that the emperor's benevolence will last. We must go to Prague, in secret, and strengthen our fallback position. For neither you nor I believe in the Templar

Order, the Rose-Cross of Berlin and all those fine talkers and ideologues who care little for rituals and symbols.'

'I shall explore every avenue to its end. I am sure the fate of the Great Magician will be played out in Vienna.'

'There are many musicians and men of influence in our lodges, but will they help him to assert himself? No matter what he does, Mozart has incited people's jealousy since he was born. He won't escape from it, even among the Freemasons.'

'This new form of purification will rid him of all naivety,' Thamos considered.

'A tough ordeal for so sensitive a being.'

'Almost impossible, it is true.'

Thamos left the laboratory first. There was no one to be seen.

Ignaz von Born walked a while behind him, then caught him up.

'Have you noticed your spy?' the Egyptian asked.

'No, he did not follow me here.'

The Venerable was not wrong. But Geytrand's servant had recruited an acolyte who now knew where the alchemy laboratory was.

# 5

*Vienna, 13 January 1785*

Given that the meeting was urgent and unscheduled, only a few Brothers from the Lodges To Beneficence and True Union attended the elevation to the degree of Master Mason of Mozart and two other Fellow Crafts.

When he had been ritually shown into the lodge, to the March of the Fellow Craft, the composer was 'tyled' at length. He was required to give the correct answers to questions about Masonic symbolism and prove that he had seen the Blazing Star rise within him. Then he presented a 'piece of architecture', his Fellow Craft masterpiece, for which he had produced a brief study on the Masonic drums and the rhythms of the lodge.

The Master Masons declared themselves satisfied, and a ritualist led Mozart to the Chamber of Reflection, the primordial cave. He was glad to return to it. What a boon to be able to mediate in total silence before facing a fearsome ordeal!

Everything had happened so fast, almost too fast. But the decision had not been his and there was no point regretting it. Now he must open himself to the Mysteries that his Brothers had agreed to pass on and shoulder the duties assigned to him.

Thamos came to fetch him and remove his profane clothes, but he did not blindfold him. When he entered the Middle Chamber, the Masters' Lodge, he bade Wolfgang observe a star in the west.

What a difference from the lodge Wolfgang was used to! This one was strange and rather sinister, its walls draped in black and almost completely dark. Only the Delta and Wisdom shone brightly.

In the middle of the temple was a coffin with an acacia branch on it. At its head was a Square, and at its foot a Compass.

The Master Masons were dressed in mourning.

'Why have we met?' asked the Venerable, Ignaz von Born.

'To recover what was lost,' answered Thamos, 'namely the true secrets of the Master.'

'Why were they hidden?'

'Because of the death of Hiram, the Master of Work.'

'A great calamity befell Freemasonry,' the Venerable told. 'It was caused by its own children. They were showered with its benefits but they betrayed it. Brother Wolfgang, are you one of those ungrateful men? Did you break your oath?'

Mozart was horrified at the very idea.

'I have kept it, Venerable Master!'

'We want proof, my Brother. The ritualist must make sure that your hands and apron are pure and untainted.'

Thamos complied.

'Venerable Master, this Fellow Craft has done nothing wrong.'

'Lead him to the Orient.'

The ritualist laid the point of a compass on Wolfgang's heart, associating him in that way with the circle drawn by the Great Architect of the Universe.

'It is our duty to practise the Royal Art,' von Born told him, 'and to pass down the essential secret by which initiates may glimpse the true joy, Wisdom. Thus, in the manner of ancient societies, our Order reveals its teaching using hieroglyphs. May the Great Goddess Isis help the initiate to come through so many perils and stand before her. May she make him speak with justice and may he contemplate her Mysteries. May she grant him true virtue by leading him along the narrow way.'

'Deep in the foundations of the temple,' recalled the First Overseer, 'is a square stone with three recesses, in each of which is a goblet. The first goblet contains the alchemical salt from which all other substances are formed; the second contains sulphur, the principle of change, and the third contains mercury, the immaterial element that is in every organism. This stone is the key to the Great Work and was brought back from the Orient.'

23

Wolfgang was taken to Hermes's palace, where he met the blacksmith and alchemist, Tubal-Cain, who showed him the emerald tablet that acted as the pivot and root of the world's axis. Sheltered from the jealousy of the vengeful god, Tubal-Cain and the initiated Master Masons fed from the fruits of the tree of Tradition, near a celestial pyramid hidden in the depths. There stood the sanctuary of Fire for preparing metals, which were purified by two columns in the temple symbolizing fire and water, the principles of male and female whose union produced alchemical gold.

'Tubal-Cain passed on his knowledge to Master Hiram,' declared the Venerable. 'And King Solomon, who was versed in Egyptian wisdom, commissioned him to build a temple to the glory of the Great Architect of the Universe. Every evening, the Master of Work took a lamp in his hand and surveyed the empty building site. You, my Brother, did you know about the plot that was being laid?'

'No, Venerable Master!'

Hiram checked that the tools had been cleaned and put away and his instructions obeyed. Finding that everything was in order, he went into the great hall, which was nearing completion.

Wolfgang saw the Master Mason standing calm and defenceless, examining the edifice he had designed. By the light of his lamp, he imagined future statues and the magnificence of the vast hall where his Brethren met.

A plot against the Master of Work ... Who could think up such dastardly schemes?

A human form loomed up out of the shadows. The first Fellow Craft dared to address Hiram with an imperious command.

'If you want to leave the temple alive, give me the Masters' password.'

# 6

*Vienna, 13 January 1785*

Outside, the Oriental night was sweet and still. The half-finished building dominated the skyline above Solomon's city and the craftsmen's encampment. It never occurred to anyone to worry about Master Hiram's safety, for no one questioned his authority and standing.

Who would have thought he was in danger, in the very heart of the sanctuary?

Yet Wolfgang saw the first Fellow Craft approach, armed with a chisel.

'You are asking the impossible,' answered Hiram firmly. 'Only the Middle Chamber can raise you to a Master Mason. Neither the Middle Chamber nor I yet consider you fit. Go on working according to the Rules and you will be called to other Mysteries.'

'I have received enough instruction,' the Fellow Craft declared. 'Tell me the Master Mason's word, immediately!'

'You are out of your mind. Get out! That is not how the secret is passed down. Away with you, or the king's justice will punish you.'

Would Hiram's firmness be enough to send the insolent Fellow Craft away, Wolfgang wondered.

But no, it provoked him! In a fit of rage, he struck the Master a heavy blow.

Wounded, Hiram realized that his attacker meant to kill him. So he tried to leave the temple by the second door.

A second Fellow Craft barred his way with a level.

'Give me the Master Mason's secret word.'

'Never!'

It was the second assassin's turn to strike.

Hiram was gravely hurt but he managed to stagger to the third door.

A third Fellow Craft was posted there.

'Don't be obstinate, speak up! Tell me the word, if you want to stay alive.'

'That is not how it is acquired,' retorted Hiram. 'You and your allies are forever unworthy to be Masons. I would rather die than reveal the secret that was entrusted to me.'

Mad with rage, the third Fellow Craft stabbed the point of a compass into the Master's heart.

As he fell to the mosaic paving, there was a clap of thunder and a violent storm was unleashed.

The Master's corpse covered three slabs.

'Let's get rid of him,' the third assassin advised. 'We must hide all trace of our crime.'

They wrapped the body in a white skin apron, then hurried through the downpour out of the city, where they dug a ditch and threw in the remains, afterwards covering it over with earth. Then, they ran off.

'Thus perished the Master, the man who was simply faithful to his Duty until death,' declared the Venerable. 'He alone possessed the secret of the Work. Don't lose courage, my Brethren. Let us go in search of it.'

The Venerable, Thamos and seven other initiates crossed the thresholds of death.

Wolfgang noticed that a sprig of acacia had just sprouted on the tomb.

'Knowledge lies in the shadow of the acacia,' recalled the Venerable.

The Ennead returned the great body of the assassinated Master to the light. Of course, there was not much flesh left on the bones and his remains were disintegrating, but the Middle Chamber banished death.

Thamos approached Wolfgang and told him the perfect points of Masonry that brought inertia to life.

Then he had the most extraordinary experience of his life, for his mind entered the celestial spheres and communed with the primordial Fire.

So Wolfgang travelled, and he became one of the Sons of the Widow Isis, who had found the scattered limbs of her husband Osiris's body, assassinated and dismembered by his own Brother, Seth. In reconstituting what had been dispersed, she had founded the principle of initiation and recreated the Master Mason, not as the body of a man but as a source of light warmed by the Widow's soul.

And so the secret of the Word and divine breath was continued, and the initiates' spiritual Mother put death to death.

The Widow became the temple and the Middle Chamber, where the Masters officiated and fulfilled their duty to build a new sun.

After the ritual, the Venerable asked Master Mason Brother Wolfgang a question: 'Where do you come from?'

'From the Orient,' he replied, 'from the place where the Light is born of itself. There, I went to seek what was lost and must be found.'

## 7

*Vienna, 14 January 1785*

At dead of night, Wolfgang took part in his first meeting in the degree of Master Mason, presided over by Venerable Ignaz von Born. Every Brother wishing to study the symbolism of the wonderful ritual and continue to progress, presented the results of his research and his thoughts on a given topic. Afterwards, the Venerable asked one of them to write up a report of the contributions, extracts of which would be published in the *Freemasons' Journal*.

The themes of the Widow, the builders' mother, and the hermetic tradition were the first to be broached. The logical conclusion of scientific thought saw matter as the only element in the universe, when not the universe itself. Soon, someone would come up with its date of birth, forgetting that creation was a continually occurring process and could not be reduced to a moment in time. According to the Ancients, Thamos recalled, the universe was both movement and repose, an exhalation and an aspiration, a contraction and a dilation. Its two 'columns' came from a third idea: the breath of Fire, which engendered mind and matter. Through the symbolism of Christ, His embodiment, entombment and resurrection, alchemical processes would turn base metal into pure gold.

'It is the task of the Master Mason, and a major aspect in the teaching of initiation, to bring the mystery to light without betraying it,' the Venerable told them.

The meeting opened up a hundred new horizons for Wolfgang. When it was over, the Egyptian walked back to his apartment with him.

'Does knowledge lead to serenity?'

'Provided you act without tension,' answered Thamos, 'and are neither passive nor impassioned. Degrees and symbols will show you how the creative forces function in constant mutation. Believing that a person can achieve perfection is a dangerous utopia, for a leopard cannot change its spots. We should practise the Royal Art by serving the Work and not ourselves. And you, my Brother Master, have a duty to develop one of the new expressions of this Art.'

The same evening, Wolfgang attended an initiation ceremony. He felt so fired by the energy of his new degree that he had not the slightest desire to sleep. So, he put the finishing touches to the sixth and last quartet* in the series intended for Josef Haydn.

* K465, in C major.

In a bold move, he opened the piece with a tortured Adagio full of dissonance that expressed the tragedy and pain of the myth he had witnessed of the death of Master Hiram.

The searing intensity of the introduction was followed by an Allegro that suggested release from grief and anguish. No, the Master was not dead! Yes, initiation opened the way to go and look for him.

But why had Hiram been assassinated? asked the dark colours of a sombre Adagio.

Why had the human race proved unable to avoid disaster?

Vigilance and Perseverance were advocated to the aspirant Freemason when he was led down to the primordial cave. Wolfgang accepted reality with lucidity and did not need illusions. He had plumbed the depths of despair, but in the abyss he had nevertheless perceived the presence of the hidden stone and regained hope.

The Minuet, a rugged allegretto, reflected the initiate's struggle to clamber out of the void to which he felt condemned because of the death of the Master of Work. But the magic of the rites and the Widow's intervention brought him back to life, and so he went on with the work and continued building the temple.

The long final Allegro evoked the power and vitality of the new Master Mason, whose determination would overcome all obstacles. Nothing and no one would prevent him pursuing Hiram's work and proving himself worthy of the immense Duty the lodge had assigned to him. Pure joy drove him on, joy that could move mountains.

Wolfgang just had time to kiss his wife and son, before dashing out to True Union Lodge, where Ignaz von Born was about to initiate Georg Spanger, conductor of the choirs at St Michael's Church, and Baron Anton Tinti, a minister at the court of Salzburg who lived in Vienna and was an excellent violinist.

The baron and Wolfgang found common ground, and the composer invited him back to his flat to play chamber music.

'What luck for our lodges that you are a Freemason,' declared Tinti. 'Will you honour us with some pieces for our rituals?'

'I described the experience of initiation in my quartet,' Wolfgang told him, 'and I am at the disposal of the Venerable Master.'

*Vienna, 15 January 1785*

'Our friend Angelo Soliman attended a fine ceremony yesterday,' Geytrand told Josef Anton. 'True Union Lodge is still expanding and gathering more and more delegates from high society.'

'Von Born is tirelessly hoeing his row,' the head of the secret service grumbled. 'Still nothing against him?'

'We are getting there, my lord, but I don't want to rejoice too soon.'

'Any interesting leads?'

'Possibly . . . We know one thing for sure: Wolfgang Mozart has been promoted to Master Mason.'

'A very swift ascent,' remarked Josef Anton.

'Generally speaking, it is the privilege of dignitaries or celebrities who live a long way from the lodge and rarely attend. Mozart is extremely diligent.'

'Why is Von Born showing him special treatment?'

'I expect he appreciates the sincerity of his commitment.'

'A privileged disciple, I suppose you might say.'

'I shouldn't worry too much, my lord. It won't be a fashionable musician that turns our society upside down.'

'In that case, why is von Born so interested in him?'

Geytrand was stumped. If Mozart was being given starring roles, he would soon find out. Since raising Angelo Soliman's wages, his informant had stepped up the flow of details about the lodges' activities.

# 8

*Vienna, 15 January 1785*

Intrigued by Wolfgang's replies to his questions about Freemasonry, Leopold Mozart wrote to say that he would soon be coming to Vienna so that they could talk more about it face to face.

To Nannerl, his daughter, he gave a different version: he had agreed to leave Salzburg because the journey was not at his expense and he could see for himself his son's opulent lifestyle. In other words, he was going to check whether the rumours of fame and fortune, which he only half believed, were true. He said nothing about the Masons, knowing that the staunchly religious Nannerl, like the deceased Empress Maria-Theresa, thoroughly detested them.

That evening, Wolfgang was invited to dinner by the Countess Thun and was surprised to find himself alone with her.

'Am I early?'

'There are no other guests, my Brother Master.'

'So . . . so you know?'

'The moment we met, I knew you would be initiated. Hadn't you been an apronless Freemason for ages? Several Brothers looked out for you as you made your way to the temple, and you replied to each of their calls.'

'Your help has been invaluable, my lady. I should never have got anywhere in Vienna without it.'

'Isn't it a Sister's duty to help her Brother?'

'You mean . . .'

'I was initiated in a decidedly lesser way into a "Lodge of Adoption". The vast majority of Freemasons believe women incapable of spirituality. To stop them making a fuss, they are allowed a watered-down initiation with few rituals and plenty of frills. They have to make do with aping men and losing their femininity without any hope of knowing the Great Mysteries. On 10 November 1782, Ignaz von Born decided the situation was intolerable. True Union Lodge invited me, and a number of other Sisters, including Madame Sonnenfels, to a banquet where we took part in a genuine female initiation. Needless to say, there was never any official report of the meeting, and the Lodge Book of Architecture makes no mention of it. All over Europe, the Sisters are considered as pretty little dilettantes whose pretensions raise a smile.'

'Why such disdain?' asked Wolfgang, in astonishment.

'Because the chain of women's spirituality was broken. One of the last known expressions of it is the series of tapestries depicting the initiation of the Lady of the Unicorn. For the past few years, I and a group of Sisters have been working with Ignaz von Born to recover the bases of the tradition: the Mysteries of Isis and the seven liberal arts as emanations of Wisdom.'

'They are directly relevant to the Fellow Craft Brothers,' recalled Wolfgang.

'We are not separate from them, but our path to the Royal Art must be specific and different, the way a king and queen take their own route appropriate to their competences but meet at the top of the mountain. If women bow to male imperatives, they are doomed to failure. Becoming true initiates in the Mysteries of Isis involves a huge amount of research.'

Impressed and excited, Wolfgang had only one thought: to join the adventure.

'How can I help you?'

'First, by belonging to the tiny number of Brethren who see the need to revive female initiation, and secondly, by evoking women's role in initiation in your operas.'

Wolfgang's head was already teeming with ideas.

'Can we collaborate, my lady?'

'With pleasure, my Brother! I shall no longer approve the masquerades where more-or-less noble ladies play at being Entered Apprentices, Fellow Crafts and Mistress Masons for the amusement of more-or-less honest gentlemen. We shall recreate a ritual based on the Ancient Mysteries. However, there is one essential condition: the work must be done in secret, outside official Freemasonry.'

Mozart's publisher, Artaria, purchased his recent Six Quartets for the handsome sum of 450 florins. On the evening of that splendid day, Wolfgang invited Josef Haydn to play through the first three with him.[*]

'I have made up my mind, Mozart. You have persuaded me to apply to become a Freemason.'

'They will feel honoured to receive a man of your talents!'

'It is lucky for you that I know you are not a common flatterer! The Order might reject my petition.'

'You can be sure that will not happen!'

'Life sometimes holds unpleasant surprises in store, my friend. I hope I am not disappointed, for what you say about the overwhelming effect of this initiation makes me want to experience it myself. And I love the idea of becoming your Brother!'

The evening overflowed with merriment, the highlight being Mozart's music and the trills and arpeggios of his faithful starling, Star.

[*] K 387, 421 and 428.

# The Brother of Fire

The weather was not too severe, and the Count of Thebes's comfortable carriage bowled along at a cracking pace. An excellent grog was proof against the cold.

'What a funny world a lodge is!' mused Wolfgang. 'Rationalists, humanists, believers, anti-clerics, occultists . . . and that's not all! How do they manage to agree?'

'It all depends on the Venerable and the orientation of the lodge,' Thamos answered. 'If it lacks coherence, it falls apart.'

'How can it be maintained?'

'By researching initiation, and nothing else. Too often, Freemasons succumb to the lure of politics, and belief and vanity in all their forms. Instead of delving deeper and deeper into the meaning of the three basic degrees, Entered Apprentice, Fellow Craft and Master Mason, they get mired in systems of higher degrees, and initiation descends into folklore. The further up the artificial hierarchies they go, the more they fall prey to an incurable obsession with lavish collars and costly regalia. Strict Templar Observance, the Golden Rose-Cross, the charitable Knights of the Holy City and all the other systems I have studied closely are going nowhere. Only Ignaz von Born and Countess Thun open the true ways. Initiation is a constant process of construction, and you are called to become one of the Masters of Work. But no route should be neglected. So, my Brother, I am going to introduce you to the Grand Cophta, Cagliostro.'

# 9

*Strasbourg, 21 January 1785*

It was hardly the dazzling temple on the Faubourg des Brotteaux in Lyons with its glittering gilt hall and three apartments, one for each Masonic degree, but Guiseppe Balsamo, Count of Cagliostro, was proud of the humble Alsatian premises where he hoped to establish his Rite of High Egyptian Masonry.

'Count of Thebes! Thank you for accepting my invitation.'

'Will you keep your promise?'

'Of course. I shall reveal to you the basics of the initiation. But you are not alone . . .'

'I can vouch for this young Master Mason.'

'Come and attend a meeting you will never forget.'

Cagliostro kept the depraved away and only admitted Freemasons on condition they keep the secret.

As he conducted the ritual, he purified the brute stone

and turned it into a cubical stone considered the mother and father of all metals. When it died, it gave birth to the triangular stone, which opened the way to the degree of Master Mason.

On the lodge tablet, a phoenix was consumed on the pyre before returning to life.

Cagliostro drew a circle. He led a pure young woman called 'Dove' into the centre and breathed on her face three times. Then he laid his hand on her head and bade her wash away his crimes and sins.

An aspirant Master Mason lay face down on the floor inside the circle. Calgiostro raised him up and breathed three times on his face, then handed him a rose.

'Contemplate the phoenix, my Brother: he is the initiate that is reborn and rejuvenated at will. If you absorb three seeds of the primordial matter I hold, you will enjoy the same powers.'

The next day, Thamos and Wolfgang were invited to attend a meeting at a Lodge of Adoption, where the Sisters regarded the Queen of Sheba as their model. Embodying twelve prophetesses, the Sibyls and seven angels, the initiates learnt to weave ritual garments.

'The spiritual part in us is male,' Cagliostro explained, 'not female. To be more precise, it has no sex. A day will come, my Sisters, when you will be distinguished not by your femininity but by your minds.'

With a crown of roses on her head, the Lodge Mistress drank the draught of immortality, while Cagliostro revealed to her a process of strong, complex physical regeneration that lasted forty days and had to be repeated every fifty years.

When the meeting was over, Cagliostro turned triumphantly to Thamos.

'Do you wish to live a long period of isolation and become immortal?'

'Too difficult.'

'Is not such a benefit worth the sacrifice?'

'Some of your initiatives are certainly interesting,' remarked the Egyptian, 'but you are straying into the perilous realm of powers.'

Cagliostro drew himself up. 'I am the Grand Cophta and I know what I am doing!'

'Are you quite sure?'

'I shall soon prove it to you, because France will recognize me as its spiritual guide.'

'Good luck, my Brother.'

Thamos and Wolfgang set out for Vienna.

'I felt very uncomfortable,' the musician admitted. 'Weren't we rather a long way from true initiation?'

'A very long way, yes. Anyone looking for power, whether psychic, magic or any other kind, will get lost in the dark. I wanted you to see for yourself so you never give in to that temptation. Cagliostro is not without scholarship and he is not quite a charlatan. But he is heading for disaster with his pursuit of fame and power.'

# The Brother of Fire

Josef Haydn's petition was accepted and True Union Lodge was preparing to initiate him to the degree of Entered Apprentice.

It was the day after Wolfgang's twenty-ninth birthday and he was looking forward to the moment when the great composer would become his Brother.

That morning, Leopold had left Salzburg for Munich. There, he stayed with his friends the Marchands whose son, Heinrich, was his favourite pupil and was to accompany him to Vienna.

Haydn tonight; before long, his own father: by becoming Freemasons and entering the world of symbols, where day by day, Wolfgang was growing and gaining in confidence, they would share the same ideal.

Of the fifty-six Brothers present, some were members of Truc Union Lodge while others were visitors, but all were delighted to welcome a musician whose fame had spread far beyond Prince Esterhazy's estate where Haydn had so far been pursuing a peaceful career. Perhaps, by offering him new horizons, Freemasonry would spur him to greater things.

At about seven o'clock, the Master of Ceremonies began to fret.

'Everything is ready, but we are missing the main protagonist! Does anyone have any news of Josef Haydn?'

No one answered.

'Has he changed his mind without telling us?' the Tyler wondered.

'Of course not!' exclaimed Wolfgang, indignantly. 'Haydn is a man of his word. Something must have held him up.'

The minutes passed.

Wolfgang talked music with the two Tinti brothers, the younger of whom, Anton, was then a very young Entered Apprentice.

At eight o'clock, most of the Brethren were showing signs of impatience.

'We shall open the meeting and initiate Franz von Hallberg, Haydn's twin,' Venerable Ignaz von Born decided. 'If Haydn confirms his intention to enter Freemasonry and explains his absence, we will suggest another date.'

Wolfgang was worried. Had Haydn come under pressure from official or unorthodox quarters? Were the powers that be proscribing his membership and, by implication, his approval of a society considered too secret?

Ignaz von Born, too, was puzzled. Was it just a chance occurrence that could soon be explained away or was it a first significant assault on the Masonic Order?

The ceremony took place in a muted atmosphere. No speech was made at the closing banquet, and the Brothers dispersed with a sense of foreboding.

# 10

*Vienna, 31 January 1785*

Josef Anton, Count of Pergen and President of the Government of Lower Austria, read Josef II's letter with relish:

> *I understand that the famous play* The Marriage of Figaro *is to be put on at the Kärntnertor Theatre in a German translation. As this work contains all sorts of reprehensible things, I am obliged to ask the censor either to reject it entirely or to amend it in such a way that he can vouch for the production and the impression it may produce.*

How fortunate that the emperor had his feet on the ground and was taking the trouble to stop the spread of subversive ideas! On 27 April 1784, Beaumarchais's work had been a sell-out at the Comédie-Française, but most of the nobility had ground their teeth at what they saw as slander. King Louis XVI had failed to stifle the deplorable intellectual ferment and Anton feared the worst.

*The Marriage of Figaro* was quick to appear in German and the translation had now reached Austria. By intervening directly, Josef II had erected a crucial barrier.

*Vienna, 1 February 1785*

Emmanuel Schikaneder trusted his instincts as a man of the theatre and felt that this *Marriage of Figaro* would be a huge success. Of course, some of the lines might raise indignant eyebrows, but you could hardly resist the zeitgeist. The whole thing was a lively romp and a gift for the players, who would make an excellent job of it and have the Viennese audience in raptures.

The Kärntnertor Theatre would have a full house every night and Schikaneder's troop could look forward to financial health again.

'Boss, you're wanted,' his stage manager alerted him.

'Not now. I'm setting the stage.'

'Your visitor says it's important and urgent.'

'Does he look serious?'

'Top brass, I'd say, from his bearing and his wig and clothes.'

Might be a philanthropist keen to invest . . . Emmanuel Schikaneder could not let the opportunity pass.

The stern face of the imposing personage was anything but reassuring.

'Baron Van Swieten, under imperial orders to examine all publications.'

'Most honoured. How may I help?'

'It appears you were intending to put on a subversive play by a French author.'

'Strong language, Baron! *The Marriage of Figaro* is an exquisite comedy and a drama of pure entertainment.'

'The emperor and I have read the play thoroughly. His Majesty does not wish this satire to be put on in Vienna.'

'A simple misunderstanding!' countered Schikaneder. 'I am sure we will find a solution. My players are quite ready and the undoubted success—'

'Beaumarchais's play is prohibited,' decreed Baron Van Swieten. 'You seem to be a likeable man, so I shall not press charges against you.'

Schikaneder realized it would be a mistake to insist: defying the emperor and his head of censorship could land him in prison.

As for Van Swieten, he had no intention of punishing a Freemason further. His personal intervention would prevent a Brother making his case worse.

*Esterháza, 2 February 1785*

Josef Haydn wept tears of rage! Heavy snowfalls and impassable roads meant that he had only just received the invitation to True Union Lodge for . . . 28 January!

Reluctant to brave the elements, the hussars who brought the post had kept to their barracks while they waited for weather conditions to improve.

How could he right such a wrong? As the missed appointment was not his fault, Haydn wrote to Brother Anton Apponyi to say that he hoped his future lodge would not hold it against him.

By good fortune, another letter brought the offer of a later date: 11 February. This time, come hell or high water, he would present himself at the temple door! 'If only it were that Friday today,' he added. 'Oh, to savour the inestimable joy of being among such a respectable circle of men!'

*Vienna, 10 February 1785*

After a work session at the home of Countess Thun, attended by Ignaz von Born and Thamos, Wolfgang finished the first piano concerto[*] he had composed since being initiated.

Tragic and uncompromising, the opening movement reflected the confrontation between the soloist,

[*] No. 20 in D minor, K466.

or individual, and the orchestra, or Brotherhood. The road to the temple had been fraught, but the initiate had harnessed his terror, controlled his instincts and held in check the waves that tried to repel him. At times, he transcended his limits and, above all, he had not given up, even while he continued to wonder: would the door to the Mysteries open?

The slow movement offered several ways to conquer despair: serene detachment; a smile in the face of adversity; the spiritual calm of one who knew his goal and did not waver. Of course, there was no knowing when and where life's violence would strike. No one could hide from its torment and agony. But that was not enough to break one's flight to Enlightenment.

The third movement conveyed the incredible sense of vitality that came from the joy of gaining knowledge at last. The dialogue between soloist and orchestra became playful, as though the pianist had managed to charm the fearsome guardians of the temple. Yes, the door was opening; yes, it was possible to enter a sacred universe where anxiety gave way to serenity.

Thamos recognized the greatness of this masterpiece; it was so much more profound than Wolfgang's previous concerti. Anyone who wanted to understand the difficulties of initiation, the efforts it demanded and the tremendous energy it afforded should listen to this score with its marriage of grace and power.

But Mozart looked downcast.

'What ails you?' the Egyptian asked.

'Josef Haydn's absence.'

'His case has been explained: it was just a problem with the post. Haydn will be initiated on 11 February.'

'That's the night I am giving my first subscription concert at the Mehlgrube on the Neuer Markt. They've already sold over a hundred and fifty seats and I can't pull out. But what a disappointment not to be at Josef Haydn's initiation! Too bad, I'll cancel the concert.'

'No, Wolfgang. That would be a disaster.'

'What is my career next to such an important ceremony?'

'You can see your new Brother at other meetings, later on.'

'But to miss his entry into the Order . . . I can't do it!'

'You are in no way responsible for this mishap.'

'I don't care! I want to be there when Haydn receives the Light.'

Thamos's voice grew firm. 'You may not realize it, but your work is now inextricably bound up with initiation. These days, a man has to have a career. The more famous you are, the further your message and the message of Freemasonry will spread. Not attending Haydn's reception is an ordeal, I grant you. But you should be prepared for others that are crueller still. At this concert, you will play your new concerto for the first time and you will be offering an unprecedented vision of the Way. That's the main thing. Accomplish your duty, my Brother Master, no matter what the cost.'

# 11

*Vienna, 11 February 1785*

Leopold and Wolfgang fell into each other's arms.

'Father, I'm so happy to see you!'

'I am not sorry to embrace you, my son.'

'Did you have a good journey?'

'Dreadful! Ice, cold, wind, roads so slippery they were all but impassable . . . I nearly turned back.'

'We have so much to talk about!'

'Could you put up my brave companion, young Heinrich Marchand, my best violin pupil?'

'Of course, my apartment is huge.'

Leopold could hardly contain his astonishment when he saw the place.

'You've done well! This must cost a small fortune.'

'My earnings allow it.'

Then Constanze appeared, quietly elegant with just a hint of make-up.

'What a pleasure to welcome you to our home, Father! I've put you in our prettiest room, and you'll have everything you need. Wolfgang and I want your stay to be as pleasant as possible. If you need anything, let us know and I'll see to it immediately.'

In spite of his prejudices, and especially Nannerl's, Leopold was touched by his daughter-in-law's warm welcome. He had to admit that she knew how to keep an excellent house and seemed the ideal companion.

'I've applied to enter the Musicians' Society in Vienna,' Wolfgang told his father. 'Then you'll be really proud of me. And I hope you'll like tonight's concert.'

It was not a futile honour Wolfgang was seeking in applying for recognition by the Society, but a kind of security for his family, for the Musicians' Society granted a pension to the widows and children of its deceased members. The composer was often ill and knew he was mortal, so he preferred to take precautions. The only trouble was that he was being asked for a certificate of baptism, which he did not possess and which he would have to send at a future date.

Behind its stone arcades, the Mehlgrube concert hall was a fine two-storey building that had once been an inn, where Mozart's admirers gathered to hear his music. His performance that evening of his Piano Concerto in D minor was intimate and dramatic.

Rapturous applause followed, and afterwards, Leopold looked into his son's eyes and said one word: 'Remarkable.'

Wolfgang could hardly believe his ears. A compliment, a real compliment from his father!

'The work is about my initiation,' he confessed.

'It sounds neither reassuring nor easy, but then, neither is life.'

'Have you decided to join me in the lodge?'

Leopold hesitated. 'I wanted to see your apartment, find out how you were living and make sure you are earning enough money and are happily married. And then . . . I wanted to have a proper talk about this Freemasonry you write so highly of.'

'I'm sorry, but we'll have to talk about it tomorrow. The fact is, I have to go to True Union Lodge to congratulate Josef Haydn: he was initiated this evening.'

In the absence of Ignaz von Born, Ludwig von Anselm, a founder member of the lodge, brought Enlightenment to Josef Haydn and his twin. Fifty-three Brothers attended the ceremony. Afterwards, the Second Overseer gave a speech in which he drew parallels between the harmony sought by the musician and the name of the lodge, *Eintract* or 'unity, concord'.

With the fees and charges waived on account of his fame, Haydn was showered with brotherly congratulations, but it was Mozart's that touched him the most.

'Will you forgive me for not attending the ritual?'

'You have fulfilled your primary duty, my friend . . . my Brother!'

'May I invite you to make music at my place tomorrow evening?'

'What a pleasure to play together, now that we are forever associated by the Light you have helped me discover!'

*Vienna, 12 February 1785*

Josef Haydn, Bartholomäus Tinti, his brother Anton and Wolfgang were playing through Mozart's three latest quartets. Leopold, Constanze, little Karl Thomas and the starling, Star, listened as the four Freemasons magnified these solemn, sometimes austere pieces in honour of Haydn's initiation.

It was a moment of plenitude and timelessness; the Entered Apprentice seemed to have been infused with new life, and his emotion was evident.

Profane Leopold would never have believed that his son was capable of taking the art of the quartet to such heights or displaying such talent as a pianist. The fêted child virtuoso of the European courts and the gallant stylist of Salzburg had vanished and in their place was a composer of astonishing originality. That day, Leopold attended the birth of the genius he had so long suspected. Seeing him burgeon in this way left him speechless.

Josef Haydn put down his bow.

'I declare to you before God,' he told Leopold, 'your son is the greatest composer I know.'

*Vienna, 13 February 1785*

At the Burgtheater, Wolfgang played his Piano Concerto in B flat* to a packed audience who sat enthralled by the pianist's assurance.

The theatre manager, however, was hardly listening, biting his nails in anticipation of the outbursts of a very special member of the audience, for the Emperor Josef II was there in person. Overriding the manager's insistence, the emperor had refused a free place. Drawing out his purse, he had paid the full price without asking for a reduction.

But what if he did not like the show? The emperor would leave the hall and blame staff at the Burgtheater for inviting untalented artists. Heads would roll.

The impresario, manager and other agents watched Josef II keenly. Mozart, meanwhile, went on scattering notes with his customary ease, quite unperturbed.

The emperor did not move until the end of the concert.

As though in a dream, Leopold murmured proudly, 'Stupendous,' and could not hold back a few tears. Thick-skinned though he was, he could not listen unmoved to such beautiful music.

Suddenly, Josef II removed his cocked hat, raised it in salute to the composer, and cried out 'Bravo, Mozart!'

What a splendid accolade for his son's accomplishment, thought Leopold! All Vienna would follow the emperor and crown the young creator as one of its heroes.

*K456.

# 12

*Vienna, 14 February 1785*

'Josef Haydn has been initiated into True Union Lodge,' Geytrand told Josef Anton.

'Another victory for the Freemasons!'

'According to my informants, it is due to Mozart's influence.'

'Him again! A gift for recruitment, it would seem.'

'At his last concert at the Burgtheater, the emperor publicly raised his hat to him.'

Josef Anton slumped in his chair.

'Untouchable, like von Born . . . Things have come to a pretty pass, my fine Geytrand.'

'We must sit it out, my lord, and be patient. I can't believe the emperor will protect the Freemasons for ever. His decisions in the past have sometimes proved unpredictable: today's protégés may be tomorrow's pariahs.'

'Any news of von Born?'

'I am proceeding cautiously, but I am getting there. Eventually, I shall know every hour of how he spends his days.'

'Still no hidden vice?'

'Alas, no, my lord. Though there is one odd fact: he seems to have a little house on the outskirts of town.'

'Does he go there often?'

'I don't know.'

'If these are secret premises, I want to know what they are for.'

'I shall find out.'

'Get on to this trail, Geytrand. We may be in for a nice surprise.'


*Vienna, 15 February 1785*


'I am absolutely fine,' declared Leopold, who had a hacking cough.

'You can see quite well that you are not,' retorted Constanze. 'You caught a chill on your journey and you need to look after yourself. That's why I have called the doctor. I haven't told Wolfgang: he is composing and rehearsing tonight's academy* performance by Miss Distler, at the Burgtheater.'

'A doctor? Out of the question! I know as much as those quacks!'

*Name given to concerts.

'I am sure he will cure you very quickly. Let him see you, Father, please.'

Constanze's melting smile persuaded Leopold.

When the doctor's visit was over, he felt better already and announced perfunctorily, 'He told me to do exactly what I would have done if I'd been left to my own devices.'

*Vienna, 17 February 1785*

After another concert at the house of the Ployers the previous evening, Wolfgang spoke to Constanze. They decided to try a risky experiment. Now that Leopold was better, his son approached him with a delicate question.

'Would you agree to dine with my wife's mother?'

'Cecilia Weber . . . I'm not saying anything!'

'The poor woman doesn't enjoy good health and she has to lead a very quiet life. She has lost her bite and would be very pleased to welcome you.'

'Aren't you labouring under delusions?'

'You'll see: she'll put herself out for us and treat us to an excellent meal.'

'Very well, Wolfgang, but I won't stand for any nonsense.'

Leopold need not have worried. Frau Weber and her daughter Sophie greeted the Mozart family warmly, and they drank to the reconciliation over a fine plump pheasant, the *pièce de résistance* of a splendid feast.

Everyone laughed and drank and delighted over Wolfgang's successes, predicting a brilliant future for him. No one spoke out of turn and Leopold kissed Constanze's mother on both cheeks.

'An incomparable table,' he told Wolfgang, as they left the Weber household.

*Vienna, 18 Feburary 1785*

On the previous evening, Constanze had served Leopold his favourite dish: whole endives boiled in meat broth. To ease digestion with a view to the next banquet, father and son drank mead made of honey and fermented water. This miraculous draught was produced by the best gingerbread baker in the city.

Accordingly, Leopold and Wolfgang turned up in fine fettle to a magnificent lunch given by Brother Gottlieb Stephanie the Younger, a member of Three Eagles Lodge. An assortment of hors-d'oeuvres was followed by oysters, pheasant in sauerkraut, and pastries for dessert, all washed down with a good Champagne.

'They're not much bothered about Lent in Vienna,' said Leopold to himself, not without pleasure. 'And if this is how the Masons go on, they can't be that bad.'

The same evening, Wolfgang gave his second subscription concert at the Mehlgrube.

'Splendid, again,' commented Leopold, who felt so many wonders would never cease.

Aside from lunches, dinners and concerts, his son was keen to introduce him to all the members of the aristocracy who had helped and encouraged him since his move to Vienna, like Count and Countess Thun, and Professor Josef von Sonnenfels.

'Do they belong to the Masons?' Leopold asked.

'Since you are my father and under the seal of secrecy, I can tell you that they are.'

'This secret society is influential, then.'

'Yes and no. By bringing such different personalities together, it allows them to understand each other better and propagates an ideal of tolerance and fraternity.'

'Some Freemasons are only interested in using their contacts to line their pockets, isn't that so?'

'Of course, and it's one of the perversions of the Order. But there are a lot of Brothers who don't approve and genuinely want to find spiritual enlightenment.'

'Are you still just as interested in Masonic meetings?'

'Increasingly so. For all people's faults, my own included, the meetings provide opportunities to collaborate on a work that transcends both the Brothers and the lodges, a work independent of human vagaries, the passage of time or the limitations of our meagre intelligence. As initiates, we are part of a vast chain that starts and ends with the Light. Our physical birth is not enough to make us conscious. It is the second birth of initiation that opens up to us a myriad of paths we never even knew were there.'

'This Freemasonry, isn't it a sort of religion?'

'It doesn't require belief, it requires knowledge.'

'A world where God would live without Colloredo . . .
That would be a fine thing! And now I am going to bed,
because night brings advice.'

# 13

*Vienna, 19 February 1785*

Countess Thun, Ignaz von Born, Thamos and Mozart worked on the symbol of Wisdom as described in *The Book of Thoth*, the Kabbalistic Hebrew texts and the esotericism of the Middle Ages. Their research shed light on the first of the Three Great Pillars* of Freemasonry and on the female equivalent of the Great Architect of the Universe.

Gradually, they began to perceive the elements of a ritual of Sisters commensurate with their own genius but that did not ape Freemasonry. But the practicalities looked a long way off and the countess doubted that they would find enough women to attempt such a venture.

'I must go to Paris,' Thamos declared. 'The Lodge of United Friends, also called the Philalethes, is organizing

---

* Wisdom, Strength and Harmony (or Beauty).

a congress to which a number of different Masonic branches have been invited.'

'Will it make up for the Wilhelmsbad débâcle?'*

'I am not very optimistic,' the Egyptian admitted, 'but I shall do what I can to help.'


*Vienna, 2 March 1785*


Leopold was exhausted by Wolfgang's routine and needed to catch his breath. On 20 February, twenty-one guests sat down to lunch at the house of the actor, Müller; on the 21st, they lunched with the Trattners and in the evening attended a concert at Count Zichy's; on the 23rd, Wolfgang played at a concert hosted by the Lebruns; on the 24th, he appeared at Auernhammer's; the 25th was the third subscription concert at the Mehlgrube, and on the 28th, he played at the second Lebrun concert at the Burgtheater, while today there was yet another appearance by the young violinist Marchand, also in the Burgtheater.

Composing, concerts, receptions, Masonic meetings . . . Where did the frail Wolfgang find such energy?

Leopold had a bad shoulder and was happy for Constanze to fuss over him and apply a soothing balm.

'Wolfgang works too hard.'

---

* Strict Templar Observance was abolished at the Congress at Wilhelmsbad.

'I agree with you, Father, but you know why?'

'Tell me, my child!'

'He wants you to be proud of him. Becoming rich and famous is a way of thanking you for having brought him up so well. Without your praise, he can't be truly happy.'

'But he hasn't needed me for ages!'

'Don't be too sure. He has forgotten none of your teaching. "Right after God comes Papa . . ." Don't you remember?'

Leopold did not give way to his feelings in front of his daughter-in-law. Of course he remembered the trusting little boy he had subjected to the bumpy roads of Europe for the glory of a child prodigy.

He had gambled dangerously but not haphazardly. Leopold knew that Wolfgang was no ordinary child and that he could make huge demands of him. No one had thought him tyrannical or abusive, and indeed, he answered to neither description; he had simply wanted to see his son fulfil his true potential.


*Munich, 2 March 1785*


After a long talk with Geytrand, who had given him a comprehensive report, the Jesuit, Frank, political adviser and confessor to Prince-Elector Karl Theodor, decided to take the plunge and try to persuade his illustrious patron to go on the offensive properly.

'Doesn't my decree govern the fate of the Illuminati?'

'They are mocking you, Your Highness. Their Order has only been superficially dissolved.'

'Explain yourself, my father.'

'The lodges are still meeting and the Illuminati have even set up reading societies to develop their subversive ideas. Adam Weishaupt, their leader, is in touch with foreign agitators, like François Mirabeau, who argues for the total overthrow of society. Unfortunately, your decree has gone unheeded because the terms are too vague. The Illuminati are exploiting the loophole.'

'Then you must close it immediately!' snapped the prince-elector.

It gave Frank immense delight to draft a detailed new decree, where vague words like 'secret societies' were replaced by 'Freemasons and Illuminati', who were now prohibited on Karl Theodor's territory.

'I detest being made fun of,' the prince added, 'and I expect my directives to be observed to the letter. You will therefore order the civil and ecclesiastic police to carry out full and swift investigations, to search the houses of all suspects, to remove Freemasons and Illuminati from official positions and to imprison the leaders.'

The Jesuit Frank rubbed his hands in glee.

*Ingoldstadt, 3 March 1785*

In his university office, Adam Weishaupt, professor of law and head of the Illuminati, was writing another vitriolic speech against the Jesuits, intending to read it out that evening at the meeting.

Suddenly, the door was flung open, and a colleague and founder member of the Illuminati burst in.

'We must leave, Adam!'

'Leave, but—'

'There's not a moment to lose, we must flee!'

'What is going on?'

'Prince Karl Theodor has just issued another decree against the Freemasons and Illuminati of Bavaria. They are being branded as outlaws and targeted by name! You have been sacked and are banned from the university. The police are under orders to arrest you.'

Adam Weishaupt tore up his speech, snatched up a handful of files and ran out of his office.

Down below, a carriage was waiting for him.

'Go to Ratisbon,' his colleague advised. 'There, another coach will drive you to Gotha where Duke Ernest II, a committed Freemason, will grant you hospitality.'

Weishaupt hesitated. 'If I flee, I shall be accused of cowardice! The Order of Illuminati will fall apart and my work will be destroyed.'

'If you stay here, you will go to prison. And you will not survive there long.'

Weishaupt needed no further persuasion. After all, he was an intellectual, not a man of action. It was better to take refuge in a safe place, be forgotten about and let the days pass in peace.

# 14

Josef Anton handed Geytrand a glass of Champagne.

'Adam Weishaupt has fled, the Order of Illuminati has been decapitated! Congratulations, my lord. You have carried off a resounding victory. In Bavaria, Freemasonry would seem to be eradicated.'

'You have been extremely efficient, my stalwart friend, and your salary will be raised in consequence. We should not believe in the annihilation of the Illuminati, however. Of course, Weishaupt's defection will halt the expansion of the Order, but Bode will take up the torch in Weimar where he knows he is safe. The authorities are leaving him free to continue his diatribes against Catholicism and proclaim himself head of the Illuminati.'

'A swan song,' said Geytrand, dismissively. 'Bode is just an impassioned orator whose influence wanes with every passing day.'

'We should keep an eye on him, all the same. He will try to rekindle the flame.'

'No chance, my lord. Bavaria is hostile to him now, and all the Masonic lodges will be suspicious of any Illuminati who attract such trouble.'

'We still have to convince the emperor to flush them out of Vienna! Alas, von Born is not on the list.'

'A number of his friends, like Professor von Sonnenfels, belong to the sect.'

'Josef II will want proof, not presumptions.'

'If you sow the seed of doubt in his mind, von Born's reputation will be undermined. We can destroy him by degrees.'

'A drop more Champagne, Geytrand?'


*Vienna, 10 March 1785*


The grand concert given at the Burgtheater earned Wolfgang 559 florins, a handsome sum that covered, in one night, the annual rent of his luxurious apartment in the heart of Vienna.

Since his fourth subscription concert at the Mehlgrube on 4 March, Wolfgang had put in considerable work on his new Piano Concerto in C major,* largely composed in February and which he played to a fervent audience.

* No. 21, K467.

Uplifting and vivacious but relaxed, the first movement expressed total self-control and an assurance that was abruptly ruffled by profound doubt that was not, however, destructive. Did life have a meaning? Initiation offered a positive and enthusiastic answer.

The central Andante revealed a world of light in a vision so sublime that the audience sat entranced.

For the first time, the composer transposed into music his perception of the temple made of living stones, beyond time and death. The dreamlike melody of the second movement evoked the mind's journey through the universe of symbols.

But no being could stay at such heights, and Wolfgang brought the music back down to earth with an elegant, spirited Allegro, although the lasting emotion of the almost otherworldly themes of the slow movement lingered as a memory.

'You were describing initiation, were you not?' Leopold ventured.

'It has become the essence of my life and, therefore, of my music.'


*Vienna, 12 March 1785*


On the morning after the fifth subscription concert at the Mehlgrube, Leopold treated himself to a lie-in and wrote to his daughter, Nannerl, describing the whirlwind he was living in with his son.

*We never get home to bed before one in the morning, we never get up before nine and we dine at two or half-past. Concerts every day! Your brother's pianoforte has been moved to the theatre or another house at least a dozen times since I arrived. He's had a great pedal-board built for him. It stands underneath the pianoforte and is sixty centimetres bigger, making the instrument extraordinarily heavy. It is transported to the Mehlgrube every Friday, and we have also taken it to the homes of Count Zichy and Prince Kaunitz.*

Wolfgang and Star liked the new instrument because of its unequalled bass and richer palette of sound. Like his father, the composer was excited by the technical progress that was taking place in music and dreamt of having enough money to acquire better instruments from piano manufacturers.

'How long is this infernal pace of life set to go on?' grumbled Leopold.

'Until the end of the Viennese season,' Wolfgang replied with aplomb. 'Isn't it marvellous to live like this, playing and composing?'

'You have realized all your dreams, my son.'

'Oh, no, Father! I want to write a grand opera and I should like you to discover the Light, for it has brought me so much joy.'

Leopold demurred. 'I need to get my breath back and give it some more thought.'

*Paris, 13 March 1785*

The Congress of the Philalethes was hoping to assemble Freemasons from the whole of Europe, as well as numerous leading personalities, like Duke Ferdinand of Brunswick, Bode, Joseph de Maistre and Willermoz.

The disappointment was on the same scale as their hopes: considerable.

'We have sent out questionnaires about the origin of Freemasonry, its heritage, the existence of a supreme Being and the immortality of the soul,' the Venerable of the Philalethes told Thamos. 'We think it essential to rediscover the primitive science of initiation and put it into practice. Unfortunately, we have received very few replies, as though such crucial subjects didn't interest our Brothers. And now here's Jean-Baptiste Willermoz, the Superior of the Knights Beneficent of the Holy City, writing: "Pointless to ask these questions – it is enough to believe in Christ." '

Thamos spoke to his Brother about *The Book of Thoth*, but the Frenchman was disconsolate and would not listen.

'Who today is prepared to challenge our errors and inadequacies? We genuinely thought this Congress would be a success and that we could start afresh on a new footing. Of course, there are lots of discussion meetings, but where are the participants? So few important people are here!'

71

'We must still try to get back to our spiritual source,' Thamos insisted. 'What future is there for Freemasonry without its Egyptian roots?'

The Venerable of the Philalethes could not hide his irritation.

'The Freemasons and most of the French have other things on their minds. They are not interested in initiation or the symbols; all they are bothered about is the total overhaul of society. Many are openly critical of the monarchy, nobility and the clergy. I fear there will be dreadful turmoil.'

'Should not Freemasonry act as a moderator?'

'What exactly does it expect? The Masons themselves do not know!'

'Without initiation,' Thamos said thoughtfully, 'no society will know true harmony. This meeting has got off to a poor start but we should try to get the most out of it, none the less.'

# 15

*Vienna, 13 March 1785*

It was testimony to Mozart's reputation as a fashionable musician that the Abbé Lorenzo Da Ponte, official librettist to the court, had agreed as a matter of urgency to write a short poem for the oratorio *Davidde Penitente*\*which the composer was conducting that evening at the Burgtheater.

Six hundred and sixty people attended the performance given in aid of the Musicians' Society, which had still not replied to Mozart's application. Using extracts from a previous Mass† and adding a few new items, he had worked at speed to complete the commission evoking David's repentance for having become Bathsheba's lover.

\*K469.
†K427.

73

Two days later, on the 15th at the second Musicians' Society concert, only twenty-five spectators turned up. The nobilities' boxes remained empty.

Nothing daunted, Wolfgang renewed his application. What else could he do to win their recognition?

His family all wanted it for him, and his father would be proud of him. He promised the honourable institution that he would continue to compose for them.

*Vienna, 19 March 1785*

The day before, Wolfgang had given his sixth and final subscription concert at the Mehlgrube. It was a musical and financial success.

'If he has no debts to pay off,' Leopold wrote to Nannerl, 'I think my son can now put 2,000 florins in the bank. The money is there, that's for sure. The household budget, including meals and drinks, is extremely economical.'

The sound of laughter interrupted his writing.

Aloysia had just returned from a tour of Salzburg and Munich and was overjoyed to see her sister Constanze again. She filled the house with noisy merriment. Wolfgang introduced her to his father, once so hostile to a possible marriage between his son and the Weber girl.

And Leopold had been right. Bubbly and coquettish, Aloysia did not have the personality that made Constanze essential to Wolfgang's wellbeing.

'We hear good things about your talents as a singer,' Leopold declared. 'I should like to enjoy them myself.'

'The proof of the pudding is in the eating! Wolfgang, sit down at the piano and play one of the songs you composed for me. Today, I am in good voice.'

Aloysia was genuinely gifted. Her audience clapped and she set off again, charmed.

'I shall have to go,' Wolfgang told his father and wife.

'A meeting?' asked Leopold.

'A Fellow Craft meeting. We are studying the Art of Tracing, the sacred geometry through which we may perceive the universe.'


*Vienna, 21 March 1785*


Although the previous day's concert at the Burgtheater with the singer Nancy Storace had been a success, Wolfgang was morose.

When he received *Rudolf Habsburg*, a libretto by a Mannheim poet Anton Klein, he had hoped it would give him the subject of a grand opera in German and, after *The Abduction from the Seraglio*, provide him with the material he needed to depict initiation. In the brief moments he had to himself, he continued to read as many texts as possible, but he had yet to find one of interest.

And it was not this half-baked poem by Anton Klein that was going to meet his requirements. He hammered out his disappointment, as he concluded his letter of refusal: *German opera will be completely ruined, at this rate. It would be a real service to Germany if we Germans would seriously think in German, act in German, speak German and even sing in German.*

*Vienna, 25 March 1785*

That Good Friday, Leopold basked in happiness. Aloysia and Joseph Lange, Mozart's Brother, offered him a splendid evening's hospitality. At the end of a delicious meal, Lange took a crayon and sketched a portrait of their visitor from Salzburg. Leopold was flattered by so much attention.

But Wolfgang could think of nothing but the first piece for his lodge to accompany the second-degree rites: a song for soloist with organ accompaniment in True Union Lodge, where the Brothers of Beneficence now met. Joseph Franz Ratschky had written a fine piece called *The Fellow Craft's Journey*:

*You, who now approach a new degree of knowledge, walk firmly along your path, certain that it leads to Wisdom! Only the man who perseveres can approach the source of Light. Pilgrims, take succour from the blessing of your Brethren! May prudence go with you always, may thirst for knowledge guide your footsteps. Exercise your judgement and never let yourselves be deluded by passive blindness. Harsh is the journey of life, it is true, but sweet is the prize awaiting the traveller who can wisely benefit from his course. Happy the man who can say, one day: the Light lit up my road.*

Wolfgang gave it to his father to read; Leopold's reaction was decisive.

'*Only the man who perseveres can approach the source of Light . . . may thirst for knowledge guide your footsteps.* Well, I lack neither perseverance nor that kind of thirst!'

'Do you mean . . .?'

'I am writing my petition to join the Freemasons.'

*Vienna, 28 March 1785*

Schwanckhardt, secretary to Beneficence Lodge, was delighted to receive from Wolfgang's hands Leopold Mozart's letter of application.

'I shall tell the Vienna workshops straight away.'

'Could we reduce the two-week wait normally required? My father will have to go back to Salzburg soon, and I should like to speed the process up.'

'I shall ask the provincial lodge administration for a dispensation,' promised Schwanckhardt.

'Do you think they are likely to agree?'

'I hope so.'

The midday dinners continued: on the 29th, at the home of the singer Adamberger, Wolfgang's lodge Brother, where conversation turned on Freemasonry; on the 30th, at Aloysia's, where they talked about opera, and on the 31st, at the Ployers', where they discussed future concerts

*Vienna, 1 April 1785*

Schwanckhardt smiled broadly.

'Our request for a dispensation has been granted!' he told Wolfgang, who had just composed an Andante for violin and orchestra[*] for Heinrich Marchand, Leopold's favourite pupil.

Meanwhile, Venerable Otto von Gemmingen announced the date of Leopold's initiation: 6 April.

The baron took Wolfgang aside.

'The Olympic Lodge in Paris has commissioned our Brother Josef Haydn to compose six symphonies.'[†]

'Isn't that good news?'

'Of course, of course, but several Brothers from True Union are raising eyebrows because they have not seen Haydn in the lodge again. He is still only an Entered Apprentice and, given his fame, he deserves to rise quickly to the next degree.'

[*] K470, a lost work.
[†] Symphonies 82 to 87, known as the 'Parisian' symphonies.

'He is a very busy man. Coming to Vienna is difficult for him.'

'We realize that, my Brother Wolfgang. When you see him, tell him we are missing him and that we should be most honoured by his presence in the temple.'

# 16

*Vienna, 6 April 1785*

When he had paid his admission dues of thirty florins and his quarterly membership fee of fifteen, Leopold Mozart, Vice-Kapellmeister in Salzburg, a free man and of good morals, received the Light in Beneficence Lodge, where his son was a Master Mason.

Like Wolfgang, he meditated in the primordial cave, the 'Chamber of Reflection', he was disrobed of his profane clothes, he was hoodwinked and he accomplished perilous journeys. From purification to purification and ordeal to ordeal, step by step, he ceased to be a total novice and was initiated into the degree of Entered Apprentice.

Long after the ceremony was over, Leopold remained silent. Back at Wolfgang's apartment, he asked for a strong drink.

'Why don't you stay in Vienna?' his son suggested.

'I could find you pupils and concerts, and you could publish a new version of your teaching method.'

'No, I must go back to Salzburg.'

'Since Nannerl's marriage, you've been living alone in that great big apartment. We are Brothers, now! Let me offer you hospitality, and let's build a future together.'

'Whatever you do, don't breathe a word of my initiation to Nannerl! My letters will talk of nothing but profane events. Your sister would not understand the step I have taken. She is very attached to the Church and ordinary belief.'

'Aren't we bound by secrecy? All the same, think my suggestion over.'

'If I stayed with you, Nannerl would feel neglected and spurned. I must treat my son and daughter fairly.'

'I don't want to pull the bedclothes too far over my side, but I won't despair of convincing you. You know, I could ask for you to be raised to the degree of Fellow Craft.'

'How long would that take?'

'Not long.'


*Vienna, 7 April 1785*


The new head of the Order of Illuminati, Johann Joachim Christoph Bode, was livid. Why was the founder, Adam Weishaupt, behaving so disreputably? Of course, the police crackdown in Bavaria was widespread, but a general should not abandon his army in the thick of the battle!

The war was not lost. The Dukes of Gotha and Weimar were sheltering the Illuminati, and Josef II was not following in the footsteps of Karl Theodor. In Berlin, Frederick II remained neutral. As for Prince-Archbishop Colloredo, he was flouting the recommendations of the Master of Bavaria and had refused to investigate the few Illuminati living in Salzburg.

So Bode was not giving up. He would go to Saxony, Hamburg, Hanover and Bremen, gather his troops and buck them up. If the intellectuals let him down, he would have great difficulty maintaining a modicum of coherence.

Nevertheless, the ideas of the Illuminati were gathering ground and would soon spread throughout Europe. Karl Theodor's offensive might be too late. His decree of excommunication only applied to Bavaria and would not halt the rise of a philosophical movement which, sooner or later, would sweep away Church and princes.

Aware of the danger, the Catholics had gone on the offensive and were endeavouring to keep the support of the authorities and take control of the Freemasons.

But Bode was on his guard. Even if he was the last bastion of obscurantism, he would not give in.


*Vienna, 8 April 1785*

'Mozart!' exclaimed Emmanuel Schikaneder, visibly delighted to see the composer he had met in Salzburg five years earlier. 'You've become quite the Viennese celebrity!'

'Don't let's exaggerate!'

'Your concerts are all sell-outs, the emperor takes off his hat to you, the critics are silent, word is spreading . . . It's fantastic!'

'And you?'

'Oh, up and down, but nothing to complain of. My band is contracted by the Burgtheater until February 1786. We were worsted by the imperial censors and have to stick to the directives. But what does it matter, so long as I can put on shows that please the public? Performing, that's the main thing! What about you: any operas in the pipeline?'

'I'm still looking for a libretto.'

'Vienna is a hive of talented artists! You'll soon come up with an entertaining text, and everyone will be charmed by your music. Maybe we'll be able to collaborate.'

Schikaneder shook Mozart's hand and all doubt was dispelled.

'Do you know the first letter?' Wolfgang asked.

'I can give you the second.'

The two men exchanged the sacred word.

'Are you going further?' the composer asked, to be quite sure.

Schikaneder gave the correct answer.

'So, we are Brothers!'

'I don't practise much,' the impresario admitted, 'but I have enormous respect for our worthy Order. Don't they open one's mind to grandiose horizons? Maybe one day our society will be better, and it will be all thanks to the Freemasons!'

Mozart and Schikaneder promised to meet again.

*Vienna, 9 April 1785*

'The news from Paris is not good,' Ignaz von Born told Wolfgang. 'The Congress only received a very few Brothers and there is endless parlaying. As I observed years ago, most Freemasons have very little interest in the aspect of initiation of their Order.'

'Can't Thamos convince them to go back to first principles?'

'He does what he can, but the Philalethes Lodge lacks coherence. French society is riven by serious tensions and Freemasonry will struggle to exert a calming influence.'

'May I ask a favour, Venerable Master? My father is going to leave Vienna soon and I should like him to know other Mysteries.'

'You want him to become a real Freemason, is that it? So, he won't go back to Salzburg.'

'That is what I'm hoping.'

'Beneficence Lodge will appoint True Union to initiate Leopold Mozart to the degree of Fellow Craft on 16 April.'

On the 11th, Leopold's 'promotion' was declared in all the Viennese lodges. And on the 12th, Wolfgang, reassured, attended a meeting for Entered Apprentices where they worked on the brute stone, one of the aspects of primary matter and fundamental to accomplishing the Great Work.

# 17

*Vienna, 16 April 1785*

At the direction of Beneficence Lodge, Leopold Mozart and five other Entered Apprentices were initiated to the degree of Fellow Craft in True Union Lodge. Von Born and Wolfgang disapproved of these mass initiations, whose only aim was to swell the numbers but which did not give candidates the chance to absorb the full meaning of the ritual.

The ceremony was therefore more conventional than the rite that had been observed for the composer's initiation. Nevertheless, Leopold was instructed in some of the basic ideas behind the Fellow Craft degree, for instance, that it provided insight into the sacred arts and the construction of mankind.

Afterwards, Brother Anton Kreil gave the first part of a speech on the theme, 'Does scientific Freemasonry exist?'. Wolfgang found much to interest him in the answers he gave, for the Ancients had known the principle of all sciences, and the secrets of the initiates were contained in the 'hieroglyphs of the three degrees'. These had been partially recovered by the Freemasons and now their duty was to pass them on.

'I can't say I follow these ideas,' Brother Puchberg muttered to Mozart, 'but I've no doubt they are worthwhile.'

The merchant had liked Wolfgang's composition for the ceremony, *The Fellow Craft's Journey* for tenor and organ.* For a few moments, the Brothers were filled with the desire to follow the path to wisdom, reject blindness and travel together towards the source of the Light.

In the lodge register, Wolfgang Mozart signed his name above Leopold's: father and son had now become Brothers.

*Klosterneuburg, 19 April 1785*

Swept up in a round of social engagements, Leopold was enjoying a fine day in the country with Baroness Waldstätten, a woman he greatly admired. The jovial baroness, with a penchant for salacious jokes, had offered Wolfgang and Constanze her protection and her support for their marriage at a time when Leopold still opposed it.

The episode had been put to rest, and the baroness was delighted by the good understanding that now existed between father and son.

* K468.

'Dear Leopold,' she ventured, 'I hear rumours that you have followed in Wolfgang's footsteps and joined the Freemasons.'

'It is an honourable society and I hold its philosophy and research in considerable esteem.'

'Will you be moving to Vienna?'

'I doubt it.'

'Don't you like our magnificent city where music occupies such a special place?'

'Of course, but I have a steady job in Salzburg, and I have spent nearly all my life there.'

'Why not try something new?'

'At my age, my lady, one's main concern is security. What would people think of me if I neglected my duties?'

'A pity, dear Leopold! You would make a perfect Viennese gentleman and we would have the pleasure of seeing you more often.'

The baroness turned to talk to Constanze about Karl Thomas, and Wolfgang took advantage of this break in the conversation to make a suggestion he hoped would persuade his father to stay in Vienna.

'True Union Lodge is going to raise you to the degree of Master Mason on 22 April.'

'Isn't that rather sudden?'

'If you must return to Salzburg, you should know the three degrees and the full extent of Masonic initiation.'

Leopold agreed on that point.

*Lyons, 20 April 1785*

Jean-Baptiste Willermoz, Grand Professional and Superior of the Knights Beneficent of the Holy City, had refused to go to Paris to attend the Congress of the Philalethes to study the origins of initiation and esoteric sciences. Such matters were pointless, because he, Willermoz, had amazing revelations to make, though only to his disciples. The Freemasons did not state overtly that they believed in Jesus Christ, and he did not trust them.

Forgetful of his promises to the Grand Master of Strict Templar Observance and no longer interested in writing the new, long-awaited rituals, Willermoz now obeyed the Unknown Agent, who dictated his orders and had charged him with leading an 'elect and cherished lodge'.

As a result, he had in his possession several manuals consisting of impenetrable signs and words that belonged to an unknown language. Finally, he had announced the great news to his Brothers: in this 'era of renewal', an authentic prophet was going to appear among them!

Every fortnight, they gathered together hoping that Christ's messenger would reveal himself. They were not in the least discouraged by his absence and were prepared to wait patiently for as long as they had to.

Sometimes, Willermoz thought back to the curious unknown Superior, Thamos, and wondered if he should have paid more attention to him.

*Vienna, 20 April 1785*

Wolfgang was so deep in his work that Leopold dared not interrupt. Constanze did not call him to dinner and the starling, Star, held his tunes in check for fear of disturbing the composer.

At last, he laid down his pen.

'I think that'll do,' he muttered.

'May I know your new challenge?' asked his father.

'I can tell you and my wife everything! I am writing a very special Masonic cantata* to the glory of Venerable Ignaz von Born. He has recently discovered a process for blending precious metals and his reputation is constantly growing in university circles. Even the emperor supports his work. Because von Born's renown is beneficial for Viennese Freemasonry, Crowned Hope Lodge wants to honour him officially. They commissioned me to write a cantata for the occasion to words† that proclaim both the merits of our Brother and those of the emperor.'

'Does Ignaz von Born support Josef II's policies?'

'His loyalty is total!'

'I was very impressed by him,' Leopold admitted. 'That Venerable is a kind of monarch leading Freemasonry along the right road.'

---

*K471.
† Written by Franz Petran.

# 18

*Vienna, 22 April 1785*

Wolfgang was expecting a lot from his father's initiation to the sublime degree of Master Mason in True Union Lodge, although he wished it had not had to be celebrated with two other Fellow Crafts. Surely a ritual of such importance should be held for one Brother alone. When would this critical reform be adopted?

Leopold experienced the betrayal of the wicked Fellow Crafts, the death of Hiram and the rebirth of the Master of Work.

Wolfgang could see from his face that his strategy had failed. As Thamos had said, it was a grave mistake to rush through the degrees. Wolfgang's own case had not been typical, because he had spent so long working up to his initiation. In his father's case, Wolfgang had found no alternative to keep him in Vienna.

The evening ended with the second part of Brother Kreil's speech on Freemasonry and science. Wolfgang was hoping to hear him expound on the hieroglyphs of the three degrees containing the essence of the science of initiates.

He was sorely disappointed. In a volte-face, Kreil declared that the Freemasons should most certainly never make the hieroglyphs, the three degrees and that kind of science the subject of their research. The Society's objectives were above all charity, equality between men, freedom of peoples and individuals, and the dissemination of the philosophy of Enlightenment.

The Masonic secret was utterly pointless! Furthermore, good Masons rejected all brotherhoods concerned with the Mysteries, in particular the Mysteries of the Rose-Cross and the Initiated Brothers of Asia.

The speech was very long and many of the Brothers were only half listening. It was late, and the Venerable avoided possible debates.

'Funny kind of ceremony,' Leopold remarked to his son. 'Can you really go through the gates of death alive and pass, fully conscious, to the other side of the mirror?'

'The ritual opens the way. It is up to us to follow it.'


*Vienna, 23 April 1785*


'Our informant, Angelo Soliman, was present when Leopold Mozart was raised to the degree of Master

Mason. His son was there, too,' Geytrand told Josef Anton.

'Is the father as active as his offspring?'

'Oh, no! He holds only a modest post in Salzburg and does not seem very dangerous.'

'This Mozart case is growing.'

'There is worse, my lord. Crowned Hope Lodge is protecting free thinkers with subversive opinions. Here are Soliman's notes.'

Anton studied them closely.

'What a pity it isn't signed "von Born"! And Josef II is still showering honours on him as though he were becoming the prince of Viennese scientists. We have enough proof that he supports the theories of the Illuminati, but there's not much to be gained by showing it to the emperor. He will say it is slander and I shall be out of favour. Patience is the greatest virtue, my good friend, but exercising it sometimes requires self-denial.'

'If the Freemasons feel too free,' Geytrand predicted, 'they will make fatal mistakes.'

The *Magazin des Muzik* was an influential journal, and Cramer's article in it summed up the critics' opinion of Mozart: 'He is the best, most accomplished pianist I have ever heard. What a pity that in his composition, which shows artistry and real beauty, he has flown too high in his search for creative novelty, for the heart and sensitivity have nothing to gain by it.'

It was a stinging review.

'You mustn't worry about that kind of judgement,' Constanze advised. 'The better known you are, the more wonderful your compositions will be and the more these little people will attack you and try to bring you down, some violently, others insidiously and by stealth.'

In the evening, Wolfgang and Leopold attended a Fellow Craft meeting where they studied the sacred numbers using Niederer's *Treatise* on the numbers Three and Seven. Three symbolized the method of thought involved in initiation, while Seven embodied the life of the mind.

Wolfgang sympathized with Emilian Gottfried von Jacquin, the brother of his pupil Franziska and son of Baron Nikolaus Joseph, a well-known botanist and a great friend of Ignaz von Born. Aside from their commitment to the Masons, the two men found they had much in common.

Leopold showed little enthusiasm for the works of the Fellow Crafts Lodge, although he agreed that the relation between numbers and music was fundamental. In any case, he had only come to Vienna to put his mind at rest and see for himself that his son was thriving. And there was no doubt that Wolfgang was prospering, happily settled in a beautiful apartment where he lived with his excellent wife and bonny, healthy son, and he was a member of the respectable Freemasons movement. He rubbed shoulders with the nobility, who would help him establish his reputation, and he was working day and night. His talents as a performer and a composer shone throughout the music season and brought him pupils from the best families, who were willing to pay a good price.

What more could one hope for? An official position at court, perhaps, though it would have to be well paid. But for all the emperor admired Mozart's music, that looked unlikely given Joseph II's financial policies. If the opportunity arose, Leopold would encourage his son not to miss it.

Although Wolfgang was taking an active part in the work of the lodge, he felt a sense of regret. Was his father really interested in the research into initiation or was he merely finding out from the inside about the secret society his son had praised so highly?

Perhaps Wolfgang, the Entered Apprentice, had been too evangelical and broken the rule of silence. But who could keep such riches to himself and not tell his loved ones about such a discovery?

If Leopold perceived the importance of the Royal Art, he would continue to frequent his lodge. Otherwise, he would go back to Salzburg and the links with his son, now his Brother, would become strained.

# 19

*Vienna, 24 April 1785*

Crowned Hope Lodge was proud to organize a fine ceremony in honour of Venerable Ignaz von Born, who had been awarded the title of Knight of the Empire by Josef II.

He received a portrait that showed him ringed by a snake biting its tail, as an emblem of the eternal renewal of cycles. Above him, an eight-point star symbolized the creative powers of the four male and female power pairs, revealed in Hermopolis, the city of the God Thoth. A palm frond and acacia sprig stood for the Great Mysteries, while a sphinx and lion* indicated the necessity of vigilance.

Two clerics, a Franciscan and a canon, waited eagerly

---

*Mozart used these symbols in *The Magic Flute*. When Sarastro appears, he is leading a chariot drawn by lions.

with the other Brothers to hear the Cantata for tenor, choir and orchestra*, conducted by Mozart himself.

To create a serious, intimate atmosphere, though not devoid of joy and serenity, wind instruments outnumbered strings: two oboes, a flute, a clarinet, a bass clarinet and two basset horns played alongside two violins, a viola and a cello.

The lodge was fortunate in having good musicians who could accompany the tenor, Brother Adamberger, the first Belmonte in *The Seraglio*. With dignity and poise, he sang a splendid opening aria: 'See how nature gradually reveals her face to the enquiring mind; see how she wisely fills the heart and mind with virtue. It is a feast for the Mason's eyes, the true, burning joy of Masonry.'

Then came a short recitative to the glory of Ignaz von Born and the emperor: 'See how wisdom and virtue are gently guided towards the Mason, their disciple, telling him: Beloved, take this crown from our eldest son's hands, the hands of Josef II. That is the celebration of the Masons and the feast of their triumph.'

Next, an Andante in the solemn key of G minor made liberal use of triplets and thirds to emphasize the importance of the number Three. The tenor led the choir of initiates in a tribute to Venerable von Born, whose talents the emperor had recognized: 'Sing, Brothers, and rejoice! Let your joyful hymns echo right to the

* K471.

innermost halls. Let them resound up to the clouds! Sing: Josef the Wise has twined laurels into a crown around the head of the man who is wise among Masons.'

It was a perfect text in praise of the sovereign, protector of the Freemasons and Grand Venerable. Nothing seemed out of place at this splendid ceremony, and Mozart's music made the evening unforgettable.

After the banquet, Leopold joined Wolfgang.

'I've had news from Salzburg.'

'Good news, I hope?'

'If I don't go back immediately, Prince-Archbishop Colloredo, the Grand Mufti, will stop paying my salary. Then he will give my position to someone else and I shall be out on the street.'

'Father, I—'

'It's useless to insist. I have no future in Vienna. I am too old and don't want to launch into the unknown.'

'Our Masonic work—'

'I'm too old for that, too. It's a universe you have to explore in depth, and I don't have those possibilities. Staying an honorary member of my lodge is good enough for me. My place is in Salzburg. I am leaving Vienna tomorrow.'


*Vienna, 25 April 1785*


At half-past ten, Leopold's luggage and his violin pupil, Heinrich Marchand, were ready. There was nothing left to do but pack them all into a capacious carriage.

'Father,' Wolfgang announced, solemnly, 'Constanze and I are coming back to your place with you.'

'What about your child?'

'A nurse can look after him.'

'That is a very bad idea. The last time you did that, it ended in disaster. You are Viennese now, and you have nothing to do in Salzburg. You must carry on with your career and your Masonic life here.'

Wolfgang did not protest. His last attempt to put off the separation had failed.

'Let us have lunch with you in Purkersdorf, four leagues from Vienna.'

'Agreed.'

Young Marchand regaled the party with stories of his work as a concert violinist and his hopes of returning to Vienna and making a name for himself as a soloist. Constanze asked Leopold how he ran his domestic life. It was ruled like orderly manuscript paper and gave him no trouble. And he would never remarry: he had loved his wife too dearly.

There was no more talk of initiation and Freemasonry. Wolfgang had the sickening feeling he was facing a Brother who was deserting his lodge and thus breaking his oath. He had opened his heart to Leopold, and Leopold was closing the door of his Salzburg apartment. In offering him the vast message of the three degrees, he had been persuaded that the Light of the Great Mysteries would revolutionize his life and make them inseparable Brothers.

He had been painfully wrong.

And now their separation had a taste even more bitter than previous ones. When they embraced, Wolfgang had the fleeting thought that he would never see his father again.

*Vienna, 26 April 1785*

'Leopold Mozart has left Vienna and gone back to Salzburg,' Geytrand told Joseph Anton.

'Has he received a mission to establish Freemasonry in Colloredo's state?'

'No risk of that, according to my informants. He'd had enough here and didn't show much interest in the Masonic rites.'

'One Mozart less!' Joseph Anton asserted with satisfaction. 'Unfortunately, we still have the son.'

'He may be dabbling in the occult works I suspect go on here.'

Joseph Anton's face clouded. 'What do you mean?'

'Neither Hoffmann nor Soliman can give me details, but Ignaz von Born appears to be organizing secret meetings with a clutch of Master Masons whom he trusts.'

'An unknown research lodge for the Masonic administration. I don't like the sound of that and I want to know more about it.'

'It won't be easy, my lord, because my informants don't belong to the happy elite.'

'They must find a way! We shall make it worth their while.'

# 20

*Vienna, 28 April 1785*

That evening, Wolfgang attended an official Master Masons' meeting. The Brothers considered the name the 'Lodge of St John' and the reasons why the Church of St Peter was separated and differentiated from the Church of John.

Peter had denied his master three times in order to save himself and had neglected his duties. Like the bad Fellow Craft, he had broken his word. And yet Peter was the rock and it was on that rock that the Church of Rome had been founded.

John, Christ's favourite disciple, and trained by the Essenians, had been kept away from the material and temporal expansion of Christianity, and so removed from the vision of initiation of the earliest ages. Yet, in the Prologue to his Evangelist, he recalled the major teachings of the wise men of Egypt: 'In the beginning was the Word and the dark did not stop it'.

Through John's secret Church, initiation had been passed down from brotherhood to brotherhood, right down to the Freemasons. And it was from his Brothers that Wolfgang discovered all the lies and posturing that had weakened the Western soul for so long.

They had to return to the source and recover the Word that had come forth, like a light so strong, it pierced every cover.

*Paris, 28 April 1785*

The only guest to accept the invitation from the Philalethes Lodge was the Count of Cagliostro, but his speech shocked the Congress delegates.

'I bring you the truth,' declared the Grand Cophta, 'and I offer you the necessary rituals. But I shall only give you this priceless gift on one condition: you must burn your library and archives! They are worthless and harmful.'

There was a cry of revulsion, but Cagliostro insisted. Either they obeyed or else Freemasonry would collapse.

During a lull in the debates, one of his disciples, his face deathly pale, spoke to him at length. His master had been arrested in an affair that was threatening to bring down the French monarchy, already in a parlous state. Heedless of the serious economic crisis that was rocking the country, Queen Marie-Antoinette, spendthrift, coquettish, irresponsible and hated by the French, had paid the jewellers Böhmer and Bassenge more than one and a half million pounds for a 2,800 carat necklace.

There were rumours that the scandal was the work of the Cardinal of Rohan, Cagliostro's disciple, who had been ostracized for several years and was keen to endear himself to the queen. The Necklace Affair gathered such momentum that the monarchy was unable to stifle it.

Since Cagliostro was implicated, he was summoned to give evidence and plead the cardinal's innocence. So he left the Congress, convinced he would quickly allay the suspicions hanging over him and soon be back in his offices in Lyons, where he would denounce Willermoz for his spinelessness.

Thamos the Egyptian returned to Vienna. Even if the meetings went on until 26 May, there was no point attending. The outcome was a foregone conclusion: the Freemasons would prioritize Christian theosophy to the neglect of the tradition of initiation. They would respect religion and avoid becoming dangerous protestors.

Many of the Brothers were disappointed and wanted to arrange another, better organized congress to discuss the fundamental principles.

But who now still believed in them?

*Vienna, 7 May 1785*

First performed at True Union Lodge on 1 May, the Cantata, *The Joy of the Mason*\*, was sung again that day

---

\* K471.

at a ceremony that brought together the Lodges Palm Tree and Three Eagles. Mozart's work was becoming a classic of Viennese Freemasonry, proclaiming the wisdom of both Ignaz von Born and Josef II, the Order's protector.

In his album, Wolfgang entered three *Lieder** to words by Weisse, who had popularized Shakespeare and was sympathetic to the Freemasons. The first song, 'The Magician', described the emotions of a young girl about to succumb to the magic of love. The second, 'Gladness', celebrated the joy and serenity of humility, which was far more important than vanity and false nobility. The third song, 'The Deceived World', involved three characters: a young woman, a good honest lad and a pretentious little master, dishonest and deceitful. The woman rejected the former and chose the latter, because the world was not only the place of deception and mistakes, but it wished to be abused and spurned goodness.

Mozart, the Master Mason, was lucid but refused to give in to fatalism; so the next day, he composed an 'Ode to Freedom',† to words by his Brother, Aloys Blaumauer.

Freedom, according to the text, was dependent on three conditions: one should not be enslaved by amorous passion, or rely on princely favours or succumb to the attraction of gold and material wealth. Initiation provided the means to accomplish this triple detachment.

---

* K472, K473 and K474.
† K506.

However much wealth and power a man might have, he was burdened by their weight, ensnared by their chains, and nothing but a prisoner shackled in a deep dungeon he had dug for himself day after day. But it was not political revolution that would liberate him, because it would only replace tyrants with other tyrants.

*Vienna, 20 May 1785*

Mozart wrote a 'Fantasy'* in the solemn key of C minor, and he used it to introduce a sonata† dedicated to his pupil Theresa von Trattner, daughter of a Brother at Palm Tree Lodge.

Almost as long as the Sonata itself, the 'Fantasy', with its constant changes of key, made a curious introduction. It was the portrait of the profane man in search of initiation, and bore the hallmark of the Master Mason offering answers suggested by numbers and rites. The tragedy of life, lucidity about human limitations and constructive doubt were not dispelled but were stages on the way to Enlightenment. Even so, death was necessary to the old man, and rebirth to the man aware of his spiritual dimension.

On 15 May, Leopold was back in Salzburg. Most likely, he would never leave it again. In vain had his son

---

* K475.
† K457, also in C minor, dating from 14 October 1784.

tried to instil in him a sense of freedom and to travel with him as a Brother.

After such a cruel disappointment, what could he have to say to him? In his enthusiasm as a new Freemason, Wolfgang had believed that his father would be sensitive to the ideal of initiation and, like him, place it at the heart of his life and thought.

But the world preferred to be deceived, his father would go on with his routine existence and, gradually, the rites he had experienced would be forgotten.

# 21

*Bad Gastein, 30 May 1785*

Ignaz von Born was suffering from chronic sciatica and had gone to take the waters, hoping to find some relief. As he left Vienna, he wondered if he was being watched.

When he sat down to dinner, Thamos came and sat opposite him.

As always, the Count of Thebes had kept their appointment.

'Did your Paris trip go well?'

'The French Freemasons' Congress is a lame duck. Endless parlaying, pointless discussions, no possibility of reviving the tradition of initiation, and limp submission to Christianity to avoid making waves. Furthermore, that necklace affair Cagliostro is involved in, combined with the social unrest stirred up by raving ideologues, is pushing France to the brink of disaster.'

'Are you afraid the monarchy will fall?'

'Evil rumours have set the people against Marie-Antoinette and they hate her. A foreign queen, scornful, Austrian and improvident! She is blamed for the economic trouble and accused of despising the poor. Meanwhile, Louis XVI has no control and is gradually crumbling under weight of the disastrous heritage left by Louis XV.'

'Do you think there might be . . . a revolution?'

'I have seen death on the prowl. Turmoil will ravage the country, because France cannot solve problems without resorting to violence.'

'What is the attitude of the French Freemasons?'

'Some preach destructive egalitarianism, others are turning a blind eye and a deaf ear. A very few lucid initiates would do better to leave. In any case, Mozart should not go to France.'

'He has just suffered a huge disappointment.'

'You mean, his father's return to Salzburg?'

'You know about it?'

'It wasn't hard to predict. Wolfgang was hoping for a new Brother, like any initiate keen to share his wonder. Now, a gulf will open up between father and son.'

'He will bear the marks of his disillusionment for ever,' von Born reflected.

'Of course, but it won't challenge his creative power. In a few months, he will pass through more stages than most Freemasons ever encounter in their whole adult life. Is the emperor still supporting you?'

'He awarded me an honorific title, but that worries me. When you want to get rid of an awkward customer, don't you grant him a complacent, laughable distinction? Anyway, I don't hide my opinions. I sent a letter resigning from the Munich Academy of Sciences, because its president dared to approve the closing of a lodge on the pretext that it is infiltrated by Illuminati. My letter is addressed to the Chancellor of Bavaria and will be made public. I confirm my pride in being a Freemason and blame him for expelling the most sensible and enlightened men by accepting a new Inquisition. That Jesuit Frank, the prince-elector's confessor, is driving us into total obscurantism.'

'You are running considerable risks.'

'As a high dignitary at the Grand Lodge of Austria, a recognized scientist and appreciated by the emperor, I must defend our Order. If I say nothing, the repression will grow.'

'You were followed here by a rather squat man in his thirties with a scar on his forehead.'

Ignaz von Born froze. 'Who ordered him to watch me?'

'I shall try to find out,' Thamos promised.


*Bad Gastein, 1 June 1785*

Like his prey Ignaz von Born, the follower in service to Geytrand had put up at the best hostelry in town. The bill was steep but he was taking enough risks to treat himself to good meals and a decent room.

His report would be somewhat slim. Ignaz von Born had genuinely gone to Bad Gastein for his health and had spent every evening in his room. The only exception had been a dinner with a passing guest. But there had been no secret meeting and no plot. In short, an ordinary patient with mundane behaviour.

Von Born left the inn and disappeared down a dark alley.

Astonished, his follower kept his distance without losing sight of him.

Just as he was passing a doorway, a powerful fist grabbed him by the coat collar, raised him off the ground and hauled him into a dark room.

'Who are you?' asked the threatening voice of Thamos, although the little man could make out nothing of his face.

'No one, no one! I just happened to be passing . . .'

'Don't lie or I'll break your neck.'

When the Egyptian's fingers closed around his neck, the prisoner realized he wasn't joking.

'I am paid to follow a man and report on his activities.'

'What is his name?'

'Ignaz von Born.'

'And your commissioner?'

'I don't know him.'

'Don't test my patience.'

'I'm telling the truth, I swear! I don't know my employer's name.'

'You must have met him . . .'

'He's tall, unprepossessing with a flabby face and dull eyes.'

'Aren't you muddying the picture?'

'No, I swear I'm not!'

'Stop swearing and tell me more, if you want to escape alive.'

'I don't know any more. He ordered me to follow von Born and report back to him on his doings and moves, that's all!'

The little man was too frightened to lie.

'Listen to me, you little creep. I agree to let you go on one condition: get out of here and never show your face again. Leave the country, and whatever you do, don't try to contact your employer. If you try to outwit me, I shall find out because I have eyes and ears everywhere. And you won't escape. Do you understand?'

'Oh, yes!'

'Will you obey me?'

'I swear I will!'

When his aggressor had gone, the follower stood petrified for several minutes. Shaking with fear, he at last managed to get up and venture into the street, convinced he would be murdered.

But the place was deserted.

The little man ran hell for leather, determined to keep his promises.

# 22

*Vienna, 7 June 1785*

'Two important pieces of news, my lord,' Geytrand announced. 'One good, one bad.'

'Start with the bad,' ordered Josef Anton.

'One of my informants who was following Ignaz von Born has disappeared.'

'In Vienna?'

'No, in Bad Gastein, where the Freemason was taking the waters for his sciatica.'

'Did your subordinate's corpse turn up?'

'No sign of the useless man.'

'Von Born must have a protector. His Brothers have traced the follower and got rid of him. These Freemasons know every trick! Without proof, we're powerless. Ignaz von Born is taking every possible precaution. What about the good news?'

'He has made a big mistake. He has written an

incendiary public letter blaming the scientific and political authorities of Munich for agreeing to the closure of an Illuminati lodge.'

Josef Anton smiled wanly. 'An official declaration at last! I shall be sure to warn the emperor, but I wonder if he'll believe how noxious this damn Freemason is? After all, he's done nothing but defend the famous free thought Josef II is so keen on. Karl Theodor's repressive policies are too reactionary for him. He might even approve of Ignaz von Born's protests. Basically, this letter doesn't help.'


*Vienna, 8 June 1785*


A violet was growing in the meadow. The flower spotted a pretty shepherdess and wanted her to pluck it so that it could adorn her breast. But the young woman did not see the violet and trod on it. Far from showing animosity as it died of its wounds, the flower sang a swan song of joy, because the shepherdess would go on to love.

As an epilogue to the *Lied*,* composed to a short poem by the Freemason Goethe, Wolfgang added: 'Poor violet! It had a tender heart.' The poem touched him because it expressed an acceptance of destiny and, better still, the capacity to overcome it through love not rebellion.

---

* 'A Violet' K476. After this date, the list of works Mozart made in his album became less precise.

The arrival of Anton Stadler lifted the mood of melancholy. Still just as jovial, he made Constanze laugh, sent Star into peels of birdsong and played with little Karl Thomas, who treated him to his sunniest smiles.

After drinking an excellent coffee, Wolfgang's childhood friend, now a highly accomplished performer, talked about the expressive qualities of the basset horn.

'I used one recently,' the composer told him.

'In which piece?'

'A Masonic cantata.'

'You're really keen, aren't you?'

'The only limits to the pathway of initiation are the ones we set ourselves. You have to go through many doors and, whatever your degree, you should never believe you've got to the top. Travelling towards Enlightenment demands constant work.'

'Too hard for me!' Anton Stadler demurred. 'All the same . . . children aren't the only ones who have to be educated. I hesitate to ask you this, but do you think a man like me . . .?'

'In my opinion, the main thing an initiate needs is loyalty to the word he has given and to the work of the community. Do you think you can do that?'

'Possibly.'

'Do you want to go beyond the world of appearances, take off your blindfold and behold the harmony of the Great Architect of the Universe?'

'I wouldn't say no. For a musician, that must be an amazing experience.'

'Unforgettable.'

'Initiation doesn't stop one wanting to laugh?' Anton Stadler asked, anxiously.

'There's no danger of that. Quite the reverse, in fact: in the worst possible moments, there is always something to laugh at, and that's our own vanity.'

'You know, I should like to join you on this adventure. Knowing you as I do, I doubt you chose this way by chance. And the reason you're following it so passionately and diligently is that it's worthwhile. So, I'd like to give it a try.'

'Think hard, Anton.'

Wolfgang had matured. His friend might only stay a Freemason for a short period. If the temple door opened, it was up to him to take his life in hand.

*Vienna, 20 June 1785*

Neither Wolfgang nor Thamos hid the fraternal joy they felt on seeing each other again.

'Did your Paris trip bear fruit?'

'I'm afraid not,' replied the Egyptian, and he described the reasons why the Philalethes Congress had failed.

Then he handed his Brother a set of Masonic songs published in Berlin in 1771.

'The first poem was written by Ludwig Friedrich Lenz in 1746 and would be ideal for the celebration of one of our major rituals, the Human Chain, at our next midsummer Festival of St John. It would help us restore to it its proper esoteric marvel and meaning. St John drank from a poisoned chalice but vanquished death and thus pointed the way by showing us how to overcome bitterness and betrayal.'

'Oh, holy bond of friendship of the loyal Brethren,' wrote Lenz, 'like the highest happiness and delights of Eden, friend of faith that is never breached, known to the world and yet so mysterious! Sing, then, Masons, tell the whole earth today that the day to which this song is dedicated is bright and beautiful, a solemn festival of faith and union.'

Wolfgang composed a simple song for tenor, organ and choir*, in which the choir repeated in unison the end of every verse after it had first been sung by the soloist.

'Virtue is our greatness,' Lenz went on: 'it makes us noble, so that our glory stretches from the North Pole to the South and Phoebus's eye sees nothing more wonderful in the two hemispheres than our lodges.'

'That's a fine hope,' Thamos conceded, 'but the author expresses a doubt: "Is this vanity, tell me, or basically calm happiness in which the Masons put their faith?" '

'I like the answer,' Wolfgang concluded: ' "No, because it is true that God Himself furnishes us with the noble instinct of brotherhood." '

'Brotherhood . . . Are we really capable of it?'

---

* 'O Hallowed Band', K148.

# 23

*Vienna, 20 July 1785*

Ignaz von Born and Thamos's efforts proved in vain and there had been no ritual of initiation for the midsummer festival of St John, because too few Freemasons wanted to change things. Why disturb their well-anchored folklore customs and try to give deeper significance to pleasant, superficial ceremonies?

One can have too much of a good thing, was the attitude of several dignitaries, who were starting to feel uneasy at the esoteric research of von Born and the enthusiasm of Mozart, his favourite disciple. The lodges were the meeting places for righteous men, not alchemy laboratories for worrying over the teachings of the Ancient Egyptians.

The Venerable nevertheless asked Mozart for two new pieces of music, one for the opening of the Master

Mason degree works, The Work of Death, and the other for the ending, The Work is Accomplished.*

Wolfgang was enjoying a time of perfect happiness. His son was a bonny, healthy little boy, his love for Constanze was peaceful and he spent delightful musical evenings with his Brother Gottfried von Jacquin.

Writing for his lodge and thus passing on his perception of initiation brought him an almost otherworldly joy.

*Vienna, 24 July 1785*

'The Vienna Musicians' Society is refusing to let me into its circle,' Wolfgang grumbled to Thamos. 'They are still examining my application but they have put me on the long finger indefinitely.'

'You mean, you won't ever get in.'

'Because I don't have a baptism certificate!'

'The typical failing of a rebellious Freemason, wouldn't you say?'

'Is it my spiritual allegiance that is making the honourable society reject me?'

'I'm sure it is.'

'In that case, all the Brothers will end up being ostracized!'

---

* These pieces, together with other scores for the lodges, have sadly been lost or destroyed.

'Very likely.'

Wolfgang was staggered.

'Why are we being hounded and marginalized when we are looking for the Light of Initiation without which there would be no moral integrity?'

'Because the world prefers to be deceived, as you yourself noted in your music.'

'Is the lust for power and money the only thing that drives the world?'

'Worse than that: stupidity does. Look how many Masonic movements tear themselves apart and sabotage themselves! The heir to Egyptian wisdom, Abbot Hermes, taught me that two opposing forces are locked in permanent combat: Maât and Isefet. Maât is justice, harmony, truth, moral rectitude, the boat's rudder and the statue's plinth. Isefet is chaos, destruction, injustice, the tendency to rot and refuse the Light, all the inherent impulses in man. The initiate's first duty is to replace Isefet with Maât, but how many Masons realize that? The perversity of Isefet consists in confusing good and evil and even in causing us to mistake evil for good and good for evil. That is why the initiates are suspected, persecuted and at times exterminated. So Isefet will reign over the earth where Maât has vanished.'

'Does human life lead to chaos and darkness?'

'Not as long as there is a Mozart to do battle with them. I am not flattering you, my Brother, because that would be the worst betrayal. I am simply telling you your duty: create wisdom, strength and harmony in

120

your compositions. If you succeed, you can expect to be attacked with unprecedented violence. The stupidity and mediocrity of our world won't be able to accept your efforts to rebuild Maât.

'The next step is this, and it is critically important: on 12 August, Venerable Ignaz von Born is to raise to the sublime degree of Master Mason Karl von König, a Venetian Freemason whose lodge has just been outlawed by the Inquisition. You must compose a piece of music for the core act of the ritual, the death and resurrection of the Master inside the alchemical athanor or sarcophagus, which the Ancient Egyptians called the "bringer of life".'

*Vienna, 25 July 1785*

At forty-one, Francesco Artaria, a native of the Lake Como region and a Brother at Mozart's lodge, was joint head, with his Brother Carlo from Crowned Hope, of a major Vienna publishing house that stood on the Michaelerplatz near the Burgtheater. He was about to publish the Cantata, *The Joy of the Mason*, and reveal Mozart's allegiance to the world.

'Aren't you afraid of negative reactions?' Anton Stadler asked, suddenly serious.

'Are Christians afraid to declare their faith? Anyway, how hypocritical and cowardly! And why might Masonic faith be lesser than Christianity?'

'You are overlooking an essential point: the number of members.'

'I am all the more aware of it because the vast majority of Christian Masons have no interest in symbolism or initiation. So what? A coherent and determined little group is genuinely looking for Enlightenment.'

'I'm sure I'm not capable of it, but I'm tempted! I wish I were there to do battle with them.'

'Think carefully, Anton, and don't do anything lightly.'

'Do you still trust me?'

'You are my oldest and most loyal friend.'

'So, the fat lady has sung! At last, you understand me!'

*Vienna, 10 August 1785*

Leopold's letter both cheered and saddened Wolfgang.

In Salzburg, Nannerl had just given birth to a boy, Leopold Aloys Pantaleon. It was a happy event, of course, but why was Leopold looking after the child and why did he have it in his care? His attention suggested his preference for Nannerl and, above all, it chained him to Salzburg and severed his links with Freemasonry. Instead of getting together with his Brothers, he was devoting himself to a baby and would never return to the lodge.

A major bond had been broken, and Wolfgang was

profoundly sorry. But his father had made up his mind and would not change it.

*Vienna, 12 August 1785*

Venerable Ignaz von Born was glad to receive Brother Karl von König, who had been expelled from Venice. A crowd of howling fanatics had burnt the heretic's possessions.

The tenor Adamberger sang two short pieces by Mozart, then, at the culmination of the ritual for elevation to the third degree, Wolfgang conducted the Master Masons' Music* for choir and orchestra.

Thamos was overwhelmed by the depth of this masterpiece. It expressed both the tragedy of Hiram's assassination and his resurrection through the creation of a new Master Mason.

It was an extraordinary piece that plunged the listener into the terror of death before opening for him the door to the Great Mysteries.

So much emotion did not stop Abbé Vittorio d'Este taking a violent swipe at the Inquisition, in Italian: 'The adversities and persecutions that beleaguer our Royal Order are the cornerstone by which the strength of the Masonic soul is proved, and which show that it must

---

* K477, known by the name of 'Funeral Music' because it was long believed to have been composed in memory of two deceased Brothers.

be its most distinctive characteristic. Today, not only is it beset by ignorance and bigotry, but also by politics and aggression. Thanks to the Great Architect, under this sky where the best of Princes reigns, our families live protected against open insult. But far away, in the Adriatic, our Time is being insulted.'

# 24

Geytrand's flabby features were set in a kind of rictus.

'A fine mess at True Union Lodge!' he announced to Josef Anton. 'Von Born has promoted to Master Mason someone who was expelled from Venice, and Mozart composed unpublished music for his ceremony. It's very rash to defy the Inquisition!'

'The emperor detests that religious institution and may be rather amused by the incident.'

'The emperor, maybe, but surely not the Archbishop of Vienna.'

Josef Anton scratched his chin. 'Send him a detailed report on the affair. An ally of that weight will be invaluable.'

*Vienna, 17 August 1785*

Archbishop Anton Migazzi pushed the copy of the Cantata *The Joy of the Mason* aside in disgust: it proved Mozart belonged to that secret society.

'And to cap it all, he's earning money from it!'

'No, your grace,' his private secretary corrected, 'because the proceeds of sales went to the poor.'

'Very clever,' remarked Archbishop Anton Migazzi. 'Mozart is substantiating the charitable vocation of his dangerous Order! Who would dare attack such a generous man?'

'Your grace fully appreciates the situation. According to trustworthy informants, Wolfgang Mozart is a member of the Lodge To True Union, a mouthpiece for some fearsome ideas.'

'The whole of Freemasonry is fearsome! It may proclaim its respect for Christian values, but its main concern is to fight religion. And unfortunately, Josef II protects this confounded brotherhood!'

'We are involved in serious talks with the emperor. If we persevere, I'm sure we shall change his mind about it.'

'What do you know about Mozart?'

'He was a musician at the court of Prince-Archbishop Colloredo and was sacked for insubordination. He had to earn his living in Vienna and has been quite successful. Unfortunately, he has taken up with the Freemasons.'

'Keep an eye on him,' ordered the archbishop. 'If Mozart gets too loud and bothersome, we will act in one way or another.'

*Vienna, 24 August 1785*

The Musicians' Society had decided: 'The decision to admit Mozart will be made on presentation of a baptism certificate.' As he could not or did not want to produce one, his application would not be accepted.

Wolfgang was disappointed but went ahead with Thomas Attwood's fourth composition lesson. The twenty-year-old Englishman had come to Vienna on a grant from the Prince of Wales and, since the 19th, had been benefiting from Mozart's tuition. The composer struck him as erratic, unpredictable and impatient, as he flitted among piles of sheet music that some visitors would have thought nothing of stealing.

Nevertheless, although sometimes despotic, he always made the subject exciting, and Attwood was hoping to be his pupil for at least two years. With him, the concept of 'music theory' was not just a matter of ready-made ideas and hard-and-fast rules. In a mixture of English and Italian, Mozart constantly went beyond mere technique to describe the very essence of creation, which no one, not even the most gifted pupil, could imitate.

Thomas Attwood was not actually learning anything, but he had the opportunity to admire a genius at work.

*Vienna, 1 September 1785*

Although Josef Haydn had not come back to the lodge, Wolfgang still held him in friendship and esteem. In the front of the edition of the Six Quartets dedicated to his Brother and published by Artaria, he set out his feelings:

*To my dear friend Haydn,*

*A father who had resolved to send his children out into the great world took it to be his duty to entrust them to the protection and guidance of a very celebrated Man, especially when the latter by good fortune was at the same time his best Friend. Here they are then, O great Man and dearest Friend, these six children of mine. They are, it is true, the fruit of a long and laborious endeavour, yet the hope inspired in me by several Friends that it may be at least partly compensated encourages me, and I flatter myself that this offspring will serve to afford me solace one day. You, yourself, dearest friend, told me of your satisfaction with them during your last Visit to this Capital. It is this indulgence above all which urges me to commend them to you and encourages me to hope that they will not seem to you altogether unworthy of your favour. May it therefore please you to receive them kindly and to be their Father, Guide and Friend! From this moment I resign to you all my rights in them, begging you however to look indulgently upon the*

*defects which the partiality of a Father's eye may
have concealed from me, and in spite of them to
continue in your generous Friendship for him who
so greatly values it.*

*Vienna, 25 September 1785*

Thanks to the ministrations of Dr Barisani, Wolfgang
was recovering from a severe bout of flu and had soon
gone back to his lessons with his English pupil.

At the first degree meeting on 13 September, Thamos
had told him that Cagliostro had been accused of
complicity with the Cardinal of Rohan in the Queen's
Necklace Affair and had been imprisoned in the Bastille.
Would adepts of his rite survive their master's fall?

Wolfgang was battling with an awkward editorial
problem. On the 10th, Torricella had started selling
manuscript copies of six early quartets,* just before
Artaria released the Haydn Quartets on to the market.
So, Wolfgang warned the public of possible confusion
between the two very different series, and Torricella, an
opportunist, was incensed.

So much time was wasted in extricating himself from
these entanglements! It was lucky that Constanze kept
the house running so smoothly and made no objection
to an oboist and a pupil living in the Mozarts' apartment

* K168 to 173.

until the end of the year. Wolfgang liked to do people favours, and Constanze made no bones about it.

Reactions to the six quartets dedicated to Haydn – the fifth and sixth of which were the first pieces Mozart had written since his initiation – were a severe disappointment.

The dissonances at the beginning of Quartet No. 6* reflected the difficulty of ritual journeys, but the critics were unanimous in their dislike. They suggested removing them in future editions, because they obviously represented serious technical errors. Prince Grassalkowicz tore up the score, and many music-lovers shared the opinion of one horrified listener: 'There are barbarians devoid of all sense of hearing but who insist on writing music.'

* K465.

# 25

*Vienna, 26 September 1785*

Wolfgang hoped that his 'get-well' song,[*] published by Artaria for the singer Nancy Storace, would serve its purpose, but he was also keen to impress the abbé and librettist, Lorenzo Da Ponte.

At his latest secret meeting with Thamos, von Born and the Countess Thun, Wolfgang had been very excited by the Egyptian's crazy idea. He could not imagine how he would bring it to fruition, but he was determined to overcome the obstacles.

After a long, fruitless search, he at last had his opera and he would not let it go.

'Delighted to see you again,' breathed the unctuous priest. 'I am, as usual, up to my eyes in work, and—'

'I have a subject and I wish you to be my librettist.'

---

[*] K477a, lost. Cornetti and Salieri contributed to this piece.

131

'Well, why not . . .? What is it about?'

'*The Marriage of Figaro.*'

Da Ponte blenched. 'Would that be the same as the play by Beaumarchais?'

'We can remove the political satire; I'm not remotely interested in that aspect.'

'The emperor has banned that play!'

'I know, but he will like ours! And you are bound to reassure him.'

'You are asking too much of me, Mozart.'

'The challenge is worth it, believe me. The opera will be put on in Vienna or somewhere else, even if the emperor grumbles.'

'You are dreaming: no one would dare defy Josef II.'

'But the subject interests you, doesn't it?'

'It does indeed,' Da Ponte admitted. 'And I'd be delighted to work with you.'

'Well then, explain to His Majesty that we're telling a beautiful, action-packed love story. The Viennese public will be highly diverted by such a romp.'

'When you put it like that . . . I shall try, but I can't promise anything.'


*Vienna, 27 September 1785*


In the presence of Michael Puchberg and Brother Mozart, Anton Stadler was admitted as a Freemason to Palm Tree Lodge.

He was very impressed by the ritual, and amazed by the temple and the symbols he discovered. As a musician, he was sensitive to the power of the Mysteries that had been passed down by the initiates. Now, he understood why Mozart was resolutely committed to this path.

Here, another sun and moon shone, a sun whose rays were those of creation and a moon that represented just action. Here, earth and sky were linked by vast pillars, and shining stars lit up the landscapes of the soul.

'How can I thank you for opening this door to me?' he asked Wolfgang, embracing him with brotherly affection.

'It was your perseverance that led you to us.'

'I won't forget to be on my guard!'

'Let's celebrate your new birth by upending a few glasses, without bitterness!'

'I like initiation more and more,' Anton Stadler admitted.


*Vienna, 1 October 1785*


'It wasn't easy,' Da Ponte told Mozart, 'but I argued your position and assured him that our only aim is to amuse the Viennese public.'

'Did the emperor believe you?'

The abbé drew himself up. 'I am experienced in making a convincing case. His Majesty appreciates my talents as a librettist and trusts my sense of propriety. I managed to gloss over reference to Beaumarchais and assured him that our *Marriage of Figaro* would offend no one. "I trust your taste in music and your prudence with regard to decency," Josef II concluded.'

Mozart's heart beat faster. 'So I can . . . compose my opera?'

'His Majesty gives it his blessing.'

'Let's make a start right away,' said Wolfgang. 'I shall tell you how to tackle the situations and characters.'

'My poetic gifts demand—'

'The libretto must serve the music. I gave you the idea and you now have the emperor's word. I assure you, I shall pay meticulous attention to the text. Are we agreed?'

Vain though he was, Da Ponte was in thrall to Mozart's authority. Indeed, given the audacious nature of the enterprise, he was really rather glad to be directed.

Wolfgang immediately changed his routine. He spent his mornings composing *Figaro* and now taught only in the afternoon. Teaching was necessary to his livelihood, but it took its toll on his energies.

He bought sheaves of manuscript paper and a quantity of ink in preparation for the first grand opera since his initiation. Before he put pen to paper, he glanced up at the main tool he would work with: a little oblong marble plinth, on which stood a silver-gilt ink pot, another pot containing sand, and between the two, a silver bell-shaped cover protecting his wax seals.

Sensing that major work was about to begin, Star struck up a happy tune.

'You're right, this venture is sheer madness: depicting the teaching of initiation in a story and an opera that everyone can enjoy, no matter what his level of perception ... So, let's have some method ... First, some pretty arias, followed by others that are both merry and dramatic, and then the main action, and finally, the lyrical passages.'

Star trilled his approval.

With encouragement like that, how could Mozart not rise to the challenge!

# 26

*Vienna, 12 October 1785*

A meeting in the degree of Master Mason on the 8th, another in the degree of Entered Apprentice on the 11th, and the preparation of *Figaro*: Wolfgang was not idle.

'The story is exactly what I need to describe the first steps on the road to the Royal Art,' he told the Egyptian.

'Those steps will lead you to represent the Great Work in music.'

'That sounds very ambitious!'

'But of course: you are the composer of *Thamos, King of Egypt*! Since then, you have ceased to see the temple from the outside world and see the outside world from the temple. Now that you live in both spheres, you can link the two together. You will need four ritual operas to symbolize the four Great Pillars at the heart of the lodge. The Pillar of Harmony is associated with the Entered Apprentice's adventure, the subject of *The Marriage of Figaro*. That will lead you to the Pillar of Strength. The second opera will deal with the tragedy caused and suffered by the Fellow Craft as he tries to discover the secret of the Master Mason. The third will deal with the secret of the Pillar of Wisdom, from the perspective of alchemy. Finally, you will fulfil the promises of *Thamos* and erect the fourth invisible but vital pillar.'

Wolfgang felt his head reel as he contemplated the task before him; yet he knew that it offered the possibility of realizing all his dreams, as a Brother and as a musician.

The Marriage of Figaro, *Act I*

'The plot looks simple,' Wolfgang commented. 'Figaro, Count Almaviva's valet, is about to marry Susanna, the countess's chambermaid. But the count wants to conquer Susanna and assert his droit de seigneur. Will Figaro and Susanna, aided by the countess, escape their predator and become man and wife?'

'To make your Figaro an Apprentice Freemason,' Thamos said, 'we will have to strip him of his polemical character that Beaumarchais was so keen on. He will embody the initiate seeking to be united with Susanna, who symbolizes Wisdom.'

'Which is why, unbeknown to Figaro, of course, the opera starts in the Middle Chamber where Susanna is holding a looking-glass – the mirror of knowledge used in the degree of Entered Apprentice – and is trying on a hat, one of the symbols of the Master Mason. The alchemical marriage is about to take place. Centre stage is a big couch with armrests representing the Venerable's throne. As an Entered Apprentice, Figaro's first task is to measure up, and his first word is "Five", the number associated with the Fellow Craft and the one he aspires to but to which he does not yet hold the key. And what is he measuring? The invisible bed, symbolizing the sarcophagus that turns death into life in the degree of Master Mason.'

'Figaro bustles about his work with all the impatience of an Entered Apprentice,' Thamos went on. 'Susanna tries to talk sense into him. She calls him a dolt and is doing her best to get him away from such a fearsome place.'

'At this point,' Wolfgang interjected, 'I shall symbolize the initiatory awakening by bells which the count and countess ring to call their servants. But the numbers are different: Susanna takes *two* steps to "surround" the countess, while Figaro takes *three* bounds, the Entered Apprentice's number, to join the count. Together, they make *Five*, the number associated with the Fellow Craft, which Figaro wants to become. Nothing is possible without Susanna. So, she asks him if he is burning to hear the rest? He replies that he is, to avoid the chill of death, and his initiation continues. "Listen to me and be quiet," Susanna demands, and she tells him the count's intentions: to seduce her and restore the old feudal right.'

138

'And so begins the inevitable confrontation between the Entered Apprentice and the Fellow Craft,' said Thamos.

' "Bravo, my noble master!" Figaro exclaims. "Now, I begin to understand the mystery." Promising to make his terrible adversary dance to his tune, he lays out his strategy: stealthily, by subterfuge and fakery, with here a joke and there a sting, he will thwart the count's schemes and discover the secret of the ritual.'

'In so doing, the Entered Apprentice gets the Fellow Craft's allies on his side, namely, Dr Bartolo, for whom "revenge is a pleasure meant for the wise", and Marcellina, who wants to marry Figaro! Legally, the count's messengers will find "matter for confusion" and reduce the Entered Apprentice to silence. "And that good-for-nothing Figaro will be vanquished!" Bartolo promises.'

'But Susanna insults Marcellina, calling her a decrepit old sibyl and a frump, until Marcellina flounces out of the room.'

'The moment has come to use the primary matter in alchemy, the brute stone on which, and with which, the Entered Apprentice works. Who are you going to use to symbolize it?'

'Cherubino,' Wolfgang said decidedly, 'a guardian angel who belongs to the celestial hierarchies. He will embody androgynous love without polarization. The count, of course, wants to expel him from the palace, because he has caught him with pretty Barberina. Only his godmother, the countess, can save him.'

'Yes, that's right: only Wisdom can make the primary matter appear.'

'Cherubino sings of pure desire,' Wolfgang went on: ' "I talk of love when waking, I talk of love when dreaming, to the water, to the shade, to the mountains, the flowers, the grass, the fountains, to the echoes, to the air and wind." And here he comes with a ribbon stolen from his cherished protector, the countess!'

'Ah, you're thinking of the officers' "ribbons" and "collars" worn by the Masons in the lodge.'

'Yes, and Cherubino is going to become a military officer. So, his allegiance to a fraternal organization will be obvious. And the ribbon will also suggest one of the love knots in the knotted cord, both the Harmony of the Universe and Union of the initiates.'

'Now comes the first interplay between Susanna, representing Wisdom, and Count Almaviva, as the Fellow Craft possessed of a Strength he thinks he can control.'

'The scene takes place in the Middle Chamber, although the count has no right to be here. Cherubino dodges behind the couch and the Fellow Craft brazenly sits down on it. He tells Susanna that he has been appointed ambassador in London, but before he leaves and takes Figaro with him, he wants to win her love. Hearing the voice of the music master, Basilio, however, he is obliged to hide in his turn. Now he will see how Basilio serves him! Susanna helps Cherubino hide on the couch and covers him up with a veil.'

'Again, the primary matter is hidden,' commented Thamos.

'Basilio advises Susanna to yield to the count but spreads so much tittle-tattle that the count springs up in a rage. He flings off the veil and uncovers Cherubino. "Things could not go worse," Susanna declares, now accused of infidelity. She explains that Cherubino had begged her to speak to the countess on his behalf so that he can stay at the palace. The count is appalled: did Cherubino overhear him declaring his love for Susanna? Figaro's entrance, accompanied by a noisy band of peasant children dressed in white, the colour of the Entered Apprentice and Fellow Craft, saves Susanna and relaxes the tension. In an ironic gesture, he gives the count flowers and thanks him for overseeing the purity of his subjects. Cherubino will become an officer and Figaro will marry Susanna.'

'Act I ends with the Fellow Craft appearing to lose face and the Entered Apprentice thinking he has won the day and is free to do as he likes.'

'Not realizing who Cherubino really is, Figaro pokes fun at him and wishes him military glory. So, at this point, he seems to be preventing the alchemical marriage by rejecting the primary matter.'

# 27

*Vienna, 15 October 1785*

Although Act I of *The Marriage of Figaro* took up most of Mozart's time, he had not stopped composing other pieces. The next day, he finished a sombre sonata in C minor* reflecting the artist's solitude as he faced the enormous challenge he had set himself.

'We have to help two Brothers,' Anton Stadler announced. 'They are basset horn virtuosi and can't get together enough money to leave Vienna and go home. The Three Eagles and Palm Tree Lodges are meeting to give a benefit concert for them.'

Stadler and Mozart threw themselves wholeheartedly into this demonstration of charity. The concert ended with splendid improvisations by Wolfgang, to the great delight of his audience.

* K457.

The two performers each made a nice little nest egg, and afterwards, Wolfgang went back to his desk.

*Vienna, 19 October 1785*

A passage in Leopold's latest letter, dated the 14th, caught his son's attention:

*Not a hundredth of what is said on the subject of the Illuminati of Munich is true. It is correct that there was an investigation and that a few stubborn characters were banished or left of their own accord; the others gave the prince-elector genuine explanations and stayed in Munich, including one of their leaders, Dr Baader. The funniest part is that a catalogue is going round listing the members of Baader's lodge. Most of the seventy-odd names on the list are priests, among them the Count of Spaur, Canon of Salzburg. The real Freemasons are very cross with these people and that is why there has been a thorough investigation into these worthy men.*

With the exception of Bavaria, where Karl Theodor and his Jesuit confessor were continuing their crack-down, the Illuminati were managing to survive. In Vienna, the most illustrious of them, Professor Josef von Sonnenfels, was not a bit concerned.

Wolfgang was lucky to live under the reign of a tolerant emperor. It was surely proof of his broadmindedness that he was allowing *The Marriage of Figaro* to be written.

*Vienna, 25 October 1785*

'It's impossible to find out anything at all about supposed secret meetings attended by Ignaz von Born and Mozart,' said Geytrand, testily. 'Hoffmann and Soliman, my best informants, don't believe a word of it.'

'Carry on digging,' Josef Anton ordered. 'Do you know that the emperor has authorized Mozart to compose *The Marriage of Figaro* after a French play that was actually banned from the stage in Vienna?'

'Masonic leverage, I suppose?'

'Apparently not. It was Abbé Lorenzo Da Ponte, a priest with no Masonic links, who persuaded the emperor. But it is my belief that Mozart will use the opera to spread Masonic ideas. Fortunately, he has no shortage of powerful rivals in the music world, including Antonio Salieri. They can't stand him and they'll do their utmost to put a spanner in the works. Maybe we shall never see this *Marriage*!'

'After a lot of trails,' Geytrand declared, 'I am now certain that Ignaz von Born has premises on the outskirts of Vienna. He goes there quite often and stays several hours. A spy tells me that he even spent two whole nights there.'

'Most odd . . . I want to know what the premises are used for.'

'Could we get an order to search them?'

'Don't even think about it, Geytrand! We're talking about von Born, not a common bandit.'

'Then, what are we to do? There's clearly something reprehensible being hidden there.'

Josef Anton slumped in his chair. 'What do you have in mind?'

'A visit from someone prowling around.'

'Von Born will lodge a complaint and there will be a scandal.'

'There will be neither pillage nor destruction, my lord, I promise.'

'Don't get personally embroiled in this.'

'Do I have your permission?'

'No false moves, Geytrand.'

*Salzburg, 4 November 1785*

Meanwhile, Leopold was still giving lessons and fulfilling his duties as Vice-Kapellmeister to Prince-Archbishop Colloredo. At the same time, he was bringing up his grandson and writing frequent letters to his daughter, Nannerl.

*In all the musical advertisements, I see nothing but the name of Mozart*, he declared proudly, regretting that he had no detailed news to pass on. A brief note was all he had received from his son, who was too engrossed in his work on *The Marriage of Figaro* to write at length.

Leopold, who knew the play and thought it laboured, was unenthusiastic. *The translation from the French must have been very freely altered, if it is going to work as an opera*, he confided to Nannerl. *God willing, the action will be effective on stage. At least the music will be good. Wolfgang will have to do a lot of running around and arguing before he gets the libretto adjusted to suit his plans and wishes.*

*Vienna, 8 November 1784*

A first degree meeting on 29 October, another the same evening and a secret meeting chaired by Ignaz von Born, then discussions with Lorenzo Da Ponte to update the libretto . . . So many calls on his time had not stopped Wolfgang composing a quartet for soprano, tenor and two basses* to be added to an opera by Francesco Bianchi. The storyline suggested curious parallels with *The Marriage of Figaro*: wanting to exercise his droit de seigneur on one of his peasant girls who was about to get married, a count had abducted her and locked her up. Luckily, her father and fiancé engineered her release.

*K479.

Ideas were freely borrowed and recycled, and Wolfgang did not mind in the least. The real subject matter of his own opera meant that it would be unique.

Loyal and quietly supportive, Constanze was aware of the intense creative power that drove her husband. By keeping the household running like clockwork and minding little Karl Thomas, she provided Wolfgang with a calm home life and the peace of mind he so much needed. And every morning, Star, the starling, greeted the musician rapturously as he sat down to begin his day's work.

# 28

The Marriage of Figaro, *Act II*

'O love,' the countess begged, 'bring some relief* to my sorrow, to my sighs; O, give me back my loved one or, at least, let me die.'

So began Act II, in the countess's private chamber, where there were three doors signifying the three degrees, and a single window that let in the Light of Wisdom, embodied by the countess. In a few words, to a sublimely pure but serious melody, she poured out her suffering at seeing the Fellow Craft recoil and betray. Either he must return the treasure of initiation, his oath of loyalty, or she would vanish.

'Only Susanna, whose name comes from the Egyptian for "lotus", can speak completely freely to the countess,'

---

* Or 'some strength', strength being associated with the Fellow Craft count.

148

said Thamos. 'As the two aspects of Wisdom, the two women try to draw the Entered Apprentice and the Fellow Craft towards them. In appearance, Susanna is the countess's servant; in reality, she is her Sister and her operational arm.'

'They even exchange clothes in Act IV and pretend to be each other. At this point in the action, Susanna tells the countess that the count wants to buy her virtue. Has he really left his wife? Of course not, because he is still terribly jealous! Ogling Susanna amounts to poor control of his power; loving the countess involves keeping Wisdom as the object and heart of his existence.'

'The two Sisters must use the Entered Apprentice Figaro's vitality to set a trap for the Fellow Craft so that he "will waste time and lose trace", in reference to the most important science of his degree, the Art of Tracing. That way, he will come to see that he is not all-powerful and learn to be humble, but first he has to overcome his infidelity, selfish caprices and possessive jealousy.'

'And don't forget Cherubino!' interrupted Wolfgang. 'After he's sung about love and being "outside himself", he is put in the Chamber of Reflection by the two sisters where, in secret, the primary matter is eternally born.'

'Dressed as a woman,' Thamos put in, 'Cherubino becomes androgynous. On his head he wears a hat like the Master Mason's, and in his hand is his commission, like the lodge commission. "I am never allowed to die," he declares, because the primary matter of the Work never dies.'

'Only one problem: the commission has not been sealed! In other words, Cherubino remains virtual. Now the trouble starts: the count comes home early and hammers on the countess's door. The door is locked! Why so, if she is alone?'

'Where can they hide Cherubino, except in his place of origin, Mother Earth, the Chamber of Reflection?'

'The countess locks him in, keeps the key and opens the door to the count, who appears in his hunting gear. He demands immediate explanations. There's a clatter from the Chamber: someone is in there: who is it? "Susanna," replies the countess, her maid, who is bothering the count far more than herself. The count orders the servant to come out; the countess tells her not to. At least she should say something! "Shut up," orders the countess. We're on the brink of scandal and ritual disorder, which must at all costs be avoided. The count persuades himself that his wife, although above suspicion, is hiding a lover! Since she is refusing to open this special Chamber, he acts as the Fellow Craft and goes to fetch tools to force the door. On his way out, he takes two precautions: he takes the countess with him, and locks all the other doors. The lover will not escape.

'So, you're evoking a typical mistake made by the Fellow Craft,' Thamos observed. 'All his energies are focused on becoming a Master Mason, associated with Wisdom, in the guise of Susanna and the countess. However, he still confuses Wisdom with ordinary power and physical force, and he tries to gain access to the mystery by Strength, the Pillar of his degree. How far will he go to get what he wants?'

'The rumpus in the Chamber of Reflection marks the start of the finale to Act II,' Wolfgang declared. 'I'll end it with the confrontation between the countess, Susanna and Figaro on one side, and the count and his allies on the other. Wisdom is in danger, and Susanna, its operational arm, must save it. The only solution is to take Cherubino's place in the Chamber. But bringing him out requires a ritual practised in some lodges during the ordeals: the leap into the void. Every exit is forbidden, and that's the only way out. Since we're dealing with the degree of Entered Apprentice, the page recalls that "one must not lose one's head"; only the perjurer can cut his own throat, in the symbolism of the degree. Cherubino is associated with the countess and cannot betray her: "I'd rather leap into the Fire than harm her." '

'How better to convey the happy outcome of the fourth and final journey of the first initiation? The leap is successful: Cherubino's function is fulfilled. Whatever happens, Wisdom has fashioned the primary matter in the Great Work of alchemy revealed to the Master Mason.'

'The plot thickens,' Wolfgang went on. 'The count now returns with the countess, carrying pliers and a hammer, so now he thinks he has the power of a Lodge Master in his hand.* As he is preparing to force the

---

* At a meeting, the Venerable Master uses a gavel.

door of the Chamber of Reflection, the countess admits that Cherubino is hiding in there and that he has been undressed and dressed back up as a woman. Mad with jealousy, the count insults his wife. He demands the key and she hands it over. He opens the door, determined to kill Cherubino.

'And there in the doorway stands . . . Susanna! The first transformation has taken place: primary matter has become one of the aspects of Wisdom.'

' "Kill this page with your sword, then!" Susanna laughs. She invites him to look around the Chamber of Reflection while she shows the countess the window Cherubino leapt from. The bewildered Fellow Craft asks Wisdom's pardon. "Your madness does not deserve to be pardoned," the countess and Susanna reply together. "I love you", the count declares, but he has a harsh sentence inflicted on him: "So this is the reward to expect for the loyalty of a loving heart." Wisdom will not recognize that this Fellow Craft is fit to be raised to the degree of Master Mason, because he has spurned her and wrongly accused her.'

'For the first time,' said Thamos, 'the count calls his wife by her name: Rosina, "Lady of the Rose", the symbol of the secret of initiation. But she answers, "I am no longer she but the wretched object of your neglect whom you love to make suffer." At the request of the count, Susanna intervenes on his behalf. How can Wisdom reject authentic love? The Fellow Craft realizes that he has just undergone a series of ordeals intended to make him aware of his mistakes. Together with the two aspects of Wisdom, he sings of the heart's call to knowledge.'

'In a brief moment of harmony, peace and happiness have been restored. But the Entered Apprentice, Figaro, bustles in! He abruptly shatters the fragile serenity,' Wolfgang suggested, 'and announces that the musicians are ready to play for their nuptials. It could not be a worse moment! "Gently, gently, not so fast!" objects the count, and he recovers his bluster because he thinks he can get the better of the Entered Apprentice by producing a compromising letter. Figaro clumsily protests his ignorance of the document, but the countess and Susanna give him decisive advice: "Don't sharpen your wits in vain, we have revealed the secret; there's no more to be said." '

'In line with the demands of his degree, Figaro manages to keep silent,' Thamos added. 'At this point, I suggest we introduce a figure the Egyptians called Bisu, "the initiator". He is a boisterous, squat, bearded fellow who loves music and jollity and presides over the birth of new initiates.'

'That'll be Antonio, the gardener,' Wolfgang decided. 'He can act as an Overseer, because he has seen someone jump from the countess's balcony. He's a bit of a tippler, of course, but no lodge forbids that practice! Even if his claim is the result of divine drunkenness, Antonio forces Figaro to make a brave declaration: "Making such a fuss for *three* pennies! Since it can't be concealed, it was I who jumped down from there." '

'The Entered Apprentice thus identifies himself as the primary matter of the Great Work,' Thamos went on. 'He assimilates Cherubino's substance, which has been carefully matured by Wisdom in the Chamber of Reflection.'

'But our Antonio sticks to his guns! To allay suspicions, Figaro offers proof: he sprained his ankle and is limping, like the opening of the initiation ceremony.'

'The role of a good Overseer consists in testing the Brother he guides,' recalled Thamos. 'So, it was not enough for Antonio to have seen someone jump. When the person fell, Antonio picked up some papers, and now he hands them to the Entered Apprentice: they must be his.'

'The count instantly appropriates them,' Wolfgang suggested. 'And then comes the fatal question: if it really was Figaro who jumped and if the documents are his, he must know what they are about!'

'Our Entered Apprentice is floored. How can he reply? The Fellow Craft is triumphant.'

'There's nothing unusual about an Entered Apprentice having limited knowledge. Because he is just and righteous, Susanna, acting as Wisdom, comes to his aid. With such powerful help, Figaro will come through his "tyling" ordeal and give the right answers. The papers are the valet's commission. What is missing? The seal. Furious, the count rips up the document, rendering it useless, and admits: "The whole thing is a mystery to me." However, a good Fellow Craft won't give up. A trio formed of Marcellina, Bartolo and Basilio now comes to his aid. "Three blockheads and three madmen," thinks the Entered Apprentice wrongly, yielding to the vanity of his short-lived victory – short-lived because Marcellina announces that she has a promise of marriage signed by Figaro himself! And it's she, not Susanna, that he must marry. Dumbfounded, the countess, Susanna and Figaro exclaim: "A devil from hell has brought them here!" '

'The long-awaited alchemical Marriage will therefore never be celebrated,' Thamos concluded. 'In its place is a horrible mess.'

'We're only at the end of Act II,' Wolfgang objected. 'The adventure is not over yet.'

# 29

*Vienna, 9 November 1785*

For several weeks, well-informed circles had feared the worst. Hostile to Josef II's policies, Frederick II was trying to rally as many German princes as possible against him. There was talk of war, thousands of deaths, fields of destruction, and horror the length and breadth of Europe.

But Josef II held off the conflict by signing a treaty and the tension was eased. Vienna drew breath, life went on as normal and everyone praised their emperor's wisdom.

Although hard at work composing *The Marriage of Figaro*, Wolfgang visited Baron Van Swieten to play through the Preludes and Fugues of Bach's *Well-Tempered Klavier*. The grand old master's indefatigable spirit gave him fresh impetus and helped him build his first great Masonic opera.

'The whole of Vienna knows you are a Freemason,' the baron told the composer. 'Your Cantata proved your generosity towards the destitute but it also brought to light your allegiance.'

'What should I have to fear?'

'The police now have you on their files as a Freemason. What's more, the ecclesiastical authorities, especially the Archbishop of Vienna, didn't like your Masonic charity. Trampling on their flowerbeds will bring you serious enemies.'

'The world is governed by stupidity,' sighed Wolfgang.

'You may be right, Mozart. All the same, you should try to keep a low profile. The emperor currently protects the Lodges against persistent harassment by the Church, but he could alter his position any time.'

'Well, I shall never alter mine! I am proud to belong to the Freemasons and I uphold its ideal.'

'Please do be careful.'


*Vienna, 11 November 1785*


'It is all going to plan, my lord,' Geytrand confirmed.

'Are you quite sure?'

'I used the services of an excellent professional who is very well paid.'

'And . . . discreet?'

'Very discreet. At the first hint of gossip, he'll be locked up.'

'How did he get into von Born's premises?'

'Through an open window so he didn't have to smash it. There is no trace of a break-in.'

'What did he see inside the building?' asked Josef Anton, impatiently.

'A splendid discovery, my lord! Retorts, alembics, several ovens, dozens of pots made of glass, metal and clay, a plethora of bottles containing miscellaneous substances, and pieces of rock.'

'Isn't von Born a mineralogist?'

'Of course, but the books in the library are all about alchemy, an occult and dangerous science, which the emperor doesn't much like.'

'An alchemist's laboratory . . .'

'Definitely, and lavishly equipped! The scholar doesn't have a fortune and his income is modest, so he must be siphoning off money from his family. If he goes on like that, he'll ruin them. Don't you find his behaviour indecent and reprehensible?'

Josef Anton filed Geytrand's report away and set off to the imperial palace, where he asked to be granted an audience with Josef II. Choosing his words carefully, he described the extraordinary details collected by his agents, although he did not specify their methods.

'Ignaz von Born, an alchemist!'

'I wouldn't go that far, Your Highness. But there are serious suspicions and gossip is rife. This illustrious scientist is of slender means, and he is despoiling his family to fund the extremely costly equipment he has accumulated.'

'Can we hush this up?'

'I'm afraid not, because they come from both profane and Masonic quarters. He is a scholar of considerable repute, learned in rational philosophy and a defender of the Illuminati, and his influence is far-reaching, so if he descends into dangerous superstition, he will take many Viennese Freemasons with him. There is a growing number of Brethren and, as you know, Your Highness, Ignaz von Born is the true head of the Grand Lodge of Austria.'

Josef II rose as a signal that the interview was over.

Although he had not voiced an opinion, the Count of Pergen felt that he was shaken. Perhaps he had just scored a decisive point against von Born and the Freemasons.

*Vienna, 17 November 1785*

In the evening, Crowned Hope Lodge organized a memorial meeting to commemorate two Brothers who had recently died.

Tobias Wenzel Epstein gave a moving speech that was published in aid of the poor. In his vision of mortality, he likened death to 'a close friend', and Mozart, who conducted a small orchestra consisting of two oboes, a clarinet, basset horn and two French horns, was touched.

Wolfgang used his Masonic Music, minus the choir. Most of the Brothers, who had come to hear this initiation into the Great Mysteries, were powerfully affected by the second version of this extraordinary work.

It opened with a kind of relentless funeral march that seemed to lead to nothingness; anguish followed, though without revolt, just resignation at the inevitability of fate; and suddenly, true and total detachment was achieved by the man on the road to Knowledge, like a beam of light in the dark. For the initiate need not fear death, since death itself was mortal, a mere stage on the journey to the Eternal Orient.

That evening, a few Freemasons realized that Mozart was not a Brother like the others but a spiritual master who opened doors and blazed trails.

# 30

*Vienna, 20 November 1785*

The starting salary for a live-in servant girl was 12 florins per year; a teacher earned 22 florins; a university professor, 300; a surgeon, 800; the director of the Vienna hospital, 3,000, and Antonio Salieri, the city's most popular composer, 1,200.

Wolfgang could congratulate himself that he was almost the equivalent of a surgeon! Of course, he had considerable outgoings to consider, such as the annual Masonic subscription fee of 60 florins. Then came his huge rent of 460 florins, taxes, which were fortunately moderate, heavy doctors' and apothecaries' bills and purchases of food for a household that enjoyed its food and drank quantities of decent wine. Clothes, too, made up a major part of the budget. Wolfgang and Constanze had to dress elegantly. A good lady's dress cost 100 florins, a gentleman's outfit at least 30 and silk stockings, 5.

And they needed numerous suits, dresses, jackets, shirts, muslin cravats, boots, shoes and, in short, everything that would allow them the fashion commensurate with their position.

In addition, Wolfgang was generous towards his friends and family and never arrived empty-handed when he was invited out.

'This month,' Constanze admitted to him, 'we are in the red.'

'*Figaro* is keeping me busy day and night, and I've been earning less money lately. Don't worry, the concert season will soon begin again. Maybe I can take on more pupils.'

'I know how much you loathe teaching.'

'Nothing worse! I shall schedule in at least three subscription concerts and ask for an advance on my fees from Franz Anton Hoffmeister, the composer and publisher, who will soon be a Freemason and commissioned four piano quartets from me.'

'Won't that hold up progress on *Figaro*?'

'Needs must, my dear.'

*I need your help*, Wolfgang wrote to Hoffmeister, *and beg you to come to my aid, just for a little while, with the loan of some money, which I badly need at the moment.*

The publisher agreed to an advance of two ducats, or nine florins, and the temporary worries were dispelled.

# The Brother of Fire

At thirty-nine, Hoffmeister already had the air of an old man. Pompous and self-assured, he saw Mozart as just one of many talented musicians living in Vienna and a potential source of money. He was obviously still popular, because the Kärntnertor Theatre had put on *The Abduction from the Seraglio* yet again, on 25 and 27 November. Pretty Aloysia Lange took the role of Constanze. A third performance was scheduled for this evening. At the Burgtheater, Francesco Bianchi's *La Villanella rapita* was playing, with two vocal ensembles[*] which Mozart had written for it. But the situation was changing.

Hoffmeister seemed edgy.

'Something wrong?' asked Wolfgang, anxiously.

'Yes, and you're the cause.'

'Why, what have I done?'

'Your quartets are not selling well. I'm losing a lot of money because of you. I think our collaboration is pointless. We had better break our contract. I shall let you have the advance I agreed to and leave you free to choose another publisher.'

'I shall repay you with another piece,' Wolfgang promised.

His Brother Artaria agreed to take over the contract. In the light of recent setbacks, however, he decided to let time pass before republishing quartets that had been so little appreciated.

---

[*] K479 and 480.

163

*Vienna, 7 December 1785*

To commemorate one of its Brethren, Three Eagles Lodge organized a meeting in the degree of Master Mason. Mozart conducted the final orchestral version of his Masonic Music, with two new parts for basset horns and a contrabassoon. His renown as a Freemason was gradually spreading throughout the lodges and everyone understood why Ignaz von Born had chosen him as his disciple.

At the banquet after the meeting, one of the Brothers, a senior administrative officer in the Grand Lodge of Austria, chatted to the composer.

'Your music is quite beautiful, but you should distance yourself from von Born. I realize he is an admirable scholar and a man of quality, but his reputation could be seriously marred.'

'For what cause?'

'Shady practices that I can't really talk about.'

'Such as?'

'He appears to be a . . . an alchemist. Don't you see? How can a rational, philosophical Mason be capable of such superstitions? The emperor has apparently found out and is not at all happy about it. To make matters worse, von Born seems to be plunging his family into financial ruin by lavishly equipping a laboratory and running very expensive experiments.'

'Who listens to such calumnies?' Wolfgang protested indignantly.

'The information seems be correct,' the functionary sighed. 'Ignaz von Born's activities could impact on our Grand Lodge of Austria and give Freemasonry a bad name.'

'Of course they won't,' Wolfgang objected. 'It's all a lot of nonsense and will soon be forgotten about.'

'Let us hope so, my Brother, but the Masonic authorities are worried, and I advise you to be extremely cautious.'


*Vienna, 8 December 1785*


'How did your interview with the emperor go?' Ignaz von Born asked Baron Gottfried Van Swieten.

'Not bad. He believes the rumours about you to be unfounded. Josef II holds you in esteem and trusts you.'

'Impossible!'

'I assure you, I—'

'The emperor doesn't believe what he says. The people who are slandering me know what they are doing; in time, they will change his attitude to Freemasonry. It was already heavy-handed of him to set up the Grand Lodge of Austria and now he is preparing directives to restrict our numbers and influence still further.'

'You seem very pessimistic to me.'

'Not pessimistic, realistic.'

# 31

The Marriage of Figaro, *Act III*

' "What a mess this all is!" exclaims the would-be-conqueror, the count embodying the Fellow Craft, baffled by the situation. The scene has changed to a hall laid out for a wedding, where there are two thrones,' Wolfgang continued, 'one for the count and the other for the countess. But he is so much a prey to human error that he doubts. The chaos, you see, at the beginning of Act III, means that nothing has been won.'

'Of course, he has not yet managed to have his way with Susanna, and she, because of her Masonic role, is not afraid to confront him. With the collusion of the countess, she offers to meet him in the garden, meanwhile telling him both "yes" and "no". And now our Fellow Craft is drunk on his own arrogance and convinced he will possess Wisdom!'

'His illusion is soon shattered,' Wolfgang interjected, 'because Susanna carelessly gives away the trap that has been laid for him. Seething with destructive force, he sings an aria of revenge and vows never to let Figaro the Entered Apprentice win!'

'How are you going to soothe his anger?'

'By having the count's allies, Don Curzio and Bartolo, intervene and force Figaro to marry Marcellina. But now come the revelations! Figaro recalls that he is of noble birth. He was abducted as a child and has never been reunited with his parents. As proof of his illustrious birth, he has gold, jewels and embroidered cloths, which the kidnappers found on the little boy, but above all, there's a hieroglyph on his arm! Figaro's future wife, Marcellina, cannot believe her ears. "A strawberry mark on your right arm?" she asks. Exactly, but how does she know? Because Figaro is her son, stolen from her near a palace! His real name is Raphael, and Marcellina introduces him to his father: Bartolo! Susanna comes in bringing a thousand gold pieces with which to buy back Figaro's freedom, and the first thing she sees is Figaro kissing Marcellina. Thinking that she's caught him philandering, she slaps him, only to discover the incredible truth. So now, they all go off to plan their weddings, Marcellina and Bartolo at the same time as Susanna and Figaro.'

'Yes, there'll be a double wedding,' Thamos agreed, 'and much alchemy will be worked. You can also announce a third marriage, because Cherubino, disguised as a servant girl, has managed to stay in the palace and marries pretty Barberina. The number Three is triumphant and the count appears vanquished. And Figaro's noble birth means the Entered Apprentice is as high-born as the Fellow Craft and is no longer a humble servant.'

'But the countess can't abandon him,' Wolfgang added. 'The role of Wisdom is to attract him to her so that he will return to moral righteousness and can be raised to the other Mysteries. Spurned, offended and betrayed, Rosina sadly recalls better moments of tenderness and pleasure, in the days when the Fellow Craft kept his word. Now, there is nothing but tears and pain, and the memory of that happiness is scarcely perceptible. But perhaps her constancy in loving him will change the count's ungrateful heart and grant him access to the Master Mason's secrets.'*

'The heart is one of the most important symbols of the degree of Fellow Craft,' Thamos recalled. 'By cheating and breaking his word and by straying from the path of righteousness, he tears his own heart out. That is what Wisdom wants to avoid at all costs.'

'Her prayer gives the Fellow Craft new strength,' Wolfgang went on. 'And now comes the ritual intervention

---

* The countess's second aria, '*Dove sono i bei momenti*', echoes and transcends the Agnus Dei and *Coronation Mass*. All musicologists, even those who see *The Marriage of Figaro* as mere entertainment and *opera buffa*, agree that the countess's arias have a religious or spiritual dimension.

of the First Overseer, who conducts a Fellow Craft's training. Antonio, the gardener, gives the count Cherubino's
officer's hat and tells him that the page, dressed as a girl,
has not left the palace. And the countess dictates a note
to her double, Susanna. The two voices interweave in
perfect harmony.'

'Like Isis and Nephtys, they are both one and two,'
Thamos concluded.

' "Write," the countess tells Susanna, "I take it all on
myself." Under the pine trees of a copse, a trap will be
set for the faithless Fellow Craft – not an ambush but
a love-knot, like those of the knotted cord symbolizing
the celestial powers. Anyway, we won't go into detail:
initiates will understand the rest! And the countess gives
Susanna a pin to seal the note, which she hides in her
bosom.'

'Anyone looking for a social message in your opera
will be intrigued,' Thamos smiled. 'A countess conniv-
ing with a chambermaid!'

'If the world would only realize that brotherhood and
sisterhood – a new word – were the only way to avoid
conflicts between castes, what progress would be made!'

'Well, there's no point dreaming,' warned Thamos,
'let's get back to the ritual.'

'Barberina, Cherubino dressed as a girl and the villagers give the countess, Rosina, roses as a sign of their
love. This little ceremony should have gone on in the
garden, between Sisters, but the First Overseer, Antonio
the gardener, recognizes the intruder, whips off his lady's

bonnet and puts the ritual hat on his head, exclaiming: "Ah, here is our officer!" '

'So, order is restored.'

'No it isn't, because the count thinks his power has been flouted and wants to punish Cherubino. Barberina interjects: "Your Excellency, Your Excellency, whenever you come to kiss me, you tell me: Barberina, if you loved me, I would give you what you desire." Ironically called "good master" by the First Overseer, the Fellow Craft bows. "I don't know what man or devil is turning everything against me," he groans. Seeing him at a loss, Figaro stupidly defies him and throws himself into the confusion. How can the Entered Apprentice dance with a sprained ankle after his fall? Now that he is initiated, he has lost his limp and is walking almost normally. But what if it was Cherubino who jumped and not Figaro? They probably both jumped, Figaro ventures, asserting, "I don't dispute what I don't know." '

'But aren't those drums they can hear in the distance? The wedding procession is coming, their argument breaks off, and it's now up to Wisdom to take over the ritual. The countess sits down on her throne with the count beside her. Rosina complains that she feels like ice, as though fearing death and the failure of the weddings, but the two couples, Figaro and Susanna, Bartolo and Marcellina, approach and pay homage to her.'

'Two girls bring the virginal veil, two others gloves and the bouquet. The couples come together, and the brides and grooms receive their ritual clothing. Bartolo leads Susanna to the count, and Figaro leads Marcellina to the countess. And the chorus sings the praises of a wise lord who has renounced intolerable rights in order to celebrate this double marriage.'

'The whole thing is all just appearance,' noted Thamos, 'because Wisdom's plan unfolds inexorably.'

'Susanna gives the count the famous note sealed with a pin and asks him to meet her in the garden. He pricks his finger, loses the pin, finds it again and sticks it in his sleeve. Feeling triumphant once more, he invites his subjects to a magnificent wedding reception. "I want everyone to know," he announces, "how I treat those I love." But the Fellow Craft has other ideas from Figaro and Susanna. If he can conquer her, won't that prevent this intolerable union?'

# 32

*Vienna, 11 December 1785*

Josef Anton did not much like being summoned by the emperor: was Josef II about to congratulate him or admonish him? For years, his secret service had been in abeyance, and the monarch could suppress it at a stroke of his pen and send the Count of Pergen back to his lands to live out a peaceful retirement.

'I have taken on board your reports and come to a decision,' the emperor declared. 'When the Empress Maria-Theresa died, there were only two hundred Freemasons in Vienna. Today, there are over a thousand. The lodges bring together aristocrats, public servants, merchants, artists, priests and even a few servants. This secret society has not stopped growing and threatens to lead to dangerous ways. I formally condemn mystic and occult tendencies and I am going to prohibit the practice of alchemy in the Austro-Hungarian states. Furthermore,

I intend to limit and control the development of the Rose-Cross. Their doctrine, with its mix of Christianity and dubious sciences, looks suspicious to me.'

Josef Anton could not believe his ears. The emperor had never taken such a clear position.

'As for Freemasonry,' Josef II went on, 'it cannot be allowed to expand anarchically. Here is the decree that provides for it.'

Josef Anton read the new law with glee:

*As, in a well governed state, there must be nothing without a degree of order, I consider it necessary to prescribe what follows:*

*The assemblies called Masonic meetings, whose secrets are unfamiliar to me and whose Mysteries I have never sought to understand, are penetrating right into our smallest villages. If they are left entirely to themselves and are subject to no kind of direction, these meetings could well lead to excesses that are harmful to religion, good order and behaviour. Above all, they may encourage their superiors, through fanatical allegiance, to deal unfairly with subjects who are not of the Order they profess; at best, they may give rise to pointless expenditure. There was a time in other countries when Freemasonry was prohibited and punished; their assemblies were disbanded because other people were not instructed in their secrets. Although I, too, am not party to them, it is enough to know that these*

*Christian Jacq*

*Freemasons' lodges have nevertheless made a real difference to poverty and have benefited education, for me to show them more clemency than has been shown them in other countries. So, although I do not know their regulations and activities, they will nevertheless be received under the protection and defence of the State, as long as they are a force for good. Consequently, their assemblies will be officially authorized. They must, however, comply with the following provisions:*

1. *In the capital of each regency, there will be no more than one Masonic lodge, or two at the most, and they shall be subject to the judge or* intendant de police, *who will be informed of the day and time at which the Brethren meet;*
2. *Lodges shall be prohibited in any other place than where the regency resides; informants against lodges established elsewhere will be encouraged;*
3. *Every three months, the lodge presidents shall be required to submit to the governor of the territory the list and names of each respective lodge;*
4. *Lodges directed in this fashion shall not be subject to any investigation or house searches; all others will be dissolved.*\*

\* Document quoted by Philippe A. Autexier, *La Lyre maçonne*, p. 42–43.

Josef Anton was jubilant. He could see that the emperor was not actually prohibiting Freemasonry, but he was none the less imposing enough strictures to reduce those idea-mongers to silence.

How would Ignaz von Born, Freemasonry's spiritual master, react to such an attack?

*Vienna, 12 December 1785*

Hoffmeister, Mozart's publisher, was not best pleased to see him again.

'Your talent is not in question, but I have the prosperity of my business to think of. In view of our recent misadventure, I am bound to be cautious.'

'I am not asking anything of you,' Wolfgang replied calmly. 'As promised, I am bringing you some music that I hope will cover your losses.'

'Ah . . . Er, what is this?'

'A very marketable piece: a sonata for violin and piano.'*

Written at speed but graceful and tender, the sonata ended with a popular, dance-like finale.

'You are a man of your word, Mr Mozart.'

'As a Freemason, I hold keeping a promise to be an essential virtue.'

*K481.

*Vienna, 15 December 1785*

A first degree meeting on 13 December passed off peaceably enough, but the banquet that followed the Brothers' concert at Crowned Hope Lodge on the 15th was troubled. Again, they had asked two basset horn virtuosi to come and play for them, and several musicians among the Brothers had made an effort. Paul Wranitzky had written two short symphonies and Stadler played pieces for wind, while Mozart played a piano concerto and an improvisation, and Adamberger sang his Cantata, *The Joy of the Mason*.

When the emperor's decree, for official publication on the 17th, was read out, the harmony was broken.

'Backs against the wall, all Freemasons!' exclaimed Anton Stadler. 'Josef II is demanding the immediate restructuring of our lodges.'

'Don't do anything too quickly,' Wranitzky advised. 'Intentions are often not followed by effects. There's no point worrying until the Grand Master of the Grand Lodge of Austria and our Venerable Brother Ignaz von Born have taken proper decisions about what to do.'

*Vienna, 17 December 1785*

Paul Wranitzky was wrong. The next day, at the request of the emperor, Prince Dietrichstein promulgated the Freemasons' Decree in accordance with the emperor's orders. They were to comply immediately and without discussion.

That evening, Wolfgang attended a Masters Degree meeting, where they examined the document that would reduce the number of lodges and profoundly alter Viennese Masonic life.

The main question was, should they obey or resist?

'The emperor has clearly been manipulated,' Thamos considered. 'We've had our suspicions about a shadowy creature sabotaging our work and plotting our downfall. The latest assault on our Brother, von Born, proves he is pernicious. But now the whole Order is under threat. Josef II is tolerating its existence on condition it dwindles and starves to death.'

'Then we must revolt and refuse to be beaten into submission!' declared a Master Mason.

'It's the ideal opportunity to close all the lodges and prohibit Freemasonry in Vienna once and for all!'

'Every Brother must shoulder his responsibilities.'

Wolfgang and Thamos ended the evening at the house of Ignaz von Born, who was suffering from chronic sciatica and a cold.

'The emperor will not retract,' he believed, 'and we will have to submit. Only two lodges will remain, the others will have to close. I was ordered to prepare this restructuring by the Grand Master and I'm closely involved.'

'In that case,' Wolfgang judged, 'all is not lost!'

# 33

*Vienna, 19 December 1785*

From now on, New Crowned Hope* and Truth† would be the only two lodges in Vienna to be officially recognized. Any other assembly of Masons was illegal and subject to police crackdowns.

A Fellow Craft meeting was held at Beneficence Lodge to discuss its future.

'We have no choice,' Venerable Otto von Gemmingen announced. 'We must bow to the emperor's directives.'

'The archives of our lodge have already been sealed,' the Secretary told them. 'In fact, Beneficence no longer exists.'

'All we can do is announce its dissolution,' the Orator declared mournfully.

---

*A merger of the Lodges Crowned Hope, Beneficence and Saint-Joseph.
† Truth Lodge brought together Brethren from the Lodges To True Union, Three Eagles, Palm Tree and Three Fires.

'If it's come to that,' said a young Master Mason, 'I'm leaving the Freemasons. I'd rather live an ideal in freedom and not under the yoke of a despot.'

'We should not react too hastily,' advised Otto von Gemmingen. 'It's up to us to use the new structure sensibly.'

'With respect, Venerable, the emperor surely won't stop there. This restructuring will be followed by annihilation.'

'I don't think so, my Brother. Josef II is not an inquisitor. He just wants to take charge of the movement of ideas and curb any dangerous ripples in society. If we continue on the road to Virtue, what have we to fear?'

'Everything, that's the point! The Freemasons will soon be considered dangerous individuals.'

When the heated debates died down, the Venerable decreed the official closure of Beneficence. Only twenty Brothers, among them Otto von Gemmingen and Mozart, were affiliated to New Crowned Hope. The others resigned.

'Who will be our Venerable?' Wolfgang asked.

'Baron Tobias von Gebler.'

The author of *Thamos, King of Egypt*, a Masonic subject that had been in his mind for years.

Saddened though he was to see so many Brothers leave the Order, Wolfgang took Thamos's advice and did not follow them.

Together with von Gemmingen and other members of the old Beneficence Lodge, who now subscribed to the new system, he attended the last meeting at True Union.

There, too, the archives had been closed and the debates were intense, but the outcome was the same: the lodge was dissolved and many Brethren left the Order.

There was one consolation, however: Ignaz von Born was to be the Venerable of Truth.

*Vienna, 20 December 1785*

For the first time since he had started gathering material on the Masons, Josef Anton drew back the curtains of his office.

A wintry sun cast its bleak light on Mozart's file, and he pored over the documents, memorizing certain details. The year was ending on a good note, because the emperor had personally dealt the Masonic Order a blow heavy enough to clip its wings severely.

What a miracle, after so much effort and so many setbacks! When, virtually single-handed, he had launched himself into this arduous crusade, Anton had never envisaged success so swift and sweeping.

Freemasonry was not yet prohibited, of course, but it had lost its room for manoeuvre. Only two lodges remained, and they contained such diverse elements that, sooner or later, they would start to flounder before ceasing to function at all. He would have to make sure there were spies among the Brethren.

According to Geytrand's latest report, more than half the Brothers had decided to leave the Order, and the lodges had been weakened by the number of resignations of leading personalities. Undermined from within and hemmed in on all sides, Freemasonry appeared condemned to extinction.

'Excellent news, my lord!' trumpeted Geytrand, with uncharacteristic nervousness. 'The Rosicrucians have just scuppered themselves.'

'What do you mean?'

'The leaders have ordered all assemblies, both big and small, to disband. It's a temporary measure but I am told by a reliable informant that their members will never hold another meeting in Vienna again. The emperor's decisions have put them to rout and no one wants to finish up in prison. So we can consider the capital shot of this occult movement. Allow me, my lord, to offer my congratulations.'

*Vienna, 23 December 1785*

*Esther*, an oratorio by Dittersdorf, was playing at the Burgtheater, in aid of the Musicians' Society. Between the two parts, Wolfgang played his new piano concerto[*] completed on the 16th. He would play it again at three subscription concerts for the enjoyment of a hundred and twenty spectators, allaying for the time being a momentary financial crisis.

---

[*] No. 22, in E flat major, K482.

As he prepared to play the opening Allegro, Wolfgang felt torn between conflicting feelings. He remembered the first anniversary of his initiation to the Freemasons and the three degrees of Entered Apprentice, Fellow Craft and Master Mason, through which he had risen so quickly, as he discovered a road without end. But how could he forget that True Union Lodge, once so powerful, had recently been dissolved and that the threat of the imperial decree hung over the work of Ignaz von Born, even while he remained, to all intents and purposes, Viennese Freemasonry's figurehead? Josef II must be trying to make him pay for his alchemical practices and force him to submit.

Ample, solemn and dramatic, the first movement of Wolfgang's Twenty-second Piano Concerto was reminiscent of *The Marriage of Figaro*. Echoes of previous themes suggested that he was looking back over his work, but he left the future open. Master of his art, Wolfgang stood back.

By giving a major role to the clarinets to satisfy his Brother Anton Stadler, Wolfgang emphasized the concerto's Masonic dimension. The serenity of the opening Allegro, symbolizing balance in the initiate's soul, was followed by a meditative Andante tinged with doubt, and even tragedy, that was nevertheless salutary if one was to remain vigilant and alert to the difficulties along the way. Then the pensive mood was lifted by the lively finish of the Finale.

# 34

*Vienna, 28 December 1785*

'So,' said Josef Haydn, 'there are only two lodges left in Vienna, and I have been automatically registered with Truth without anyone asking me my opinion! The emperor and Masonic administration both look unacceptably autocratic to me.'

'In the face of adversity,' Wolfgang asked him, 'isn't it better to fight with one's last energy?'

'There speaks the voice of youth and vigour, my dear Mozart! I've spent my life seeking a minimum of freedom. At my age, I had hoped to find perfect serenity in Freemasonry, and now this respectable Order is in turmoil! I have no desire to take part in a war in which the conqueror is already known.'

'You're not thinking of resigning?' Wolfgang asked, anxiously.

'I am exempt from the subscription fee, and I benefit

from permanent excuses because my house is so far away, but they are not sufficient reasons to continue to belong to a lodge I don't attend.'

'Wouldn't you rather give it some more thought?'

'No, Mozart. This story will come to a bad end and I intend to preserve my independence. You don't blame me, I hope?'

'Of course not! Many Brothers share your feelings about the situation and are leaving the Masons. Your decision changes nothing about our friendly relations.'

'I'm glad to hear it, Mozart, very glad.'


*Vienna, 2 January 1786*


While a revival of *The Abduction from the Seraglio* was taking place next day, Constanze was singing the countess's first aria from *The Marriage of Figaro*, to the great delight of her child and Star. She had learnt all the arias by heart and in that way participated in the composition of her husband's enlightened and near-perfect opera. Mozart's music provided an antidote to all weariness and despondency, erasing a hundred daily irritations and rejuvenating the soul.

Work with Da Ponte was going well. The abbé provided the words and Mozart adapted them to fit the music and the underlying theme of initiation, of which the librettist had not the first idea. He was immensely proud of his poetry and focused exclusively on the brilliance of the language and the rhythm of the dialogue, and that suited the composer perfectly.

There was no disagreement between them. Da Ponte accepted the rules of the game Mozart set, and he appreciated his quick wits and extraordinary capacity for work. Never vague and always precise, the musician was the ideal manager.

*Vienna, 6 January 1786*

Josef Anton and Geytrand were taking stock of the situation.

Josef II's decree had caused huge ructions. The maximum number of Brothers per lodge was now 180 and the lodges were reduced to two. There were therefore no more than 360 Brothers duly on file and controlled.

'They have been resigning in droves,' Geytrand told Josef Anton. 'Some have left in disgust, others are afraid of trouble. Freemasonry and its beautiful brotherhood has been spectacularly blown apart. You have brought off an astonishing feat, my lord. The emperor realized the danger and has taken the right decisions.'

'All the same, there are still two lodges and a number of subversive elements that nothing can intimidate. What does not kill the adversary makes him stronger, my good friend. Ignaz von Born is still the Freemasons' spiritual leader and he is not a man to retreat.'

'The revelation of his alchemical practices has

tarnished his reputation irrevocably: an occultist, a bad husband, a bad father . . . That pillar of respectability has been toppled. No one, however robust, can come out of a well-planned smear campaign unscathed. And then, von Born's power looks abusive. We should continue our underground work to destroy his reputation inside and outside the Freemasons.'

'There's still Mozart . . . Josef Haydn has resigned but not he.'

'Why does a mere musician bother you?'

'Because the emperor is protecting him. He is a Freemason and a disciple of von Born, but he is allowed to write *The Marriage of Figaro* and disseminate Masonic ideas through his operas!'

'He won't dare,' said Geytrand. 'He'll just produce a nice little show, like *The Abduction from the Seraglio*.'

'I've read that show you're talking about, and it was already a call to freedom even before Mozart was initiated. *The Marriage of Figaro* will be the work of a Master Mason. How could it possibly be inoffensive, especially if it makes use of a provocative theme?'

His argument gave Geytrand pause.

'If Mozart commits a huge *faux pas*, he will be heckled by Viennese audiences and never be allowed to compose another opera.'

'If only!'

# The Brother of Fire

Tobias von Gebler, the reluctant Vice-Chancellor and Venerable of the new lodge, New Crowned Hope, had commissioned two settings of poems from Mozart, for the opening and closing of the inaugural meeting. There was nothing in the texts that might shock the Emperor.

The opening* advised the Brothers to overflow with transports of joy and songs of merriment because Josef II had again showered them with benevolence. The three-fold flame of Wisdom, Strength and Harmony shone in their breasts and hope remained intact.

And the chorus responded: 'Let us join our hearts and voices to sing this hymn to Josef, to the Father who has strengthened our union. Charity is the finest duty. He saw us practise it with passion and has crowned us with his loving hand.'

'We've just had our wings clipped,' Wolfgang remarked, 'and we're having to thank him!'

'You are not entirely wrong,' Thamos acknowledged, 'but we must play the game. The Brother tenor then pays tribute to our predecessors who taught us moral righteousness and fraternity. The second and last chorus then evokes our fervent aspiration to raise ourselves to their level.'

'I like the conclusion: "With threefold strength" – referring to the three degrees, Three Great Lights and the Three Great Pillars – "let us get down to the supreme

---

*K483.

187

business and cease this joyful song." In other words, let's stop praising the oppressor and get on with initiation!'

'As you show, a poem can be read in a number of ways, even an official eulogy.'

'The poem for the closure of the works is actually quite interesting,' Wolfgang admitted. 'The soloist thanks our "new masters" – namely Ignaz von Born and Tobias von Gebler – for their loyalty and asks them to keep us constantly proceeding along the path of virtue, rigour and respect for the Rules, so that each Brother may rejoice in the human chain, which links them to better beings and sweetens the cup of bitterness of our existence. Then it calls on our Masters to bear us up on wings of truth to the throne of Wisdom, so we can reach the sanctuary and prove ourselves worthy of the initiates' crown. True charity consists in ridding ourselves of all profane aspirations.'

'The choir of Brothers twice declares its basic commitment to our Venerables,' Thamos went on: 'By this holy oath, we, too, solemnly promise to work like you in constructing the great edifice.'

Building the temple . . . By contributing to the work through his music, Wolfgang was keeping the promise he had made. So, he set to work with his usual enthusiasm and the certainty that New Crowned Hope Lodge would at least have a fine birth.

# 35

*Vienna, 14 January 1786*

Wolfgang was looking forward to attending the inauguration of his new lodge that evening, where his latest pieces would be played at the opening and closing of the works.

Since getting up that morning, he had not felt at his best but had nevertheless been working on *Figaro*.

'Before I have lunch, a walk will do me good,' he told Constanze.

'Don't catch cold!'

'I won't be long.'

By the time he got back to his luxurious apartment, Wolfgang was racked by a violent headache and stomach ache. He could not eat and drank herb tea with honey.

Unable to leave his chair, he owned up to his malaise.

'There's no way I can attend the meeting,' he admitted miserably. 'Bring me something to write with, please.

I'm going to send a note to the Venerable to excuse myself.'

*Dear Brother, for an hour since I came home, I have been truly ill with a terrible headache and stomach pains. I was hoping to feel better but unfortunately the opposite is the case and I can see I am in no state to attend the first ceremony today. Please do your best, my dear Brother, to offer apologies on my behalf. No one is losing out more than I. I remain your very sincere Brother.*

*Vienna, 26 January 1786*

When he was back on his feet, Wolfgang took part in two Master Mason meetings, on 24 and 26 January. Given the circumstances, the Brothers of the Middle Chamber decided they should hold serious debates about the future of Viennese Freemasonry.

Each Master Mason freely aired his hopes and fears. The wealthy nobility urged total obedience to the emperor, who, from one day to the next, might close down the two surviving lodges. Confronting or criticizing him would lead to disaster.

Baron von Gemmingen voiced an opinion that was widely shared: Freemasonry could only hope to survive by being a low-key movement of ideas and offering permanent support for the sovereign's policies. Indulging in mystic and esoteric practices was strictly banned.

In future, the subject of lodge works would be submitted to the police and would not overstep the bounds of acceptability. Restricted freedom was better than no freedom at all.

Thirty-two-year-old Count August Clemens Hatzfeld, an amateur violinist, was sorry that authoritarianism had caused so many Brothers to resign. Would not the reduced numbers lead to the lodges drying up?

He and Mozart struck up a friendship.

'I admire your music,' the count declared. 'You know the human soul better than anyone and you take us to real wonderlands.'

'Initiation broadened my horizons! I should have been lost without it!'

'Why is such an ideal so violently opposed?' wondered Hatzfeld.

'People are scared of freedom,' Wolfgang opined. 'The world wants to be deceived, men love their chains and are loath to shoulder their responsibilities. They think it better to blame the powers that be and stage revolts that don't change anything.'

'Should one just resign oneself, then?'

'Absolutely not! Initiation requires us to change the way we look at things and makes our vision more intense. Then the blindfold falls.'

'Vigilance and Perseverance,' said Hatzfeld, thoughtfully. 'A whole life is not enough to put the extraordinary lessons learnt in the Chamber of Reflection into practice.'

'Each degree provides a new birth and a new life.'

When the debates recommenced, Venerable Tobias von Gebler invoked the weight of his sixty years. He had not been thrilled to be appointed head of New Crowned Hope, at the discreet request of the emperor. Most of the Master Masons had heeded the monarch's wishes and had voted for him to avoid provocation. But von Gebler was no longer interested in exercising any power whatsoever, and he stressed that only Ignaz von Born could guarantee the coherence of the Order.

No objection was raised by the Brothers, in spite of the rumour that was challenging the mineralogist's reputation.

*Vienna, 27 January 1786*

Baron Gottfried Van Swieten was thunderstruck. Of course, he was still the head of censorship and could continue to deflect trouble with the Freemasons, but he had had no inkling of the emperor's intentions and feared it spelt the worst for the Society.

Having concluded that there could be no secret service charged with spying on the Brethren, he now doubted his judgment. Knowing the Order only from the outside, the sovereign had obviously been swayed by one or more counsellors. One of them had managed to persuade him to adopt Draconian measures in order to quell the rise of Viennese Freemasonry.

Thamos advised Van Swieten to do everything in his power to find the creature of the shadows that was influencing Josef II; if he was unsuccessful at first, he should not be put off.

Then the Egyptian dressed himself in clothing the colour of stone walls and prowled around the precincts of New Crowned Hope, a good hour before the Brothers arrived.

He first spotted a police officer hidden in a doorway, shivering with cold. A second officer sat in a carriage, his eyes fixed on the lodge entrance. The pair of them were counting the Brothers going in.

Far more discreetly, another team was spying on Ignaz von Born's home. The laboratory, too, was attracting the attention of the police. Under the emperor's decree, the Freemasons were the subject of rigorous surveillance programmes.

The Egyptian would advise von Born to keep a normal calendar of meetings so as not to arouse the authorities' suspicions. They would have to take extra care to organize Master Mason meetings with total security and keep up sound relations with the research lodge in Prague.

Although the genius of the Great Magician was deployed writing *The Marriage of Figaro*, the future of initiation in Vienna looked extremely uncertain.

## 36

The Marriage of Figaro, *Act IV*

Wolfgang spent his thirtieth birthday working with
Thamos on the last part of his first great ritual opera,
where subtle games of Apprenticeship and Fellowship
were played out.

'Figaro now thinks he has won his battle with the
count,' Thamos recalled, 'and can celebrate his marriage
in peace. But his adversary's power remains intact. Eager
for conquest, the Fellow Craft is hoping to add Susanna
to his hunting trophies. He does not know that Wisdom,
in the double guise of the countess and Susanna, is working out her strategy.'

'I'll start the last act at dusk with the only aria in the
opera in a minor key,' Wolfgang declared. 'In a few bars,
Barberina tells us in annoyance that she has lost the pin
she used to seal a letter intended to trap the Fellow Craft.
She reveals to Figaro that she was supposed to give it

to the count from Susanna. And this "seal of the pine trees" will seal the young woman's consent to the lord's desire!'

'So, the tomb of fidelity lies under the pine trees,' remarked Thamos. 'And for adepts of the Royal Art, this pin will symbolize the acacia thorn associated with the lost word.'*

'Thinking that he has been betrayed, Figaro declares: "I am dead," as if identifying himself with Master Hiram. Marcellina remonstrates with the despairing Entered Apprentice, who is about to burn his boats: "Calm down, calm down. This business is serious and we need to think it over."'

'Like any Entered Apprentice at some point along the way,' Thamos said, 'Figaro is no longer listening. Instead of keeping quiet and watchful, he talks and thinks he knows everything.'

'Knowing that Susanna is innocent, Marcellina warns her that Figaro is on the rampage and planning to avenge all husbands! The Entered Apprentice's "mother" evokes happy marriages celebrated in nature: the union of the billy-goat and nanny-goat; the sheep and ram never fight; even savage animals leave their mates in peace and freedom. Only men treat women cruelly and treacherously, because the human male is a wicked oppressor. And Marcellina is absolutely right! As long as this world

---

* It was an acacia tree that revealed the location of Hiram's tomb to the Master Masons.

refuses to allow women the dignity of their own route to initiation, men's road will be incomplete.'

'Your *Figaro* will be the first leg of that long journey,' observed Thamos. 'I wonder if anyone will notice that the pastoral symbolism, here, comes from *The Zohar*, the main text of the Kabbalah? So, the nanny-goats are the disciples of the Master Mason responsible for instilling Wisdom in them.'

'Let's get back to our pretty Barberina. We find her in a bushy garden where there are two pavilions. Hearing someone coming, she murmurs: "I am dead!" and runs off stage-left towards the pavilion. Along comes Figaro dressed in a cloak, peering into the dark by the light of a lantern in his hand. He bumps into his father, Bartolo, Basilio and a group of workmen.'

'Just the place for the lodge Brethren to meet!'

'Catching sight of Barberina, the Entered Apprentice walks towards operations. He decides to show them what he is worth. He orders the "workers" not to go far and tells them to help him when he gives the signal . . . so now Figaro takes the role of the Master! Left alone, Basilio and Bartolo, Officers of the Lodge, examine Figaro's case, as happens at the elevation to a higher degree. But they cannot agree: Bartolo thinks Figaro is right to rebel, while Basilio considers that he is possessed and should put up with what plenty of other people have to go through. Rubbing shoulders with the high and mighty is always dangerous in this world – give them a hundred and they'll only ever give back ninety and win every time!'

'Basilio offers an important revelation about Masonic dress, which we don after shedding our profane clothes, thereby becoming Brethren on the path to knowledge,' Thamos continued. ' "In those days when reason mattered little," he explains, "I also had that fire, and I was a madman but I no longer am. With time and perils, Dame Patience arrived; she stopped me being whimsical and gullible. One day, she led me to a little hut and took down an ass's skin from the wall of that peaceful place. 'Take this, my dear son,' she said, and then she turned from me and vanished. I stared silently at her gift. The sky grew dark and there was a clap of thunder. Rain and hail started to hammer on the roof. I was fine in my shelter and I wrapped myself in the ass's skin. The storm abated, and I had just stepped outside when a horrible beast with a gaping maul reared up right in front of me, close enough to touch me. All my thoughts centred on escape. But the stench from my cloak so disgusted the beast, that he lost his appetite and turned away revolted, and slunk back into the forest. Thus, fate taught me that with an ass's skin, one can escape from shame, danger, dishonour and even death." '

'How better to suggest the significance of our initiate's apron?' Wolfgang commented. 'So many Brothers see it as nothing but an old-fashioned accessory!'

'The garden where the alchemical works go on till midnight is tended by the First Overseer, Antonio. He sees and knows everything, because he imbibes celestial dew, the secret of the garden.'

'And now Figaro launches into a great tirade against women who are unfaithful! "Everything is ready, it will soon be time," he declares. On this dismal night, Susanna is giving him a good deal of trouble. Trusting women is utter folly: they are goddesses and witches, but they are also thorny roses and comets so bright they blind men; their hearts are pitiless . . . and Figaro stops there, because everyone knows the rest!'

'Beaumarchais had this character declaim a political satire. In your case, you can highlight the Apprentice's mistakes by making him bark up the wrong tree and expose himself to the risk of never celebrating his marriage.'

'He hides, hoping to catch Susanna and the count in the act, but Marcellina tells Susanna that her fiancé is hiding and will be able to hear her even if it is too dark to see. Out loud and intelligibly, the countess announces that she is going to bed, after changing clothes with Susanna. Disguised as the countess, Susanna sings a hymn of pure love beyond human passions. Earth, sky, night and silence are allies. She calls to her beloved, without naming him, so that she may crown him with roses.'

'The Entered Apprentice will then gain access to the secret of his degree,' confirms Thamos, 'provided he recognizes Wisdom, whom he nearly lost for ever. Not knowing if he is asleep or awake, he is troubled by the arrival of Cherubino, who thinks he is looking at Susanna although it is really the countess. This intrusion of unfocused desire threatens to jeopardize everything and cause chaos.'

'The count, described as the "bird-catcher", is chasing after Susanna. Da Ponte can have some fun here, and write some snappy scenes full of misunderstandings. Cherubino wants to kiss the countess, whom he takes for Susanna, but Almaviva gets in the way and receives the kiss. Thinking that he is hitting Cherubino, he slaps Figaro. And the count, believing that he is courting Susanna, addresses his wife.'

'Suddenly,' Thamos suggested, 'the countess sees the flicker of torches. The flames dispel the darkness. The count tries to lead her over to one of the pavilions, and he tells her, "It's not to read that I want to go in there." '

'Figaro's intervention forces him to withdraw. Disguised as Susanna, the countess enters the pavilion. "All is quiet and peaceful," thinks our Entered Apprentice. "Beautiful Venus has entered. Like a modern Vulcan, I shall be able to catch her and her handsome Mars in my net . . ." And now he faces the countess and finds that her voice is . . . Susanna's! He then pretends to court Rosina and receives a series of delightful slaps from his fiancée to punish him for his infidelity. Now comes the real awakening of the Entered Apprentice. Truth is revealed: "Peace, my sweet treasure, peace, my tender love," sing Susanna and Figaro together.'

'Bewailing the fact that he has been disarmed, the count calls his people to him to tell them that the countess is cuckolding him with Figaro and that she deserves a fitting punishment.'

'How dare the Fellow Craft project his own betrayal on to Wisdom?' asked Wolfgang.

'Because he is driven by vanity, passion and desire for personal power. Brandishing torches, the initiates witness the Fellow Craft's revenge. Out of a pavilion come Cherubino, then Marcellina and finally Susanna, wearing the countess's clothes.'

'She begs his pardon, and they all kneel imploringly before him with her.'

' "No, no, don't hope!" says the Fellow Craft, pitilessly. Five times, according to the number of his degree, he refuses.'

'The countess comes out of the other pavilion and wants to kneel, too. But the count won't let her. "I hope that I shall obtain their pardon," she says. Stupefied, the count no longer knows what to believe. In that moment, he accomplishes the right action with the true nobility of an initiate, begging Wisdom to absolve him.'

' "I am gentler than you," she answers, "and I grant it to you." '

When Wolfgang played the melody for the culmination of the ritual, where the countess captured a moment of perfection, Thamos shivered. Reviving a theme sung by the bass in *Thamos, King of Egypt*, his opera of 1779, Mozart had touched on the sublime.

'I shall amplify the countess's declaration and develop a polyphony of five voices, the Fellow Craft's number,' added Wolfgang. 'And I'll use a chorus of ten people to exalt the number Five by doubling it and signify the end of the Apprenticeship and the fulfilment of the Companionship.'

'The desires have been purified,' noted Thamos, 'and true love transforms the Entered Apprentice into a Fellow Craft. The powers are now in their right place.'

'The ritual ends in harmony,' said Wolfgang, 'and the whole community celebrates this glorious moment: "Thus, we are all happy. Only love can end this day of torment, caprice and madness in joy and merriment. Husbands and wives and friends, dance and play, set off fireworks of joy and let us all run to celebrate, to the sound of a joyful march." '

'However,' Thamos concluded, 'this is only the first stage. In reality, the alchemical weddings have been announced but not celebrated. It is now up to the Fellow Craft to find the way in to the degree of Master Mason in an encounter with Fire.'

# 37

*Vienna, 28 January 1786*

At a first degree meeting, the Freemasons of New Crowned Hope had the privilege of hearing two new works by Brother Mozart: a march played by two basset horns and a bassoon,* and an adagio for five clarinets.† Among the performers was Anton Stadler, still working on the hitherto unexplored possibilities of the clarinet, especially in the lower registers.

Deep and contemplative, the two pieces were ideal for rituals and gave the initiates glimpses of previously hidden meanings. Mozart's music brought out the significance of every action performed in the lodge and every word spoken.

'How can we thank you?' Venerable von Gebler asked him, in a whisper.

*K410, in F major.
† K. 411, in B flat major.

'Please don't thank me! Every Brother must give his best, isn't that so?'

Tobias von Gebler looked very embarrassed.

'The emperor wishes our lodge, like Truth Lodge, to keep its work quiet. However, you are a public figure. Your music could displease both the sovereign and some of the Brothers, because you are starting to become too important. Evil rumour is spreading that our meetings are turning into concerts to your glory.'

'That is not what I intend!'

'You must keep a low profile, my Brother. The emperor can use any excuse to restrict our freedom. Ignaz von Born himself is no longer in a position of strength. Under the instructions from the powers that be, I must reduce our running costs and the part music plays. Please stop composing for the lodges.'

It was a severe blow, but Wolfgang would continue to pass down Masonic thought in his other works, starting with *The Marriage of Figaro* but also including his instrumental music.

'Why do people want to stifle us like this, Venerable Master?'

'Officially, it's a drive to promote austerity, which the emperor sees as the supreme virtue. And music makes our assemblies too attractive.'

*Vienna, 30 January 1786*

'Venerable von Born and von Gebler are applying the emperor's instructions to the letter,' Geytrand told Josef Anton. 'It looks as though von Gebler has been beaten into submission.'

'What about von Born?'

'No move out of place and no stormy declaration. That business with his alchemy laboratory has broken his spirit.'

'This victory looks too good to be true. Have you got hold of any information about secret meetings?'

'I'm afraid not.'

'But I feel sure they are taking place. What has observation of von Born brought to light?'

'Nothing exciting. He leads a life of discipline and entertains very little. His timetable is limited to scientific work and his Masonic activities.'

'Are his spies constantly vigilant?'

'I don't have qualified staff, so, of course, there are a few gaps . . .' Geytrand admitted.

'Then von Born is exploiting them! Given how he has been targeted, he is bound to have stepped up precautions. Neither he nor Mozart has yet fallen into disgrace. The emperor has even commissioned the composer to write a little piece to be put on at the Schönbrunn! The Freemasons are still influential, Geytrand, and these two lodges will be difficult bastions to destroy.'

# The Brother of Fire

Wolfgang had gone back to his composition lessons with Attwood, his English pupil, and soon produced a short one-act *Singspiel, The Impresario.*[*]

Aloysia Lange, Caterina Cavalieri and the tenor and Freemason Adamberger performed on the play's opening night at the Orangery in the Schönbrunn Palace, in the presence of Josef II and guests of honour who included his brother-in-law, Albert, Duke of Saxony-Teschen, governor-general of the Austrian Low Countries, and his wife, the Archduchess Maria-Christina.

Wolfgang was glad to pocket the sum of 50 ducats, half the amount paid to Salieri for his production *First Music and then the Words*, which came after Mozart's vigorous satire on the artistic world.

The plot involved a hapless impresario, charged with putting on a show in a culturally backward city (Salzburg, obviously), and who had to make an awkward choice between two prima donnas, each as vain and excitable as the other. Frau Herz – Mrs Heart – queen of sopranos, sang a languorous aria and was answered by her rival, Fräulein Silberklang – Miss Silver-voice – in a lively rondo. In vain, the tenor Vogelsang – Mr Birdsong – tried to soothe the two enemies. Instead of placating them, he set off a jerky trio, full of nervous energy. The

*[*] Der Schauspieldirektor*, K486.

impresario managed to restore a kind of harmony in a final showdown that was sardonic rather than joyful.

The piece was variously enjoyed, and some of the courtiers were quick to mutter that Mozart was using a rather trivial fable to criticize the emperor and his court. They had not expected the amiable composer to poke fun in this way.

However, no prohibition was announced and, on the 11th and 18th, Mozart and Salieri's pieces were staged at the Kärntnertor Theatre. Even some Freemasons considered their Brother's sketch ambiguous and likely to sully his reputation.

Not least among those to relish the criticisms was the Archbishop of Salzburg. Why was the emperor commissioning music from a notorious Freemason? The monarch should learn his lesson from this incident!

# 38

*Vienna, 19 February 1786*

In the grand ballroom of La Redoute, respectable Viennese society liked to don fancy dress and enjoy unbridled fun at masked balls. One of these involved a kind of feast of fools and included among the revellers Anton Stadler and Mozart, the latter disguised as an Indian philosopher.

He was handing out pages on which were written riddles and wise words attributed to the sage Zoroaster,* born in the sixth century BC. One of the clues proved particularly popular: 'We are several sisters. Having us and losing us hurts. We live in a palace that could also be called a prison, since we are shut up in it to feed men. The oddest thing is that the door is often opened for us, both day and night, and that we never go out. What are we? Teeth!'

* The Venerable in *The Magic Flute* is called Sarastro.

Another riddle appealed to the Freemason Stadler: 'We live for man's pleasure. If he has to do without a single one of us, he is imperfect. What are we? The senses!'

Some of Zoroaster's writings conveyed more serious ideas: 'If you are poor and stupid, you should enter the Church. If you are rich and stupid, become a farmer. If you are a poor noble and stupid, do what you can to get bread. And if you a rich noble and stupid, do what you want, but, please, don't pretend you are a man of intelligence.' And Wolfgang insisted on an indisputable maxim: 'Being modest doesn't suit everyone, only great men.'

That night, imperial austerity was put aside, and everyone tried to believe that it was possible to have fun and forget the world's troubles and tomorrow's distress.

*Vienna, 3 March 1786*

At his second subscription concert, after a first concert on 24 February, Wolfgang gave the first performance of his new Piano Concerto in A major.* While he was finishing *The Marriage of Figaro*, the musician wanted to formulate his vision of initiation into the Great Mysteries.

Wisdom, Strength and Harmony were united in the concerto, and Thamos felt transported to Egypt and

* No. 23, K488.

relived the most intense moments of his own trajectory. Here, in Vienna, the Great Magician had succeeded in conveying the ineffable.

The serene first movement recalled the good times, when the initiates had built the temple and celebrated the old rites. Despite the seriousness of their project, life had seemed carefree, because the gods' words were in the stone they worked and in the formulae of knowledge. Every day, the right actions performed at the right moment gave them a sense of profound inner joy.

Then came the most extraordinary slow movement Mozart ever wrote. In a brooding Adagio in F sharp minor, he transcended nostalgia, sadness and despair, which the initiates confronted sooner or later, to offer genuine hope. Yes, the Light shone in the darkness and initiation dispelled the shadows. The music's incredible purity expressed celestial love, the love of intellectual creation beyond human turpitudes.

No living being could stay at such heights, however, and the final Rondo released energies that brought the initiate down to his earthly embodiment, yet he did not lose the memory of what he had experienced beyond the visible world.

Mozart was no longer just a genial composer; now, he was also a spiritual master whose words continued the work of the Great Architect of the Universe.

*Vienna, 13 March 1786*

Lessons with the Englishman, Attwood, a third subscription concert, and, that evening, a performance of *Idomeneo* given by a company of amateurs in the private theatre of a prince. Although he had only just put the finishing touches to *The Marriage of Figaro*, Wolfgang realized how far he had come, as he conducted this older opera, now with two new pieces inserted, the second of which included a violin part especially for his friend and Brother, Count Hatzfeld.

At the end of a successful evening, conversation turned to the event that was threatening to shake the empire: the war against the Turks.

'The emperor is right,' Hatzfeld considered. 'They want to invade Europe again and force conversion to Islam. Confrontation is the only possible answer.'

'They are awesome warriors,' remarked the prince, 'and our nobility could be decimated.'

'Is not the defence of freedom the most exalted of duties? In countries where Islam reigns supreme, freedom doesn't exist. Women are considered inferior beings that must be hidden under veils and stoned if they are unfaithful, polygamy is legal and slavery permitted. Josef II must fight off such barbarity.'

'And you, Mr Mozart, what do you think?' asked the nobleman.

'I share the opinions of my friend, Hatzfeld, and I shall fight, after my own fashion, by composing a war song that boasts our army's courage.'

'Soldiers are always sensitive to music. In the old days, Greek troops were intoxicated by musical chanting to make them forget their fear.'

'My contribution will be far more modest,' said Wolfgang, quickly, 'but I shall emphasize my commitment and my hope for victory.'

'At what price?' the prince asked, in alarm. 'We shall lose most young men who would have been tomorrow's elite. And then the enemy's massed ranks trouble me. Won't their sheer number be decisive?'

'We must on no account give up,' Hatzfeld said, decidedly. 'In the face of obscurantism, we must stand up for our values and defend them without yielding an inch of land.'

When he got home, Wolfgang hushed little Karl Thomas, who was teething.

'You look tired,' observed Constanze.

'Worried, mostly.'

'Are performances of *Figaro* to be banned?'

'No, I'm concerned about the war against the Turks.'

'Are they about to invade Vienna?'

'That's what they intend.'

'The emperor won't let them! Our army is the one of the best in Europe. God will sustain us and let us bring up our second child.'

'So, it's definite?'

'Absolutely definite, my dear. I am so happy to be pregnant again!'

# 39

*Vienna, 24 March 1786*

After accompanying his friend, the singer Josefa Duschek at her concert on the 14th at the Burgtheater, and giving his fourth subscription concert on the 17th, Wolfgang gave his first performance of his new piano concerto at the fifth concert.[*]

What an extraordinary contrast with the serenity of the previous one! Of course, there was the anguish of the war and the uncertainty about the staging of *The Marriage of Figaro*, still scheduled for early May, however. But what the Great Magician wanted to express went well beyond these passing troubles. This time, he touched on the tragic aspect of the Master Mason and the ordeals the candidate faced as he tried to get out of the destructive fire alive.

[*] No. 24, in C minor, K491.

The turbulent opening of the Allegro conveyed his struggle to find a way into the heart of the temple. Vigilance and Perseverance helped him overcome the obstacles without losing his initial enthusiasm. No assault could erode true youth, the youth of the spirit. The initiate parried the violent blows of fate with the strength of his endeavour. Neither ecstasy nor blessing, but a physical struggle with the dark.

This rough tussle of uncertain outcome was followed by the Larghetto, a slow, solemn march to the temple. Lost in the vastness of profane turmoil, the small voice of desire for initiation nevertheless made itself heard and, weak as it was, pierced the dark clouds. No, the tomb of Master Hiram was not lost for ever! Thanks to the ritual journey, the Brethren found the place of mystery where death was turned into life.

Then the final Allegretto erupted with wild elation, in affirmation of the pure, direct will that nothing could deflect. Such joy was not of this world.


*Vienna, 6 April 1786*


A few days after the official first and second degree meeting of 30 May, the Master Masons of New Crowned Hope assembled in the Middle Chamber to assess the situation. Only the star of Wisdom shone.

Gaunt, bowed and deathly pale, Venerable Tobias von Gebler did not hide his bitterness.

'My Brothers, we are being closely watched and have no more opportunity for growth. Our Order today is reduced to two lodges.'

'We are still celebrating our rituals and deepening them with our research,' Mozart reminded him. 'These are hostile times for us, but the future may be more clement.'

'I doubt it.'

The day before, Mozart had attended a secret meeting at the home of Countess Thun, together with Thamos, Ignaz von Born, Anton Stadler and Hatzfeld. Thanks to their study of *The Book of Thoth*, they were able to go back to the basics of Masonic initiation. Revivifying the Tradition in New Crowned Hope was a crucial mission.

'Our first duty is to obey the emperor to the letter,' declared Brother Angelo Soliman, 'and support the reforms he deems necessary. It is thanks to his protection that our Order has survived and not become mired in alchemy or the occult sciences.'

'Is that a criticism of our Venerable Brother Ignaz von Born?' snapped Wolfgang, indignantly.

'It is down to Josef II and no one else to establish the ground rules of our activities and set the bounds within which we must stay. Anyone who tries to ignore them in the name of so-called freedom would be stupid and a rebel.'

214

## The Brother of Fire

*Vienna, 7 April 1786*

'The Masters' meeting at New Crowned Hope was pretty heated,' Geytrand told Josef Anton. 'The Brothers divide into those who wholeheartedly condone the emperor's decisions and those who reject them.'

'Do you have the names of the protestors?'

'Of course, my lord. Angelo Soliman played devil's advocate precisely to trigger their reactions.'

'Is there a ringleader?'

'It has to be Ignaz von Born. In his absence, his first disciple stands in.'

'Mozart?'

'The same.'

'I've had my suspicions about that troublemaker for a while now! Fortunately, his latest works have not been so well received. He is stepping out of line and attracting more criticism.'

'But *The Marriage of Figaro* is set to go on,' Geytrand lamented.

'First, there is no guarantee of success, and secondly, Antonio Salieri is jealous of Mozart's talent and is plotting behind the scenes to nip it in the bud. That chap is clever, cunning and determined. Unbeknown to him, he is becoming one of our best allies. If he can ruin Mozart's career, that confounded Freemason will go back to his native Salzburg and have no more influence.'

'I shall spread as many rumours as possible,' Geytrand promised. 'Dissolute life, a string of mistresses backstage, tippling, profligacy . . . Many music-lovers will be shocked.'

'According to your last reports, Venerable Tobias von Gebler seems to be increasingly disillusioned.'

'He is permanently afraid of esoteric trends, Rose-Cross in disguise and underground Templars. Anything bordering on occultism makes him uneasy and he blames himself for not managing to root out the weeds. To be honest, he is looking for an excuse to resign and escape the weight of duties he is finding intolerable.'

'A new Masonic drama in view! We should rejoice.'

# 40

*Vienna, 7 April 1786*

In spite of Mozart's recent success at the Burgtheater, Thamos felt extremely unsettled. Gossips were spreading evil rumours about the musician, and his latest concertos were considered too deep and too difficult.

It was not really alarming, because the world of music was a hotbed of constant rumours, name-calling and slander. Antonio Salieri's activity in this vein, however, was both relentless and surprising.

Born on 18 August 1750, rich, famous and considered the official composer at the imperial court, he intended to dominate Viennese music single-handed, leaving other composers he deigned to protect nothing but a few crumbs.

But there was Mozart, who knew his own mind and was his own man. Not content giving concerts, he had dared to take on an opera. And now the librettist, Abbé

Da Ponte, who had a finger in every pie, was collaborating with him. As he also had the emperor's ear, he was unassailable.

Mozart, the little upstart, irritated Salieri profoundly, and he took a very dim view of the approaching opening night of *The Marriage of Figaro*, which he still hoped to scupper. For all he was a brilliant pianist, Mozart did not know how to compose Viennese operas. And the contentious subject he had picked, from a play that had been banned, would be bound to cause trouble.

There was criticism from the Freemasons, too. Some Brothers were disparaging of Mozart's originality and disapproved of his connections with Ignaz von Born, a dabbler in alchemy who riled believers and rationalists alike.

Thamos tried to stave off the attacks as best he could, but he was worried that the Great Magician would not have the strength to withstand them without losing his creative spontaneity.


*Salzburg, 12 April 1786*


While on tour in the city of Prince-Archbishop Colloredo, Josepha Duschek and her husband, Franz Xaver, a pianist, teacher and composer, called on Leopold Mozart. They found him aged and irascible.

'Wolfgang hasn't written to me for ages,' he grumbled. 'Is he really so busy?'

'It would be impossible to work harder!' Josefa assured him. 'He is teaching, giving a series of subscription concerts and about to finish his grand opera *The Marriage of Figaro*.'

'The synopsis is terribly complex and I doubt the Viennese will like it. Why did he choose such a difficult subject?'

'I have to tell you, Mr Mozart, that a small army of musicians led by Salieri is trying to undermine your son.'

'Oh . . . Will his opera be banned?'

'According to people in the emperor's circle, Josef II has no intention of vetoing it. But his reactions can be unpredictable.'

'Wolfgang isn't depressed by it all?'

'No, he is composing with his usual enthusiasm! We arc hoping that his *Figaro* will be a huge success and that he will visit us in Prague where his fame does nothing but grow.'

Leopold felt partially comforted. His initiation into the Masonic movement was now just a distant memory, and he had no inkling of his son's spiritual adventure, aware merely of his artistic and material success. But he felt that Wolfgang was spending an inordinate amount of time on this opera which had, after all, an uncertain future.

*Vienna, 15 April 1786*

'The mystical virus has infected our lodges,' Baron Tobias von Gebler declared to Mozart. 'Occultism has not been eradicated by the emperor's new regime. I didn't want to take on the job of Venerable and I wish I had never accepted it. It is impossible to do anything any more.'

'Freemasonry needs you.'

'No, my Brother. I am old and ill and demoralized. Of our seventy-two active Brothers, over a quarter will soon resign, and I have had to send a dozen Brother Servants packing because they cost too much. Worse still, we are getting no petitions for initiation. In the eyes of the great and good, Freemasonry has become suspect. My hands and feet are bound and I have no more physical strength to shoulder an unbearable burden: I am giving up and leaving the Order.'

Wolfgang felt that no argument would make the author of *Thamos, King of Egypt* retract his decision. Von Gebler's Masonic chapter was ending on a sad note.

*Vienna, 20 April 1786*

Salieri was livid. In spite of all his efforts and his generous bribes to courtiers to ruin Mozart's reputation, he could not stop *The Marriage of Figaro* going ahead, or programme in other operas that would defer the first night indefinitely.

Salieri was still relying on the unconditional support of Count Rosenberg, the Master of Shows. Although he had links with Freemasonry, Rosenberg hated Mozart and despised Da Ponte. If he intervened, *The Marriage of Figaro* might be cancelled once and for all.

*Vienna, 25 April 1786*

As the premiere approached, Wolfgang stepped up the pace at rehearsals. His excitement was infectious, and the singers and orchestra strove to master the difficulties of the score.

Wolfgang reassured the nervous and gave each performer the individual attention he needed but without giving ground. As they were rehearsing the hazardous finale to Act I, Lorenzo Da Ponte burst into the Burgtheater, in obvious distress.

'There's trouble brewing, I'm sure of it,' he announced. 'Rosenberg wants to see me urgently. You know he hates both of us, so it can't possibly be to congratulate me.'

'Stick firmly to your guns,' Wolfgang advised.

# 41

*Vienna, 25 April 1786*

Full of his own importance, the Master of Shows, Count Franz Xaver Rosenberg-Orsini, looked the Abbé Da Ponte up and down: the arrogant Venetian should be banished from court. Why had the emperor got involved with this sleazy, unctuous poet?

'I have read your libretto and consulted Mozart's score,' he declared laconically. 'Nothing shocks you, eh, Abbé?'

'Nothing.'

'In Vienna, we have laws.'

'I don't understand, my lord.'

'In the finale to Act III, Susanna slips the count a note . . . in a fandango, and the scene is accompanied by a ballet! Do you not know that, on the order of the emperor and following the prior recommendations of the great Antonio Salieri, it is illegal to include ballet in operas?'

'This one is very low-key and very short. I don't think it really breaks the law.'

'It breaks the law!'

'Couldn't we come to an agreement?'

'*That* is my agreement!'

The count grabbed the two guilty pages of Da Ponte's libretto and tore them into a thousand pieces.

'Be aware, Mr Poet, that I am all-powerful!'


*Vienna, 29 April 1786*

Mozart's first impulse was to strangle the Master of Shows. Then, consenting to listen to Da Ponte, who advised him not to ignite a destructive fire, he decided to act rather than *re*act, not least because, to everyone's astonishment, the emperor attended the dress rehearsal.

'This is most unusual,' fussed Da Ponte. 'He is checking that there is nothing shocking in either the libretto or the music. If we have put a foot wrong, *Figaro* will be banned!'

Dressed in a cocked hat with gold braid and a crimson pelisse, Wolfgang conducted his opera undaunted. Although there were minor imperfections, the overall performance was good and the musicians' reaction heart-warming: '*Bravo, maestro!*' they cried in Italian. '*Viva, grande Mozart!*'

None the less, when Josef II stood up and approached the quaking Da Ponte, the composer feared the worst.

'Why, at the end of Act III,' asked Josef II, 'do we see the count and Susanna gesticulating in that ridiculous manner?'

'Because Mozart and I had intended to insert a ballet, Your Majesty, and Count Rosenberg forbade it because he is all-powerful.'

'It is clearly indispensable: please put it back.'

*Vienna, 1 May 1786*

At last, the great evening had arrived: the opening night at the Burgtheater of the first Masonic opera by Mozart, the Master Mason, directing from his own pianoforte.

Da Ponte was reassured and pocketed 200 florins, the composer 400: a pittance given what the theatre hoped to make.

Most of the audience sat spellbound. Undemonstrative and precise, moving little and gesturing only when necessary, Mozart nevertheless produced such dazzling music that even Thamos was carried away by its magic.

However, in the first interval, Wolfgang gathered his singers together in concern.

'Some of you are making mistakes and are far less convincing than in rehearsal. I demand explanations.'

'Can I speak to you alone?' asked one of the performers.

Wolfgang drew him aside.

'Forgive me, maestro, but Salieri has offered me a handsome sum not to give my best. I feel terribly ashamed!'

'Speak to your colleagues who are in the same position and fulfil your duties properly. Then, let's forget all about it.'

The English woman, Nancy Storace, his Susanna, and Michael O'Kelly, his Don Curzio, did not let him down. Other singers, on the other hand, were more concerned about their careers and their fortunes than about the work of art.

Nevertheless, the magic won the day and Salieri's plot was foiled. All the performers did their best, right up to the sublime forgiveness that Wisdom, appearing as the countess, granted the count, embodying the Fellow Craft. And the apprenticeship of Figaro, future husband of Susanna, another aspect of Wisdom, was completed harmoniously.

Thamos was bowled over.

How could a mere mortal achieve such perfection? Not a single weak point, not a single fault in the design or production. Figaro was steadfast, the count was strong, Cherubino tender-hearted, Susanna witty and intelligent, the countess sublimely dignified and the ensembles majestic and powerful . . . Every aria, every duet and every chorus was enchanting and spoke straight to the simplest heart and the mind of every initiate.

Mozart had portrayed the road from Apprenticeship to Fellow Craft and unveiled the need for the alchemical marriage, still a long way from being accomplished.

*Vienna, 2 May 1786*

Although Mozart conducted the second performance of *Figaro* without incident, the principal Viennese critics shared the opinion of Roehliz and the court: here was an insignificant composer who, in ten years' time, would have been forgotten. Meanwhile, Count Karl Zinzendorf, an official chronicler of Viennese cultural life, noted in his diary: 'At seven o'clock in the evening, to the opera: *The Marriage of Figaro*. The work bored me.'

Mozart's fate looked sealed. By trying to rival the great composers who knew how to entertain the Viennese public, he was showing his limits; the work would be coolly received and soon withdrawn.

However, Antonio Salieri wore a long face.

'We may not have stopped this trifling work being performed,' commented Count Rosenberg, wryly, 'but we can congratulate ourselves that it has flopped. The critics have savaged Mozart and the public will follow suit.'

'I paid a good few scribblers handsomely,' Salieri reminded him.

'Why are you so upset?'

'Because I listened to *Figaro*. If he lives long enough, Mozart will reduce us all to penury. His music is so superb that it will show up the inferiority of other musicians.'

'Are you not the emperor's favourite?'

'My glory could well be confined to my lifetime. Mozart's, on the other hand . . .'

'Are you saying you like his music?' blustered the count.

'You do not understand. Either Mozart disappears, or else he will eclipse us all.'

'You surely don't intend to—'

'Let us hope Mozart goes from failure to failure, disappointment to disappointment, and that he gives up composing,' declared Salieri. 'If he fades out naturally and ends up as a third-rate performer, no one will need to intervene.'

# 42

*Vienna, 3 May 1786*

'Nothing is more important than your health, my darling,' Wolfgang said to his wife, clasping her tenderly in his arms.

'I am absolutely fine and so is our little boy! Were you pleased with last night's performance?'

'Musicians and singers were both excellent and the public was attentive. *Figaro*'s future is now assured.'

'Nothing shocked the emperor?'

'Nothing at all. Everything is in order, so I need have no more worries and I can let another conductor direct it. We have earned a long walk in Augarten Park.'

After long months of relentless work when Wolfgang had allowed himself no respite, Constanze was reunited with a once more kind, loving husband.

# The Brother of Fire

*Vienna, 4 May 1786*

'In spite of Tobias von Gebler's resignation,' Geytrand groaned, 'the Lodge To New Crowned Hope has not stopped recruiting new talent. It is running lectures for Freemasons and sympathizers to boost the Brethren's hopes and improve their training.'

'Mere internal flurry and much ado about nothing,' was Josef Anton's opinion. '*The Marriage of Figaro* concerns me a lot more.'

'It's not been a resounding success, the reviews are poor, and the emperor said he couldn't hear the singers because the orchestra was too loud.'

'Indeed, like most of the audience, he heard nothing at all! Now that Mozart is forbidden to compose for his lodge, he is using his music to spread the word of initiation. This opera is not like anything else. Do you know why, Geytrand?'

'I'm not that interested in music, my lord.'

'Then you should listen to Mozart's: it is an awesome weapon! His *Figaro* is not your average play but an artfully veiled ritual. I have detected dozens of significant details.'

'But the public doesn't know, so what difference will it make?'

'Magic doesn't work according to reason. How many Freemasons genuinely understand the rituals and symbols? All those analyses and exegeses . . . They lead nowhere. Mozart's genius lies, not in his ability to communicate with the Brothers or the uninitiated, but in his ability to tap into the very soul of the universe: he creates light-waves that can touch everyone and guide them to the Light of initiation. Nothing was ever more subversive or more dangerous.'

Geytrand would have liked to think that his master was mad; but he had been initiated before defecting, and he knew that Anton was not wrong.

*Vienna, 9 May 1786*

On 3 and 8 May, *The Marriage of Figaro* was performed again at the Burgtheater, under the baton of Josef Weigl, who had had to give several encores.

Antonio Salieri was on the verge of a nervous break-down and went to complain to the emperor.

'Your Majesty, this situation cannot go on! The very art of music is in peril.'

'How so?'

'Several parts of *Figaro* were played as an encore and the interruption to proceedings on stage was catastrophic. If this practice is tolerated, neither the composer nor the librettist or performers will be able to work properly.'

'What do you suggest?'

'An official ban on an appalling distraction!'

'I have heard you, Salieri.'

Mollified, the musician was sure he had dealt Mozart another blow. Future audiences would not be able to show their enthusiasm.

# The Brother of Fire

*Brunswick, 9 May 1786*

Duke Ferdinand of Brunswick, Grand Master of Strict Observance, sat slumped in a chair, watching the rain fall. His bones ached, he was feverish and anxieties played on his mind.

A Templar, a member of the Golden Rose-Cross and Illuminati and a Freemason, he no longer believed the Order had a future, although he was still its head. Why had he not listened to the unknown Superior, that Egyptian from the Orient, instead of organizing a hopeless Congress and putting his trust in that French mystic Willermoz?

Willermoz was never going to send him the rituals he had promised that were supposed to reactivate Freemasonry. Ferdinand of Brunswick had been fooled and had not been sufficiently on his guard, although Vigilance was a prime virtue recommended from the first steps on the pathway to initiation.

What remained of the splendour of the Templar Order that should have reigned throughout Europe? The lodges and Brethren were like rats leaving a sinking ship.

'Prince Charles of Hesse would like to see you,' his secretary informed him.

The Duke of Brunswick could not refuse his assistant, whose convictions were still intact.

'Grand Master, the future looks golden!'

'What makes you so optimistic, my Brother?'

'Because Christ in person has communicated the mystical virtue of the words uttered at the Last Supper. Our way is clear: we must return to our Christian origins, restore the secret Church of John and pass on Jesus' true teaching. Only Strict Observance can fulfil this mission.'

'It is in its death throes, Charles.'

'Only in appearance! Our unshakeable faith will rekindle the dying embers, and hundreds of lost Brothers will join us.'

'May God come to your aid.'

'Do you authorize me to act in your name?'

'Take over the management of the Order and save whatever can be salvaged. I need to rest.'

*Vienna, 24 May 1786*

On 10 May, a new production of *The Abduction from the Seraglio* opened at the Kärntnertor Theatre, and on the 24th, the Burgtheater put on *The Marriage of Figaro*. Mozart's renown appeared unaffected by the calumnies of Antonio Salieri and his friends. The opera had been coolly received and the critics were hostile, but the opera ran, nevertheless.

During a secret meeting at the home of Countess Thun, the countess thanked the composer fulsomely.

'Your female characters are a splendid expression of Wisdom. You have given the countess and Susanna leading roles and brought new life to women's initiation.

This is a decisive step towards an essential revival if our world is not to deteriorate further.'

'There is still so much to do!'

'You have placed Countess Rosina at the crux of the ritual and changed the way it is conceived. This vision will profoundly transform the sensitivities of initiates, now and in the future. At last, we have grounds for genuine hope! When the countess sings and grants her pardon, wisdom turns into love.'

# 43

*Vienna, 3 June 1786*

Thamos told Wolfgang that, after ten months of investigations into the Marie-Antoinette Necklace Affair, Cagliostro had been acquitted and banished from French territory and that he had set sail for England where he would establish his rite, with its mixture of Freemasonry, magic and occultism.

Cagliostro was not, however, the spiritual master of the kingdom of France, and the royal couple, although innocent of the accusations held against them, had come out of the scandal considerably weakened. The people hated the Austrian queen, seeing her as spendthrift and frivolous. She led an opulent life and despised the poor.

Wolfgang was completing the first piece he had composed since *The Marriage of Figaro*, an intimate and meditative piano quartet* that betrayed a calm seri-

*K493.

ousness and, here and there, the influence of Johann Sebastian Bach. The slow movement suggested a contemplation of the Mysteries, specifically, the ritual scene at the opening of the works, when the Venerable, two Overseers and the Master of Ceremonies lit candles and unveiled the stars.

Then Wolfgang wrote a rondo* for solo piano, a piece both ethereal and severe. The soul aspired to heaven but earthly reality reminded it that there were still many battles to be fought.

He, Brother Mozart, Master Mason, would remain steadfast.

*Vienna, 22 June 1786*

Because of Tobias von Gebler's resignation and the cancellation of the midsummer St John festivities that year, the mood at the first degree meeting at New Crowned Hope Lodge was grim.

'Let us celebrate the festival anyway,' Mozart suggested. 'It is part of our ancestral tradition.'

'We cannot possibly defy the emperor,' replied an old count. 'Restraint is the condition of our survival.'

'Given that our numbers are dwindling and that we are no longer initiating anyone, don't you think this survival is somewhat illusory?' asked a Fellow Craft, anxiously.

---

* K494, which formed the finale to Sonata K533 in 1788.

'I am not denying how serious the situation is,' acknowledged Wolfgang, 'but we must keep to the path to initiation. As soon as the temple door is hermetically sealed and our metals are purified, we hear the voice of the symbols and work on the brute stone, that mysterious primary matter that contains all our potential.'

Thamos revealed one of the lessons of *The Book of Thoth* relating to the cutting of blocks by initiated builders, then he reminded them of the importance of the pyramid. This primeval stone embodied divine love and allowed creative energy to circulate between heaven and earth.

That evening, the Brothers forgot the emperor, Vienna and the uncertainties of the future.

*Vienna, 30 July 1786*

The summer was blissful. Constanze, Karl Thomas and Star were in excellent health, and there were more performances at the Burgtheater of *The Marriage of Figaro* on the 4th and *The Abduction from the Seraglio* on the 21st. Salieri's attacks had done nothing to dampen the enthusiasm of Vienna audiences for a favourite musician, and Mozart speedily wrote a horn concerto* for Joseph Leutgeb, who sometimes tired of his job as a cheesemonger. Despite the throwaway

---

* K495.

nature of the piece, Wolfgang slipped in an allusion in the first theme to the joy of initiation, already celebrated in a cantata.

And because he was forbidden to write overtly Masonic compositions for his lodge, he used profane titles. Thus, five Divertimenti,* though not particularly diverting, included slow movements suitable for ritual marches. As for the twelve duets for two basset horns,† they were used at research meetings in the Jacquins' villa, attended by Thamos and a few other Master Masons who knew how to hold their tongues.

On the 8th, Wolfgang finished his first real piano trio. The result was a brilliant polyphony that showed his debt to Bach and Handel but also his ability to take the art of variation to new heights. Moments of gravity, however, recalled that Brother Mozart's thoughts were no longer those of a gallant virtuoso intent on seduction.

*Lyons, 30 July 1786*

For all he was imbued with the spirit of Christ and his own high moral purpose, the mystic Jean-Baptiste Willermoz liked the company of women. Some of his disciples were aghast at his propensity for enjoying the pleasures of the flesh, but the Superior of the Grand

* K439b.
† K487.

Profess had no intention of moderating his conduct at others' behest.

In theory, he obeyed no one but the 'unknown Agent', whose messages he alone understood. And on this particular day, his occult contact advised him to restructure the Masonic rituals of the first to fourth degrees and to tell the Duke of Brunswick, Grand Master of Strict Observance Lodge, of his decision.

The unknown Agent was a bit late because that had been one of the major objectives of the disastrous Congress at Wilhemsbad.

Willermoz felt a pang of remorse but was certainly not of a mind to do anything about it; all the same, he wrote to the duke to reassure him. The old man was, in any case, ill and despairing about the collapse of his Order.

In France, the situation remained febrile. The Affair of the Queen's Necklace had stirred up anti-royalist feeling even among the Freemasons. Fortunately, the unknown Agent and his interpreter would keep the Benevolent Knights of the Holy City on the road to Christ.


*Vienna, 8 August 1786*


The first hot, sunny days of August saw the birth of two pieces, in the Jacquins' shady garden. First, came a piano sonata for four hands* which explored the

---

* K497.

keyboard's full potential. With more than a nod at the heritage of J. S. Bach, the opening Adagio suggested the candidate's meditation before the temple door. Dark forces threatened to cast him back out into the profane world and had to be dominated. Wolfgang depicted with honesty the storms that every Brother faced on his quest for Enlightenment, which had never been definitively fulfilled.

Then, while he was playing skittles with his Brothers, the idea came to him for a trio scored for piano, clarinet and viola* and dedicated to the Jacquin family, especially Franziska. With this unusual combination of instruments, Wolfgang created a hymn to wonderful moments of true brotherhood untainted by anguish. Yet it was not mindless gaiety the trio captured but the happiness of maturity experienced in sweet and peaceful times.

Already, such times were vanishing, for Wolfgang had to think how to maintain properly his family, soon to be added to, with the arrival of a second child.

---

* K498, called *The Kegelstatt Trio*, which Mozart drafted while staying in the Jacquins' house before writing up the final version.

# 44

*Vienna, 8 August 1786*

Neither *The Abduction from the Seraglio* nor *The Marriage of Figaro* made enough money to cover the Mozarts' expensive lifestyle, so Wolfgang fell back on more composition lessons with his English pupil, Attwood, still just as fussy and untalented but unfailingly respectful.

A position at court? Antonio Salieri's hostility made it pointless to think about it. Wolfgang sent a detailed proposal to Joseph Maria Benedikt von Fürstenberg, Prince of Lichtenstein.

The mail brought a request to purchase four symphonies, five concerti and three pieces of chamber music. Eager to do as much work as possible, Wolfgang was disposed to meet the Prince's demands by composing symphonies, concerti and quartets in exchange for an annual salary that would allow him to compose in peace.

Peace . . . That was what the musician so much longed for, to be able to devote himself to Freemasonry and music and be free of material worries.

*Vienna, 15 August 1786*

'Personally,' Venerable Ignaz von Born told Mozart and Thamos, 'I cannot go on. I refuse to lower the level of Masonic work and I know that my schedule will be censured by the authorities. Truth Lodge can no longer function freely. What with Josef II and the archbishop's spies, and half-hearted or hypocritical Brothers, Masonic research is no longer practicable. The smear campaign against me has succeeded and a number of Master Masons now blame me for being a misguided occultist and a bad father. We have to face the facts: I am held in disrepute and my authority is no longer recognized. If I were to continue, the Church would be quick to accuse me of heresy and my condemnation would have repercussions for the entire Order.'

'Wouldn't the emperor defend you?' asked Mozart.

'Josef II is double-dealing. Liberalism prevents him closing Vienna's two remaining lodges, but he is hoping they will soon collapse.'

'You are unfortunately right,' agreed Thamos. 'Most Master Masons in Truth Lodge are ready to vote against you and replace you with a docile, subservient Venerable.'

'New Crowned Hope looks less corrupt. You, my Brother Wolfgang, must stay and fight. As for me, I am giving up all my Masonic offices and going underground. So that no one in our circle need worry, I am going to stop publishing the *Freemasons' Journal*. Continuing to use it as our mouthpiece is a danger to authors and lodges.'

Wolfgang was distraught.

'Spread your ideas through people's hearts, my Brother Master. Our Prague lodge will continue to function and you will take part. Why don't you compose a piece – a symphony, for instance – that would give you an excuse to visit?'

'Maybe the police will relax their surveillance of you,' said Thamos, hopefully. 'Once you no longer have a position, you will cease to be a threat to the regime. All the same, we must be on our guard and meet in the house of Countess Thun, because the authorities don't know her real role. We shall form a secret lodge, the way people used to do in former times.'

'The emperor wants Freemasonry to be completely controlled,' said von Born. 'If it loses its initiatory dimension, it will be nothing but an assembly of sanctimonious intellectuals in his service.'

'How can we fight against that?' asked Wolfgang.

'First, by being lucid. Then, by gathering around you a few Brothers stalwart enough to withstand the pressures from within and without. Whatever you do, don't stop celebrating the rituals: communing with the symbols will give you the necessary strength. And you will touch base at the secret meetings. Don't forget, my door is always open to you.'

'Your departure,' remarked Thamos, 'will affect Viennese Freemasonry for a long time to come. It is no bad thing if it looks directionless to the profane world and in danger of extinction. That is why I shall advise the Secretary not to announce all the dates of the meetings.'

'Become the secret Venerable of the lodge,' Ignaz von Born advised Wolfgang. 'Don't worry about the title: all that matters is what you do.'

'Am I capable of it?'

'Your Brothers will recognize you as such.'

'Now, more than ever, we need to pass on the message,' added Thamos. 'Your work will allow Egyptian initiation to survive and embellish the message of initiation. *The Marriage of Figaro* was the first stage. Your task now is to remain an esteemed and recognized composer so that you can stage a new opera.'

It sounded an immense undertaking.

There was the issue of accepting the calling to initiation in a hostile environment with added, unofficial responsibilities but without attracting attention; and then there was the need to remain a public figure and avoid being devoured by the outside world or falling foul of the emperor. And aside from so many ordeals and difficulties, the need to compose!

'I knew the path would not be easy,' Wolfgang confessed, 'but I did not think it would be this hard!'

'I share your concern,' Thamos sympathized. 'I was so happy in my monastery in Upper Egypt under the direction of the Abbot Hermes. I had almost forgotten how close evil and chaos are and that they were constantly hammering at the magic wall that sheltered us. When he asked me to leave that wonderful realm and go in search of the Great Magician, I thought my life forever after would be one long nightmare. And then, I discovered you and, with the conscious and unconscious help of a few Brothers, I led you to the temple door. Hermes the Priest has left this earth, but from the Eternal Orient, he communicates the Secret Fire to us without which no great work would be accomplished. Embattled on all fronts, Venerable von Born is now leaving official Freemasonry. We are losing a guide and a leader who could have advanced the Order and played a part in the harmonious development of the society. The forces of destruction will remove all obstacles to their progress. Let us change tack and strive, now, to nourish the spirit of initiation, for it is vital in encouraging love of Enlightenment. Your duty is vast, my Brother Wolfgang, because you alone are a genuine creator capable of achieving this goal.'

# 45

Neither Josef Anton nor Geytrand could bear the heat and light of summer. The curtains were drawn and the Count of Pergen's office remained in darkness.

'Ignaz von Born has laid down his arms,' Geytrand announced, with a smirk.

'Has he . . . resigned?'

'Better still, he is leaving his lodge and Freemasonry. Our main opponent is floored. We won't be hearing any more about him. Allow me to congratulate you, my lord, for this decisive victory.'

'Don't count your chickens! How can a Freemason of his standing stop practising initiation?'

'Our slander campaign and an insiders' plot have ruined von Born. He no longer enjoys general esteem and he has decided that he would not manage to turn the Grand Lodge of Austria into a major institution and a spiritual centre. Given Josef II's attitude, the lodges are condemned to rein themselves in and recruit only innocuous characters. I understand von Born's disappointment and despair: the grand temple he was hoping to build has been reduced to a pile of rubble! Our long and patient work has borne fruit.'

'You will receive a bonus, Geytrand, but I am still sceptical. I cannot believe von Born will give up all Masonic activity.'

'He will shut himself up in his alchemy laboratory and go mad researching the Great Work.'

'I am convinced he will start up a secret lodge. If he has gone into hiding, he will be more cautious than ever and difficult to keep tabs on!'

'We have issued such violent blows that he will not get over them. And his health is waning.'

'Has Mozart resigned, too?'

'Not to my knowledge.'

'Ignaz von Born outside Freemasonry, in touch with alchemists and members of the Rose-Cross, while his main disciple is inside! Von Born will continue to instruct Mozart, who will act in his place and carry out his commands: that is their plan. The war is not yet over, my good Geytrand. These Freemasons have another trick in their hat.'

That same evening, Josef Anton heard that Frederick II of Prussia had died. Europe held its breath, as it wondered what direction the realm would take; she was equipped with a powerful army.

*Vienna, 23 August 1786*

Wolfgang was struggling to get over Ignaz von Born's decision and the terrible consequences it involved, and he had composed nothing but the Allegro for a piano sonata for four hands,* which he never completed. Then he poured out his distress in a brooding, ironic string quartet,† taut and almost tuneless. The opening Allegretto was all tension, the Menuetto troublingly heavy, the interminable Adagio was plangent and sorrowful, while the final Allegro expressed the irritation of a caged beast. There was not much chance that Hoffmeister would make his fortune publishing this cry from a tortured soul!

'A cousin to Salzburg is asking to see you,' Constanze told him, concerned to see her husband on the verge of depression.

'Who is he?'

'Gilowsky, a doctor. Maybe he can help you.'

'Show him up.'

The practitioner congratulated Mozart exuberantly, as though he were his oldest friend.

'Salzburg was sorry to lose you, my dear Wolfgang, and it congratulates you on your success. You have become its most famous child.'

'Why did you want to see me?'

---

* K357.
† K499.

'You earn your keep admirably and probably don't realize that a poor soul like myself, devoted as I am to working with the sick, struggles to make a living. I am going through a difficult time and wondered if you might lend me a little money . . . Maybe a hundred florins. You would be helping me in my hour of need, although your purse would barely notice the difference!'

Wolfgang yielded. Gilowsky was not the first to borrow money from him, and he would not be the last never to repay him.

*Rouen, 26 August 1786*

'Welcome, my Brother.' Thamos was greeted by the Superior of the Scottish Templars, charged with establishing a new Grand Chapter in France. 'You come from the Orient, we from Heredom, the mountain beneath which the first Masonic Lodge was formed, well before the English Grand Lodge of 1717. Now, they claim to be its leaders. Heredom is also the name of the heirs responsible for receiving the message of the last Templars to take refuge in Kilwinning, a small town in the county of Ayr.'

'So you do not recognize Strict Obervance?'

'Superfluous! An Unknown Superior is bound to be conquered by our rite.'

Always sensitive to the slightest enthusiasm for initiation, Thamos hoped that the new structure might instil hope.

When he understood the principles, he was less keen.

The corner stone was called Jesus Christ, the son of God, in whom the Freemasons placed their faith. The system of high degrees would therefore be chivalric and Christian, the same as Strict Observance and Willermoz's system.

*Vienna, 30 September 1786*

On 28 August and again on 22 and 23 September, there were more performances of *The Marriage of Figaro* at the Burgtheater. Although not rapturously received, the opera continued to please a section of the Viennese public. Wolfgang had bounced back and composed twelve pretty and relaxed variations,* which Hoffmeister included in his *Notebooks for Piano*.

Above all, in return for 119 florins, he had sent the Prince of Fürstenberg six commissioned pieces, namely three symphonies† and three Concerti.‡ Unfortunately, the worthy nobleman did not appreciate chamber music and did not want annual, regular deliveries.

That door was closing. Wolfgang was not gaining the financial peace of mind he so much wanted and had to go back to toiling over teaching that bored him and concerts where he had to charm his audience.

*K500.
† K319, 338 and 425.
‡ K451, 459 and 488.

*Vienna, 18 October 1786*

It was cold and snow was falling. Winter had come early, but Wolfgang hardly noticed. All his thoughts were focused on Constanze, who was giving birth after a tranquil pregnancy.

'It's a boy,' announced the midwife. 'Mother and child are doing well.'

Wolfgang happily cradled Johann Thomas Leopold, whose godfather would be Brother Johann Thomas Trattner, publisher, printer and bookshop owner, just as he had been for Karl Thomas, now nearly two years old and thrilled to have a baby brother.

Star greeted the happy event with a cascade of trills, although they failed to suggest the theme of a concerto to the musician.

Constanze was radiant.

'You didn't suffer too much, my darling?'

'Our little man was so keen to come into the world and make his parents happy! The pain is forgotten and all that remains is happiness.'

# 46

*Vienna, 30 October 1786*

'Our Brother, Venerable Tobias von Gebler, is dead,' Ignaz von Born announced to the few Master Masons gathered secretly in the house of Countess Thun. The countess had turned one of her drawing rooms into a temple. 'I suggest we celebrate a memorial meeting for him and pray that he is received into the Eternal Orient.'

Wolfgang felt deeply sorry.

Tobias von Gebler, the librettist of *Thamos, King of Egypt* and his first conscious contact with the world of initiation. The opera had not ceased to haunt him, and in composing countless other works along the way, he sensed that he was gradually moving towards it, so that he could give the subject the full scope it deserved.

With the death of von Gebler, the dreams and illusions of his youth were fading. Now aged thirty, Wolfgang was a musician in full possession of his art, a grown man and a Master Mason charged with a difficult mission.

Torn between esoteric research and fashionable rationalism, between his attraction to the Egyptian Mysteries and his rejection of the traditional sciences, von Gebler had not been a great initiate and an excellent Venerable, but Wolfgang owed him his formative awakening.

At the banquet, Thamos told his Brothers about his pointless journey to Rouen and briefly outlined the contents of *The Letter to the French People* recently published by Cagliostro.

'The Great Cophta is foretelling the demolition of the Bastille, the end of *lettres de cachet* and random imprisonments, and the convocation of a States General. Nevertheless, he is preaching a quiet revolution involving patience and good sense.'

'Utopian or visionary?' asked Wolfgang.

'A bit of both. French society is in the grip of serious unrest and the Freemasons are divided. Some are keen to uphold traditional values, others are eager for major changes.'

'Even if it means blood and violence?'

'We have not yet come to that.'


*Vienna, 1 November 1786*


'Baron von Gebler has died,' Geytrand told Josef Anton.

'A detail. He had lost hope and had never been a

dangerous leader. Von Born, however, is still very much alive!'

'But deprived of all power.'

'I should like to be sure. For all he congratulates me on my work so far and wants me to go on spying quietly on the Freemasons, the emperor has ordered me to leave Ignaz von Born alone.'

Geytrand was indignant. 'What a regrettable mistake! You must continue your observation, find out how he spends his time and—'

'We cannot take that risk, Geytrand. If the official police find one of our men on von Born's trail, we shall be in serious trouble and our service will be disbanded. The good mineralogist has left the Freemasons and is concentrating on his beloved research. Josef II has given him his blessing.'

'The emperor is in error!'

'Of course, Geytrand, and that confounded alchemist is a fiendishly skilful negotiator. He is outside the Order, so he has freedom of movement.'


*Vienna, 9 November 1786*


The director of the Burgtheater looked put out.

'Organizing a concert this autumn is proving well-nigh impossible, Mr Mozart. We regularly put on your *Marriage of Figaro*, although it is hardly a favourite with the Viennese, and you must understand the demands of our schedule.'

'I shall play new pieces at a concert, including a concerto.'

'The last ones were a bit heavy-going, although there's no denying you are an excellent pianist. Believe me, I shall do my utmost to be agreeable to you.'

Antonio Salieri was waiting for the impresario in his office.

'Did Mozart set on you?'

'Of course not! He is a man of refinement and well brought up.'

'What a disappointment for him!'

'Indeed, he was not expecting me to refuse.'

'Thank you for your kind collaboration, dear friend. You shall be rewarded for it.'

Salieri rubbed his hands. *The Marriage of Figaro* would gradually sink into general indifference, and Mozart would never be played again at the Burgtheater. He would have to find more modest places, and his reputation would wear thin.


*Vienna, 10 November 1786*


'Salieri is seeing me off from the Burgtheater,' Wolfgang told Thamos. '*Figaro* will run for a bit longer as a supporting piece in the programme, but I can organize no more big concerts. I shall have to fall back on the Trattner Hall and subscription concerts.'

'I shall try to mount a counterattack,' the Egyptian promised. 'In the meantime, why don't you go over to England for a while?'

Wolfgang had always felt himself to be an 'Englishman at heart' and spoke the language of Shakespeare, one of his favourite authors, correctly, so he did not dismiss the idea, provided that the stay was brief and well organized.

But there was one major obstacle.

'I should like to send my two sons to my father. That way, Constanze can come with me and I shall be able to show her what a beautiful country England is.'

Having just finished an Andante with five variations for Piano Duet,* Wolfgang felt in need of a break. Composing *Figaro* and the recent Masonic upsets had taken their toll, and travel would bring him relaxation and the chance to work on future pieces.

So he wrote to his father, Brother Leopold, asking for his help.

*Vienna, 15 November 1786*

While Wolfgang was working on a piano trio,† a piece suffused with tranquillity and joy symbolizing the return of inner balance, fate struck a cruel blow.

*K501.
†K502.

In obvious distress, Constanze slowly entered her husband's study, where he was transcribing a majestic, serene melody that transcended all emotion.

'Our baby is dead,' she murmured.

'No, Constanze, no . . .'

'He had the most terrible convulsions. There was nothing anyone could do.'

Johann Thomas Leopold Mozart, third child of Wolfgang and Constanze, was buried on 17 November at the Saint-Marx cemetery. That same evening, there was a repeat performance of *The Marriage of Figaro*, but it was a different opera that won the special applause of the Viennese audience, a production by Martini.

Moreover, Wolfgang suddenly had to cope with being let down by his father, his ex-Brother, who wrote him a firm letter telling him that he refused to give his two sons board and lodging. What could his son have in mind, except, as he put it, to take advantage of the carnival season to go off on a jaunt to England? Leopold could not agree to such distractions.

Wolfgang was profoundly hurt by his attitude. How could a father be so cold-hearted? However, the musician put aside his resentment and chose to end the trio with only a hint of sadness. No cry, no revolt, just the dignity of a man accepting fate without collapsing.

Initiation and music helped him stifle grief so intense it might have led him to despair. But what did the troubles of his life matter compared with the Duty he had been entrusted with?

# 47

*Vienna, 5 December 1786*

In Trattner Hall, Wolfgang gave the second concert for Advent after a crowning success at the first, on 28 November. He played his new piano concerto,[*] hot off the press from the day before, while he worked day and night on a symphony, mindful of his future and a crucial trip to Prague for a meeting in a lodge that had escaped the control of the imperial police.

Constanze was getting over her grief and consoling little Karl Thomas, heartbroken not to see the baby any more. His mother explained that he had returned to the Good Lord and was playing with the angels.

Thamos was impressed by the assurance and majesty of the concerto's first movement. He recognized the Master Mason's evocation of the building of the temple,

[*] No. 25 in C major, K503.

257

at the opening of the works. The spirit guided the craftsman's hand and allowed him to perform his task to perfection: the living stones assembled themselves.

In the slow movement, the Egyptian could see his Brother's intentions: to celebrate one of those outstanding moments when the initiates lived in communion beyond time and space because the metals, ritually laid at the temple door, had been transmuted. Piano and orchestra comprised a peaceful brotherhood beyond the reach of external events. And the final Allegretto conveyed the sentence spoken at the closing of the works, when they had been duly accomplished: 'Everything is right and perfect.'

*Vienna, 12 December 1786*

At his third Advent concert in Trattner Hall, Mozart conducted the symphony he had finished on 6 December.*
And Thamos had good news for him.

'Your *Marriage of Figaro* has been warmly received in Prague. Audiences there are sorry that the Viennese are not more enthusiastic, and they are looking forward to your visit. To avoid arousing police suspicion, Truth and Union Lodge has declared its attachment to Christian morality and respect for religion, but it has refrained from questioning candidates about their thoughts on this

---

* K504, known as the 'Prague'.

or that dogma. We shall work in peace with Brothers who are loyal to von Born.'

'Do you think it will be possible to write a second ritual opera?'

'Isn't the symphony to become known as the "Prague" the introduction to it? How better to describe the degree of Fellow Craft, evoke its gravity, passion, desire to conquer and boundless energy but also the tragedy of the initiate, torn between the sacred and profane? Yes, my Brother, you are already preparing your second ritual opera. In Prague, you will find the way to do it.'

*Vienna, 25 December 1786*

After more performances of *The Marriage of Figaro* on the 18th, *The Abduction from the Seraglio* on the 19th and the last Advent concert in Trattner Hall on the same day, Wolfgang received two fine Christmas presents: first, a lively, intelligent little dog called Gaukerl, and then a letter from a 'society of serious connoisseurs and amateurs' who invited him to Prague to attend a performance of *Figaro*.

The musician smiled. The Brothers of Truth and Union were indeed great connoisseurs of Masonic symbolism!

'Are you pleased about this journey, my darling?'

'We could both do with it,' answered Constanze. 'Leaving Vienna and this apartment will do us the world of good. We need to shake off the shadow of death and regain our confidence in the future.'

*Vienna, 27 December 1786*

'Is your decision final?'

'Yes, Wolfgang,' replied the singer Nancy Storace. 'I am dying to go to England.'

'You gave supreme performances as Susanna in *Figaro* and I could have given you other roles.'

'I don't doubt it, but I am terribly homesick! O'Kelly and your pupil, Attwood, are also feeling it.'

'All my English friends are abandoning me! When are you thinking of leaving?'

'Late January, or some time in February, as soon as we are ready. You must come and visit . . . You would be fêted in London!'

'I have excellent memories of my stay there and I see England as a beacon to genuine freedom. I nearly went there not long ago, but fate decided otherwise.'

'You are working on another grand opera, are you not?'

'In the meantime, I shall give you a farewell present: a concert aria entitled "How could I forget you?" '*

He sat down at the piano and sang her an enchanting song, which Nancy Stoarce was keen to join in, before kissing on both cheeks this man who was so unfailingly generous.

She dared not admit that her husband, a violinist, beat her. The scandal had come to the knowledge of Josef II: he was demanding that the brute leave.

* *'Ch'io mi scordi di te'*, K505.

# The Brother of Fire

'Why did you want to see me urgently, Soliman?' Geytrand asked, in surprise.

'I have decided to leave Vienna.'

'Where are you thinking of going?'

'France. Society here is still too rigid. Things are happening over there. Men like me fit in better.'

'But you were totally accepted!'

'Let us say . . . tolerated. An African is always an African.'

'And the tutor of two princes!'

Angelo Soliman smiled ironically.

'That has allowed me to blacken Mozart's name and spread a hundred calumnies about him that will be distilled in high society: dangerous Freemason, poor husband, bad father, womanizer, alcoholic, squanderer, shallow musician, and that's just to start with! People adore gossip and are only too keen to believe it.'

'Why do you hate your Brother so much?'

'Because he has talent and I love mediocrity! When you hear his music, everyone else's sounds insipid and vacuous. In the lodge, even when he is silent, he takes up an enormous amount of space and puts the dignitaries in the shade. One day, they will get rid of him.'

'I shall miss you, Soliman.'

'You will find other informants.'

'If I gave you a rise, would you stay?'

261

'No, I can't bear this country any more. Your emperor is reactionary, in spite of his liberal reputation, and he will be swept away by the revolution from France.'

'The lodges are pinning their hopes on him, I suppose?'

'They are still too Christian! But a few Brothers, especially the Illuminati, are striving to open their eyes.'

'What do you know about possible secret meetings?'

'Nothing at all.'

'Could Mozart be an occult Venerable?'

'Frankly, that wouldn't surprise me.'

# 48

*Vienna, 8 January 1787*

At five in the morning, just before leaving for Prague, Wolfgang opened the commemorative notebook of his Brother and cousin by marriage, Franz Edmund Weber,* actor, musician and director. He wrote two lines: *Apply yourself, avoid laziness and never forget. Your cousin who loves you fondly*, and he signed off with an upside-down triangle, and three dots. Freemasons who read these words would see in it another symbol of two basic virtues of initiation: vigilance and perseverance.

Then he went to join his travelling companions, now more or less awake, starting with Anton Stadler, who was already seated in the carriage. Not wanting to subject little Karl Thomas to the rigours of the journey, Constanze had taken a nurse to look after him. Josef,

* Father of a few months to Carl Maria von Weber, the future composer.

Mozart's valet, was checking the baggage, and the dog, Gaukerl, capered about his master in delight at the prospect of adventure.

'I was dreaming of England,' Wolfgang admitted to Thamos, 'but we're off to Prague.'

'Important revelations await you there.'

'The subject of my second Masonic opera?'

'We shall discuss it in the lodge. You can't imagine how pleased our Prague Brothers will be to welcome us.'


*Prague, 11 January 1787*


The journey passed off peacefully, Gaukerl's behaviour was exemplary throughout, and at midday, the travellers arrived in Prague where they settled in at the Three Gold Lions Inn. Then Wolfgang, Constanze, Anton Stadler and Thamos were invited to dine with a local nobleman and enjoy an hour and a half's music.

After walking Gaukerl, whose satisfaction with the hostelry and food were obvious, Wolfgang began a letter to his mother-in-law, but was interrupted, at six o'clock, by Thamos, accompanied by the forty-two-year-old Josef Canal, a secret imperial counsellor.

'My Brother Mozart, let me introduce you to our Brother, the First Overseer at Truth and Union Lodge, responsible for instructing Fellow Crafts.'

The two Freemasons exchanged the brotherly greeting.

'It is a joy and an honour to welcome you to Prague,' said Count Canal, clearly moved. 'We have scheduled several working meetings, but tonight I have a surprise in store for you. We are going to Baron Bretfeld's weekly ball, and you will love the music you hear there.'

Wolfgang was indeed amazed.

He was too tired to dance or chat, claiming 'native stupidity', but was content to look on with satisfaction at all these people plainly enjoying themselves immensely as they twirled about him to music from his *Figaro*, arranged for formal dances and contredanses.

'Here,' Count Canal told him, 'people talk of nothing but *Figaro*. We play, breathe, sing and whistle *Figaro* and only go to the opera if it's *Figaro* and more *Figaro*!'

*Prague, 13 January 1787*

The day before, Count Thun had invited Mozart to stay and, better still, had placed at his disposal an excellent fortepiano, which was immediately put to use to accompany a witty trio.

That morning, at eleven o'clock, Father Karl Unger, head of the Clementium Library and Seminary, opened his premises to Mozart. They barely talked about religion, because although a cleric, Unger was the Second Overseer of Truth and Union Lodge, and he insisted on showing his Brother a number of symbolic and esoteric works that he intended to turn to advantage.

Then the two Freemasons lunched at the house of their Brother Count Canal in company with Thamos. The Prague contingent told Mozart how their workshop functioned and suggested a programme of meetings where they would celebrate rites that had been developed and studied, thanks to the Egyptian. Afterwards, they would study certain major aspects of each of the three degrees, such as ternary thought, the Art of Tracing and the myth of Master Hiram.

'Don't forget your journey has a musical objective,' Count Canal reminded Mozart. 'You have several public appearances with which to pacify the imperial police. Tonight, we shall attend a performance of an opera by Paisiello.'

Usually, Wolfgang listened attentively to other composers' works and memorized salient passages that might provide inspiration for his own pieces. But this chap Paisiello was so insipid and dull that he carried on talking to his neighbours to keep himself awake.

*Prague, 15 January 1787*

Wolfgang wrote a cryptic Masonic letter to his Brother Gottfried von Jacquin to tell him what he was doing in Prague. He expressed nostalgia for Vienna, and above all 'for the Jacquins' house', code for the secret meetings where they could work unobserved by the emperor or archbishop's spies.

The day before, Wolfgang had been glad to meet up with Ignaz von Born, venerated by the Brethren of Truth and Union Lodge. Under his direction, they strove to uncover the Mysteries of Osiris on which Masonic symbolism was based. When stripped of the parasites and rags it had been saddled with by deplorable aberrations, initiation was revealed in all its power.

There was an enormous amount of work to be done. Wolfgang was aware of the difficulties and dangers, but he had come to Prague precisely to find the forces he would need to accomplish his Task.

*Prague, 20 January 1787*

On the 17th, Wolfgang attended a splendid performance of *The Marriage of Figaro*, and on the 19th, he gave a concert at the main theatre. The programme included his Symphony in D Major[*] and three improvisations. During the last of these, an admirer cried out '*Figaro!*' Instantly, the pianist launched into a series of fiendishly difficult variations on the famous aria from the end of Act I, 'Little love-sick butterfly, you won't go strolling around the pretty girls day and night any more, disturbing their rest',[†] and the audience burst into rapturous applause.

[*]K504.
[†] '*Non più andrai*'.

The excitement that evening reached new heights, with the composer himself conducting *Figaro* by popular demand from an impassioned audience. What a joy and what a privilege it was to see Mozart in person directing his own masterpiece!

As he approached his thirty-first birthday, Wolfgang was at the peak of his glory and creative power. Refusing to let himself get carried away by this spectacular trip where everything seemed so easy, he made ready to face a stern ordeal.

An ordeal that would be revealed to him by Thamos at one of the Truth and Union Lodge meetings.

# 49

*Vienna, 1 February 1787*

Joseph Anton, Count of Pergen, should have relished so much excellent news.

To begin with, Leopold-Aloys Hoffmann, former Secretary to the defunct Beneficence Lodge, which had delayed Mozart's initiation by its dilatoriness and incompetence, was now engaged in pitched battle with the last Illuminati. He, Brother Sulpicius, was distributing anonymous hostile pamphlets, bent on ruining his friends' reputation once and for all.

Furthermore, Hoffmann, a professor of German literature and Venerable Otto von Gemmingen's secretary, could use his inside knowledge of Freemasonry to sell Geytrand first-hand news.

Then, the two ministers of the Golden Rose-Cross, which had been thoroughly established in Berlin, were enforcing a general *silanum*, which meant the total extinction of their Order.

Panicked and afraid of disgrace and its terrible consequences, they preferred to abandon ship and get back into line. Their adepts scattered and, with no further direction, gave up their practices or took refuge in lodges themselves under threat.

The Illuminati were in their death throes, the Rose-Cross was obliterated and Viennese Freemasonry reduced to a fraction of its former self and severely restricted. Really, Joseph Anton should have been delighted.

Yet, no sooner had Geytrand appeared, than he quizzed him mercilessly about his overriding obsession.

'Have you caught up with Mozart?'

'He is living in Prague where *The Marriage of Figaro* is a triumph.'

'Who invited him?'

'Local aristocracy and music-lovers.'

'You mean the Freemasons!'

'Not necessarily . . . Mozart is far more popular in Prague than in Vienna.'

'A smoke screen!' blustered Anton, digging out of his archives a thin file on Prague Freemasonry.

'We don't have much control over the local lodges,' Geytrand admitted, 'and my informants don't seem very committed.'

'We know that Truth and Union receive Illuminati and don't publish the dates of their meetings. Why else, except because their activities are subversive? And Mozart can meet his Brothers away from prying eyes.'

'Don't you think you're attaching too much importance to him, my lord?'

'Von Born is working underground and training his disciple, Wolfgang Mozart, to take his place. The emperor appreciates his talent but doesn't see him as a leader of men and the Freemasons' mastermind. But I do! Look at him: he's a conductor with the power to make totally different, when not actually sparring, individuals play together! Mozart could be the Grand Master of an esoteric Freemasonry and a tireless militant. He's not interested in honours and recognition by the high and mighty. He's also a genuine creator capable of passing on initiation. Turn your attention to Prague, Geytrand. I want to know everything about what the lodges really get up to.'

*Prague, 6 Feburary 1787*

The magic visit was sadly drawing to a close. Apart from his musical success and such encouraging popular acclaim, Wolfgang had attended a number of useful meetings. He took away with him memories of research into the symbolism of the elements, especially Fire. The tradition of alchemy in Prague was still very much alive, and the composer now had a better vision of the various phases of the Great Work, expressed in the Masonic degrees.

But he had to return to Vienna where *The Abduction from the Seraglio* was playing that day, and Wolfgang rapidly composed four German dances for orchestra* to be played in the ballrooms of La Redoute.

After bidding the customary farewell to all the Freemasons of Truth and Union Lodge, he still had one last appointment to keep.

The impresario, Pasquale Bondini, was delighted to see him.

'Your *Marriage of Figaro* is a sensation, Mr Mozart. Not a person in Prague who isn't humming its arias! I want to make you a proposal: would you agree, in return for 1,000 florins, to compose a grand opera that we could put on this autumn?'

Wolfgang could barely contain his joy. But there was one issue he needed to settle.

'Do you already have a libretto?'

The director looked astonished.

'We wouldn't dictate the subject matter to a musician of your standing! Everyone knows you had considerable influence on the libretto for *Figaro*, even if it was officially by Da Ponte, an accomplished writer and in the emperor's favour. Of course, you are entirely free to choose your libretto and I shall not interfere in any way.'

Wolfgang could not believe his ears. Prague really was starting to look like Paradise.

'Do you accept my proposal, Mr Mozart?' Pasquale Bondini repeated, anxiously.

'The opera will be ready for October.'

*K509.

The impresario's face lit up in a broad smile.

'What a wonderful gift! The Prague audiences will look forward to it immensely when they find out.'

Constanze had finished packing and Wolfgang took Gaukerl for a walk. Thamos soon joined them.

'Are you happy with the terms our friend Bondini made you?'

'You are behind all this, of course!'

'Didn't I tell you Prague would be a decisive stage?'

'I am going to write the second ritual opera and take up my characters where I left off.'

'Figaro and Count Almaviva are now one: the Fellow Craft Freemason with all the powers of his degree. The time has now come to face his own destiny and become a Master Mason.'

'We need to find a really good story to convey the revelation of the mystery without giving it away.'

'Have you thought of one of Molière's plays?'

'I'm not so keen on his comedy. There is one play that caught my attention, and that's *Don Juan*. But it would have taken Shakespeare to deal fully with such a tormented figure!'

'Might that be your task?'

Wolfgang stopped in his tracks. Sensing that something momentous was about to happen, Gaukerl turned from one man to the other.

'Molière used a myth that had been rewritten by countless authors before him,' Thamos added, 'and Da

273

Ponte will have no qualms about mining those resources and, under your direction, putting his own spin on them. Choice of characters will be fundamental and it won't be easy to handle the matter of the ritual.'

'Don Juan's power, his desire for conquest, the Fellow Craft's adventure, his encounter with death . . . Do you think I have it in me to juggle all those elements?'

'Your Brothers think you do,' answered Thamos.

# 50

*Vienna, 12 February 1787*

Constanze, Wolfgang, Gaukerl and their servant Josef left Prague on the 8th, arriving in Vienna on the 12th, after a journey without incident, despite the rigours of winter.

Wolfgang joked and chatted, but all the while he was thinking of the difficult, almost agonizing subject of his next opera.

The first news to greet the composer was the death of his Brother, the violinist Hatzfeld, in Düsseldorf on 30 January.

'My best friend and a man of integrity,' he said to his wife. 'We hadn't known each other long, but our fraternal bonds had brought us very close. He was thirty-one, like me.'

Seeing how hard her husband was hit, Constanze brought Karl Thomas to him. The little boy threw himself about his father's neck.

Then, and only then, did Star, the starling, welcome home the Mozarts with a tune that even Gaukerl liked.

*Vienna, 20 February 1787*

In Vienna, there were only nine performances of *The Marriage of Figaro*; in Prague, the opera would be played continuously throughout the winter. More seriously, right in the middle of the music season, Wolfgang found himself unable to organize any subscription concerts, as though the public no longer wanted to hear him.

Trouble had struck just as he and Thamos were poised to tackle *Don Giovanni*, a project whose proportions sometimes filled him with dismay even while he felt irresistibly attracted to it. The more he thought about it, the more he realized that here was the ideal story for his second ritual opera, where, through the ordeals of the Fellow Craft and their alchemical meaning, several forms of death would play major roles.

Thanks to Constanze's excellent household management, there were no unnecessary outgoings. But the Mozarts had to live in a style befitting to their rank, and cover an enormous rent, settle the bills of doctors and pharmacists, and keep an open table for Brothers and musicians, who thought nothing of borrowing significant sums, afterwards forgetting to pay off their debts. For, lack of generosity would be a contemptible fault. It was up to Wolfgang to earn as much money as in the previous two years.

*Vienna, 21 February 1787*

'Mozart is in Vienna,' Geytrand announced to Josef Anton. 'He has come back with his wife and a few friends, including his Brother, the clarinettist Anton Stadler.'

'Any news about the Prague lodges?'

'Not yet, my lord. It's going to be a very difficult milieu to infiltrate. The Bohemians are suspicious of the Viennese and unwilling to open up. As I have no top-flight agent in Prague, I am treading cautiously.'

'Go to Prague and set up a proper network.'

'I'm not much of a traveller.'

'It's the only solution.'

Geytrand sulked.

'On my side,' said Josef Anton, brightening up suddenly, 'I have good news! I am dining today with Johann Baptist von Puthon, director of the National Bank of Vienna.'

'Is he about to increase the budget for our department?' asked Geytrand, sarcastically.

'On the emperor's recommendation, von Puthon has just been elected Venerable of Truth Lodge.'

At forty-three, the industrialist and wholesale merchant, von Puthon, knighted in 1773 and appointed Grand

Treasurer of the Grand Lodge of Austria in 1784, had amassed a tidy fortune and flattered himself that he had Josef II's confidence. Managing the National Bank amounted to controlling the empire's finances and maintaining its prosperity. Aware of his importance and mindful of his heavy responsibilities, Johann Baptist von Puthon could have done without taking on the fate of Viennese Freemasonry. Now that Tobias von Gebler and Ignaz von Born had gone, and so many other Brothers resigned, the Order had lost its good reputation.

'Thank you for answering my invitation, sir,' said Anton, politely.

'It is a pleasure to meet the President of Lower Austria, Count of Pergen. The court is proud of your administrative abilities and sound government. We know how the emperor appreciates people who are careful with money.'

'Like you, I make sure that his policies are enforced and the necessary reforms carried through. It will take more than the Turks, or countries in the grip of rioting hoodlums, to destabilize us.'

'Of that I am convinced! But we still need to keep up strict moral standards.'

'Doesn't Freemasonry actively contribute to that?'

'Of course, my lord!'

'But I understand that some Brothers are suspected of supporting the dangerous theories of the Illuminati while others indulge in occult practices?'

'There are black sheep in any group of people.'

'You must flush them out,' suggested Josef Anton.

'Indeed, that is what I intend. I can assure you that the restructuring of Freemasonry, which the emperor decreed, has had excellent results. The two last lodges, New Crowned Hope and Truth, follow the law and religion to the letter.'

'I do not think that goes for Brother Mozart.'

'The musician?'

'Von Born's favourite disciple, they say, who propagates illicit ideas, like those conveyed in *The Marriage of Figaro*.'

'Do you have specific accusations to make against him?'

'Not yet, and I hope it does not come to that. According to the Archbishop of Vienna, he is a slippery character to control. Let us hope he does not rise in the Masonic hierarchy; he could ruffle the calm waters of that Order.'

'I shall make sure he does not, my lord, for we insist that our leaders and dignitaries are above suspicion.'

'I did not doubt it, sir, and thank you for your vigilance.'

Von Puthon bitterly regretted his involvement in this affair. Von Pergen was clearly speaking for the emperor and the archbishop, and ordering him to keep further tabs on the Freemasons. The Masons had brought him influential contacts, but they were threatening to become a handicap.

How could the head of the National Bank extricate himself from this burden?

# 51

*Vienna, 23 February 1787*

This time, the English contingent was really returning to London. Attwood thanked Mozart fulsomely for
his composition lessons, and that evening, Wolfgang
accompanied Nancy Storace on the piano at her farewell
concert at the Kärntnertor Theatre.

'Come to England!' *Figaro*'s first Susanna enthused,
not for the first time. 'There, you will know what it
is to have real glory. They will sound your trumpets
even more loudly than in Prague. Remember the
careers of Handel and Johann Christian Bach! When
my country adopts a musician, she raises him to lofty
heights.'

'I have not given up on England, but I have lots of
commitments here and I should not want to neglect
them.'

'A project for a grand opera?'

'Prague offered me a thousand florins and left me free to choose the subject. Will you be passing through Salzburg?'

'Of course.'

'Can you deliver this letter to my father?'

'By all means, and I shall give him your news.'

Wolfgang described at length the death of his friend and Brother Hatzfeld, and his profound grief.

'I hope to see you soon in London.'

'If God wills, Nancy.'


*Salzburg, 26 February 1787*


Increasingly peevish and complaining of a variety of ills that the doctors were failing to cure, Leopold neverthe-less agreed to receive Wolfgang's English friends again.

'How is my son doing?'

'Never better,' Nancy Storace told him. 'He has come back from Prague and been given a handsome sum to compose a grand opera. He is considered a genius over there!'

'And my grandchildren, Karl Thomas and Leopold?'

The young English woman's face clouded.

'Karl Thomas is growing up into a fine little man, but you . . . you don't know?'

'What ought I to know?'

'The baby, Leopold: he died three months ago.'

For a long moment, Wolfgang's father said nothing. So, his son had not thought to tell him about such a tragic event, as though he no longer expected words of comfort from his father and Masonic Brother.

How had they come to this, after receiving the Light? Wolfgang's refusal to talk was a sign of deep disappointment, perhaps even tinged with despair. By no longer attending his lodge, Leopold, the Master Mason, had broken an essential bond with his son.

'Wolfgang gave me a letter to give to you,' Nancy Storace broke in.

'Oh . . .'

The singer searched for the letter everywhere.

'I'm sorry, I seem to have lost it.'

'It doesn't matter. Perhaps he will write again.'


*Vienna, 11 March 1787*


Breaking a three-month silence, sterile apart from a handful of German dances, Wolfgang composed a brief rondo for piano,* whose calm, serious mood reflected his ability to detach himself from the calls of everyday life.

It was an everyday life that was hostile, because despite his efforts, Wolfgang had not managed to organize any more concerts. In contrast, the Mozarts' overheads continued. Refusing to give in to pessimism, he went to see Lorenzo Da Ponte, still overwhelmed by work.

* K511, in A minor.

'A new project, Mozart?'

'Do you have time to work for me?'

'I shall find it! I know *The Marriage of Figaro* was hardly a dazzling success, but no one questions your talent. And Prague adores you, I hear.'

'Indeed, my new opera is intended for Prague.'

'What subject do you have in mind?'

'The story of Don Juan.'

'The seducer who dares to defy death and is dragged down to hell! Bertati's *Stone Guest* was put on in Venice this January to music by Gazzaniga. Not a masterpiece but a cheerful mix of comedy and tragedy. I can pick out some of the best bits, but our own version will be a lot better!'

'If I understand correctly, the theme inspires you?'

'A nobleman who conquers every woman he comes across and is interested in nothing but his own pleasure: what a fascinating figure!'

'He is just a libertine,' Wolfgang objected. 'A stone man comes back from the dead and invites him to a banquet where visible and invisible clash.'

'Tragedy, seduction, fantasy, mystery, a hero who both attracts and repels . . . I'm enjoying myself already! When does it need to be ready?'

'October.'

'I have several libretti to finish as a matter of urgency, but that should do.'

The prospect of working for Mozart delighted him, and adapting for stage the myth of the strange figure of Don Juan, already depicted so often by more or less reputable authors, struck him as a superb challenge.

'As soon as I can,' Wolfgang assured, 'I shall give you precise details.'

Da Ponte liked being guided in this way. At least, with Mozart, one would be kept on track.

# 52

*Vienna, 30 March 1787*

In the album of his lodge Brother, the language teacher
Johann Georg Kronauer, Wolfgang wrote down his
thoughts of the moment in English: *Patience and peace
of mind contribute more to cure our distempers than the
whole art of medicine.* He added: *Member of the Very
Respectable New Crowned Hope Lodge, in the Orient
of Vienna*, and he signed off with his signature of two
crossed triangles, symbolizing the necessary marriage of
heaven and earth.

On 1 April, he decided to start his own album to collect
the thoughts and signatures of his Brothers, starting
with those of the first Osmin in *The Abduction from the
Seraglio*, Fischer, for whom he had recently composed
two arias* sung at concerts on 18 and 23 March.

* K512 and 513.

Then, it was the turn of his Masonic Brother and impresario, Joseph von Bauernfeld.

'I hear rumours that a small theatre on the outskirts of Vienna is about to come on to the market,' he told the musician. 'By all accounts, it is not in too bad a state, and, if the price seems appropriate, I intend to buy it. Maybe it will be useful to us some day. Nothing to compare with the Burgtheater, but one shouldn't spurn the popular public.'

'I have total respect for it,' declared Wolfgang. 'In Prague, simple people who are neither critics nor musicologists sing arias from *Figaro* perfectly well. And I am not relying on specialists to make good music famous!'

*Vienna, 2 April 1787:* Don Giovanni, *Act I, Scene i*

'Da Ponte seems happy about our new collaboration,' Wolfgang told Thamos. 'He thinks the character of Don Giovanni can be reduced to a profligate intent on pleasure.'

'That's all we need ask of him. You can bring out the Strength of the Fellow Craft, a prey to the will for power and the desire for possession.'

'It is night-time,' said Wolfgang, 'and Don Giovanni's manservant, Leporello, dressed in a great coat, is pacing up and down in front of the magnificent palace of Donna Anna, daughter of the Commendatore.'

'The Commendatore is the opera's central character,' suggested Thamos. 'He embodies Hiram, the Master of Work. Donna Anna represents the Pillar of Wisdom which Don Giovanni, the Fellow Craft, wants to conquer by Strength in order to obtain the Master Mason's password.'

'Leporello will be seen just as a servant, but in fact he is the First Overseer, responsible for guiding Fellow Crafts through their initiation. Throughout the ritual, he conducts Don Giovanni and leads him to his ordeals, until the final confrontation with the Commendatore. Unknown to everyone, Leporello masterminds the plot. He is the "little hare"* and he knows the truth. At the end of the opera, when he leads Fellow Craft Don Giovanni to the Secret Fire, the First Overseer goes to fetch a "better master", in other words, a new Fellow Craft that he will guide on the same path. Like Don Giovanni, Leporello is a baritone, and in his first aria he stands outside Wisdom's house and bewails the demands of his task! And any First Overseer who has had responsibility for a Tracing Chamber full of Fellow Crafts, puffed up with pride at not being Entered Apprentices any more and thinking only of rising to the next degree, will understand his colleague's lassitude! Wearing himself out night and day with never a word of thanks from Don Giovanni, putting up with the vagaries of life and constantly having to look out for him! Leporello would like to leave service. But there's someone coming: the ritual begins. Abruptly recalled

* *Lepre*, in Italian.

287

to duty, the First Overseer hides in the shrubbery and keeps watch.'

'The plot thickens,' continued Thamos. 'The Fellow Craft is obsessed by the idea of getting hold of Wisdom, Donna Anna, the only "woman" he cannot touch with impunity. Having vainly tried to seduce her using Force, all he can do is disappear.'

'Donna Anna catches up with him, grabs his arm and warns him, while he hides his face: "If you don't kill me, don't expect me to let you escape." She accuses him of breaking the Masonic oath he made when he swore to abide by the Rules and live according to the Light. Don Giovanni has one hope: if no one can identify him, his fault will have no consequences.'

'His assault on Wisdom and the breaking of the oath provokes the appearance of the Master Mason, the Commendatore, who vouches for Masonic integrity.'

'He orders Don Giovanni, the indignant Fellow Craft, to leave Wisdom alone and draw his sword in self-defence. Blinded by vanity and his Strength, which he imagines is invincible, Don Giovanni jeers at the Master Mason, considering him a negligible adversary because of his age.'

' "So," says the Commendatore, "you think you can escape me?" '

'Then the Fellow Craft kills the Master Mason.'

'And this is the first time, my Brother Wolfgang, that an initiated musician will recreate the ritual assassination of the Master of Work.'

Mozart sat down at the piano and composed an aria for the death of the Commendatore, and the Egyptian felt the hairs rise on the back of his neck, as he recognized echoes of *Thamos, King of Egypt*.

Gravely wounded, the Master Mason feels his soul departing, and Don Giovanni sings of death at the same time as his victim.

In spite of the brutality of his death, the Commendatore remains curiously serene, whereas Don Giovanni is suddenly horrified at what he has done, although he does not fully realize the seriousness of the assassination.

Meanwhile, the First Overseer, Leporello, watches the rite unfold and listens to the thumping of his heart – one of the main symbols of the degree of Fellow Craft – and he foresees what will follow: from now on, no more conquests for Don Giovanni and a fatal step in the direction of the flames of the hereafter, be they destructive or transformative.

# 53

*Vienna, 4 April 1787*

Wolfgang embraced his wife.

'Suppose you brought a little girl into the world? Wouldn't that be wonderful?'

'I shall pray to God for your wish to be granted. My pregnancy will be fine, I'm sure of it. But not a single concert, right in the middle of the music season!'

'Don't worry. Thanks to you, we have enough money to maintain our lifestyle. And then, the people of Prague will like my next opera. On the other hand, my father's health worries me. I must write to him without delay.'

Wolfgang took up his pen.

*I have just this moment heard news that distresses me, particularly as I had supposed, from your last letter, that you were, thank God, in excellent health. I now learn that you are gravely ill. I need not tell you how keenly I am now waiting for news that will comfort me, and I am counting on it even though, in these circumstances, I have grown accustomed to imagining the worst. Since death, when we consider it closely, is the true final goal of our existence, I have become so familiar in recent years with this best and truest friend of mankind, that not only do I see nothing frightening in its image but, on the contrary, I find it soothing and consoling. And I thank my God for graciously granting me the chance (you know what I mean) to learn that death is the key to our true felicity. I never go to bed without thinking that perhaps, young as I am, I may not live to see the next day. Yet there is no one, among all those who know me, who can say that I am sad or wretched in my conversation. For this felicity, I thank my Creator every day, and it is what I wish for all my fellow men from the bottom of my heart. In writing this, I hope and trust that you are feeling better. If, however, contrary to all expectation, you are not getting better, then I beg you not to hide it from me, but write to me or have someone write the pure truth to me, so that I can be in your arms as soon as is humanly possible. I entreat you to do this, by all that is most sacred to us.*

The letter was couched in such terms that it would not arouse the suspicion of the police. But the last words clearly pointed to Masonic brotherhood in a way to retie the knots with his father. Would he be sensitive to his prayer?

Since his initiation into the Great Mysteries of Master Mason, Wolfgang saw death as a counsellor. Death heightened one's consciousness, enabled one to tell the essential from the futile and encouraged a love of life in all its dimensions, even beyond the material and visible world.

Don Giovanni, *Act I, Scenes ii to vi*

'Let's get back to our assassin, Don Giovanni, and the First Overseer, Leporello,' said Thamos. 'He bemoans his misfortune at witnessing a tragedy he knew was inevitable. Then he asks Don Giovanni an odd question: "Who has died? You, or the old man?" '

'The Fellow Craft, Don Giovanni, thinks the question is stupid, but he is wrong!' said Wolfgang. 'Because the Commendatore's murder will lead him to his own death.'

'Leporello balefully concludes: "Two charming enterprises: raping the daughter and killing the father." '

' "The Commendatore was asking for it: too bad for him!" scoffs the Fellow Craft, arrogant and unrepentant. He even threatens the First Overseer, who makes a show of backing down. Leporello wants nothing, unlike the Fellow Craft, who wants everything.'

'The two men go off stage, and Ottavio, Donna Anna's fiancé, appears. He embodies pure love, beyond all passion, and he holds the ritual sword, ready to avenge the Commendatore's death. Overwhelmed by the sight of the corpse, Donna Anna faints and thinks she is dying. But Wisdom cannot die, and Ottavio brings her round by persuading her to remain on earth and promising her he will be both a husband and a father to her and take over from the Commendatore.'

'As she comes back from the abyss,' Wolfgang went on, 'Donna Anna thinks she is looking into the face of her murderer! Her hallucination passes and Wisdom demands Ottavio take the Master Mason's oath: he must punish the Commendatore's assassin.'

'By adding his voice to Anna's, Ottavio seals the Fellow Craft's fate. Whatever happens, the murderer will not escape.'

'It is still dark,' Wolfgang continued. 'Leporello and Don Giovanni are walking down a dark alley. The First Overseer wants to talk to the Fellow Craft about his crime. Don Giovanni turns a deaf ear, and Leporello exclaims: "You are leading the life of a knave!" and accuses him of neglecting his initiate's word. Despite these harsh but just rebukes, Don Giovanni continues to be Leporello's friend. How could it be otherwise, since the servant is, in reality, the Master Mason?'

'At this point in the ritual,' suggested Thamos, 'shouldn't you introduce the symbol of the senses, associated with the Fellow Craft?'

'Suddenly, Don Giovanni notices the smell of a woman. Through the darkness, his piercing gaze detects a beauty! "What an eye!" Leporello declares. Already, the Fellow Craft is aflame. Donna Elvira appears in travelling dress. Although she was only with Don Juan for three days – the number associated with the Entered Apprentice – he nevertheless called her his wife before setting off on the Fellow Craft's road, eager for countless conquests. In an aria at once virulent and nostalgic, Donna Elvira sings of her desire to find the traitor and tear out his heart!'

'That is, accomplish the gesture which, in the ritual of initiation to the degree, will punish the dissolute, treacherous Fellow Craft.'

'Don Giovanni is off his guard and doesn't recognize Donna Elvira. Believing that he is seducing a new prey, he is severely disappointed, as foreseen and arranged by the First Overseer. Don't forget, after killing the Master of Work, the Fellow Craft keeps coming up against barriers. Only the initiatory death and purifying fire will wash away his crime.'

'Elvira makes a terrible accusation,' decided Thamos. 'Don Giovanni has failed in the sacred duty to heaven and earth. So, fate has put him in her way so she can be avenged. Will he be afraid and beg her forgiveness?'

'Of course not!' answered Wolfgang. 'Donna Elvira is trying his patience, so Don Giovanni asks Leporello to tell the unhappy woman the real reason for his behaviour: the constant need to extend his list of conquests, "because in this world a square is not round," says the First Overseer, whose task is to teach Fellow Crafts

sacred geometry, and he shows Donna Elvira the catalogue of Don Giovanni's successes with women. The
predator exercises his talents in every country and all
social classes and preys on women of all ages. True,
the young debutante is his chief passion but he does not
spurn old women. Whether they're rich or poor, beautiful or ugly, dark or fair, it doesn't matter: he wants them
all. And Leporello updates the list.'

'We are getting to the nub of the Fellow Craft's adventure,' added Thamos: 'the desire to add to his conquests,
experience everything, know everything, possess everything, exhaust the inexhaustible. Endless and boundless,
the list proclaims the formidable powers of the Fellow
Craft, who believed them invincible until he tries to rape
Wisdom, Donna Anna, and in that way obtain the secret
of the Master Mason.'

'Why,' asked Wolfgang in amazement, 'does the way
to knowledge of the Great Mysteries have to go through
such tragedy?'

'Because mankind has neglected his spiritual duties
and forsaken his purpose. Initiation can help us recover
our true nature, arduous though that enterprise is, and we
have to confront several kinds of death before we can
know life in its plenitude.'

'That is why Elvira, who symbolizes Beauty, one of the
Three Great Pillars in a Masonic lodge, cannot forgive
the depraved Fellow Craft, who scorned her love. How
can we end Don Giovanni's capacity for destruction?'

# 54

*Vienna, 7 April 1787*

Having hastily written a rondo for horn and orchestra based on a previous draft to earn his keep, Wolfgang went back to giving lessons, his main source of income in the absence of concerts.

While the musician was trying to teach two pupils how to play piano duets, a young man of slovenly appearance turned up at his apartment. At the visitor's insistence, Constanze interrupted the lesson.

'Mr Mozart,' the intruder blustered impulsively, 'I wish to receive your instruction.'

It seemed to cost him an effort to bring out his request, but the young man had such admiration for some of Mozart's works that he wanted to benefit from the advice of so extraordinary a creator.

'What is your name?'

'Ludwig van Beethoven and I come from Bonn. I

have decided to be a composer and devote my life to music.'

'You will have to face stern tests.'

'I am ready for them.'

'In the meantime, will you play something so that I can see what stage you're at?'

Beethoven sat down at the piano and improvised exactly as he should not have done for Mozart: he sought to stun him with a brilliant technique.

The Master's verdict was terse.

'Graceful, but mechanical.'

Beethoven was vexed and asked his teacher for a theme to develop. This time, his improvisations were less conventional and his playing more sensitive.

'I shall take you on as my pupil,' Wolfgang agreed.

Ludwig van Beethoven bid him good day and left. Although nettled, he told himself that he would come back.

'Keep an eye on him,' Wolfgang advised his two pupils. 'He will have something to say.'


Don Giovanni, *Act I, Scenes vii to x*


'A merry band of villagers is preparing to celebrate the marriage of two young people,' said Wolfgang.

'We're back to the theme of *The Marriage of Figaro* and the subject of alchemy in your ritual operas,' recalled Thamos, 'the union of Man and Woman.'

'Let us call the affianced pair Masetto and Zerlina. Masetto, based on the root *mas*, meaning "male", will be "the little male", and Zerlina, "the little mistress". They form the little couple, destined for a little union, that is, the first stage of the Great Work. Count Almaviva, the first embodiment of the Fellow Craft, prevented Figaro from marrying Susanna; Don Giovanni, the Fellow Craft at the peak of his powers, is opposed to the union of Masetto and Zerlina. No woman will escape his domination!'

'One essential point,' continued Thamos, 'is that the same singer, a very deep bass, should sing the roles of both the Commendatore and Masetto. What is below is also above, so this young peasant is the earthly expression of the Commendatore.'

'Masetto and Zerlina are looking forward to enjoying themselves: to singing and dancing, playing games, and, in short, to simple, peaceful pleasures. But they reckon without the intrusion of Don Giovanni led in by the First Overseer. Leporello mutters: "In the Number – an important subject of study for the Fellow Craft – there will surely be something for me." And he agrees to protect all the girls invited to the party, while Don Giovanni learns the names of Zerlina and Masetto, "an excellent-hearted man" in the words of his fiancée.'

'Again,' observed Thamos, 'Don Giovanni's power is checked by an unknown force: Masetto's. Because he wants to add Zerlina to his list, the Fellow Craft tries to get rid of this killjoy. What should he do? He decides to play the generous nobleman and ply the villagers with chocolate, coffee, wine and cooked meats; he even offers to open up the gardens of his palace to them. Leporello can show them the gallery and chambers! Don Giovanni, meanwhile, will lead Zerlina away.'

'Masetto objects,' countered Wolfgang. 'His fiancée should not go off without him!'

'The Fellow Craft finds a decisive ally: Zerlina herself!'

'An ally . . . or a trap?'

'How could the bearer of Strength think for a minute that a weak woman could manipulate him? What has Zerlina to fear from a knight, for whom honour and righteousness arc essential virtues?'

'Don Giovanni settles the matter by bringing out his sword: if Masetto does not clear off, he will be sorry. The poor man sings an aria that borders on tragedy and pours out the bitterness of his defeat.'

'Left alone with Sister Zerlina, the little mistress, the Fellow Craft, Don Giovanni, is in no doubt he will quickly seduce her.'

'He calls her "my heart",' interjected Wolfgang, 'and assures her that he will make a clean sweep and that he could not bear such sweet freshness to be thrown away on a lumpish peasant. As he approaches Zerlina, he feels as though he were touching milk and breathing the scent of roses.'

'She holds the secret of primary matter, like Cherubino in *The Marriage of Figaro*. All the Fellow Craft's senses are awake, according to the ritual of the degree, and now he just has to take hold of this boundless treasure.'

' "Let's not waste time," Don Giovanni insists. To overcome Zerlina's reticence and concerns, he promises to marry her. Is not nobility written in his eyes? And he bids her accompany him to a little pavilion nearby where they will consummate their union.'

'Will she yield?'

'She does and doesn't want to,' Wolfgang answered, 'because she would be happy to meet a true Master. But Don Giovanni is only a Fellow Craft, so unfitted to find the Great Work.'

'All the same, Zerlina weakens. The Fellow Craft embraces her and leads her away.'

'Then Donna Elvira bursts in! She grabs hold of Don Giovanni and cries: "Stop, you scoundrel! Heaven brought your treachery to my ears. I have come in time to save this poor innocent creature from your barbarous grip." '

'Does Don Giovanni repent at last?'

'Not yet! All he wanted, he declares, was to have fun, he "a tender-hearted man", like any Fellow Craft worthy of the name. He mutters to Zerlina that the wretched Elvira is infatuated with him and that he has to feign love for her! "Flee the deceiver!" Elvira advises Zerlina, dragging her away from this liar. Frustrated yet again, the Fellow Craft grumbles: "I feel as though the devil is playing with me today and thwarting all my pleasant pastimes. Nothing is going to plan!" '

# 55

*Vienna, 19 April 1787*

Between two work sessions on *Don Giovanni*, Wolfgang had tried to compose a string quintet, but the sardonic opening was leading nowhere. He reread a piece his Brother Gottfried von Jacquin had written in his album on 11 April: *A heartless genius is an absurdity. For genius is not made from the elevation of intelligence or imagination alone, or even both combined. Love! Love! Love! That is the soul of genius.*

Wolfgang felt as though a great weight had been lifted off his shoulders, and he launched into a splendid quintet for two violins, two violas and a cello.* Severe and intimate, the work was pervaded by a sense of death experienced now as a struggle, now as an escape towards the Light. Agony had no dominion at any point. On the

*K515, in C major.

contrary, the sometimes desolate space of the quintet was suffused with the breath of life, and despite assaults from the darkness, its creative vigour never waned, till the very lure of the abyss seemed to have had its neck wrung.

When Mozart next received Beethoven, the young man looked both annoyed and embarrassed.

'I should have liked to receive your instruction,' he assured him, 'but unfortunately, I won't now be able to.'

'If there's some financial problem . . .'

'No, my mother has just fallen gravely ill, and I must hurry back to Bonn. Believe me, I am truly sorry.'

'Good luck, Beethoven.'

Don Giovanni, *Act I, Scenes xi to xviii*

Wolfgang returned to Don Giovanni and found him dismayed by the appearance of Donna Anna and Don Ottavio.

' "This encounter is the final blow!" exclaims the Fellow Craft.'

'Anna asks him a ritual question,' put in Thamos. ' "Do you have a heart and a generous soul?" '

' "Has the devil set her on my track?" worries Don Giovanni. Maybe she suspects he is her aggressor. He hurriedly offers her his possessions, his sword and his blood, daring even to ask her why she is crying and who could have been so cruel as to ruffle the peace of her life.'

'Then Donna Elvira intervenes. "The black soul of this perfidious monster must be judged," she declares.'

'Do you know how Don Giovanni is going to give himself away? When he takes leave of Ottavio and Anna, he calls out, "Farewell," and the Commendatore's daughter recognizes the perpetrator . . . by his voice!'

' "I am dead," Anna tells Ottavio. But as the embodiment of the Pillar of Strength, Ottavio keeps Wisdom alive. She tells him of her terrifying ordeal when she narrowly escaped being raped. Anna's cry for help summoned the apparition of the Master of Work assassinated by the Fellow Craft. She demands revenge.'

'The First Overseer, Leporello, warns the Fellow Craft that things are not going well. Don Giovanni refuses to face the truth and he sings his first aria, a swaggering invitation to all his guests to get drunk on wine and sing and dance at a great feast. By morning, a dozen pretty girls will have extended his list! Carried away by infectious and unbridled excitement, he even invites Masetto and Zerlina, still intent on seducing the peasant girl.'

'At this point,' Thamos advised, 'bring in the masked personifications of the Three Great Pillars of the lodge, with Anna as Wisdom, Ottavio as Strength and Elvira as Beauty. They turn up at the Fellow Craft's party in order to reveal his guilt. "By his face and voice," they sing together, "we know the traitor." Don Giovanni opens one of the windows of his house and invites them in. Guided by heaven, the three masked characters find themselves in a brightly lit hall laid out for a ball.'

'Don Giovanni brazenly declares that he is free to do as he likes and orders three small orchestras to play an aristocratic minuet, a bourgeois contredanse and a rustic allemande. The three themes reflect the whole of humanity. Believing that he is endowed with absolute power, the Fellow Craft is bent on seducing Zerlina. But the Three Great Pillars remove their masks and reveal their identity. Taken aback, Don Giovanni identifies Ottavio and Elvira but not Anna, Wisdom, who is beyond his powers of perception. The trio calls him a "traitor" and recalls that his deeds are already ritually known. Now, because of his crime, revenge must take place.'

'Does the Fellow Craft finally give in?' asked Thamos.

'His mind is confused, he admits, he no longer knows what he is doing, and a storm is brewing. All the same, he is cool-headed and does not think he is lost or undone. Even if the world collapses, he boasts, his courage will never forsake him.'

'The First Overseer repeats these words and they conclude Act I. Will the Fellow Craft conquer the adversity that he himself has unleashed?'


*Vienna, 24 April 1787*


Wolfgang walked sadly through the grand rooms of his magnificent apartment in Schulerstrasse, which he had occupied since 29 September 1784. With so high a rent but so little income in recent months, he could not possibly continue to live here.

The composer was sorry to leave his home, with its spacious studio, Rococo stuccowork and fine drawing room that allowed him to receive passing guests in style. But priority had to be given to other expenses and he had no choice but to move into more modest accommodation, at 224 Landstrasse.

'Don't be downhearted,' Constanze told him. 'I like our new apartment, and so do Karl Thomas, our starling, Star, and Gaukerl. I think it will be more practical than our old one. We were happy here and we will be even happier there.'

'But moving while you're pregnant . . .'

'It's not me who'll be moving the furniture!' she joked. 'Come, it is time we were leaving.'

In his album, Wolfgang wrote a double canon and added: 'Ah! How brief is this short life!' How could he forget that here, in Camesina House, he had written *The Marriage of Figaro*, his first ritual opera bursting with youthful enthusiasm?

While he had lived here, he had been initiated into the degrees of Entered Apprentice, Fellow Craft and Master Mason, and had discovered the immensity of the Great Mysteries.

This house would be forever the place of his spiritual awakening, of material success and recognition. And given the uncertain future of Viennese Freemasonry and his first financial difficulties, the happiness of these things might be ebbing away from him.

# 56

*Vienna, 25 April 1787*

'Mozart has just moved to a more modest apartment,' Geytrand told Josef Anton. 'He hasn't managed to organize a single concert during the music season, and his income has dwindled. He is reduced to giving lessons again. Nevertheless, he is composing a new opera for Prague with the librettist, Abbé Lorenzo Da Ponte.'

'What's the subject?'

'The story of Don Giovanni, his passion for women and his crime and punishment.'

Josef Anton scratched his chin. 'Mozart will use this old fable to propagate Masonic ideas, like *The Marriage of Figaro*. Da Ponte will just be an oblivious tool in his hands, the way he was before. Have you got hold of information on the Prague lodges?'

'My spies have hit a blank, and I have gleaned nothing but official information of no interest whatsoever.'

'The Prague Freemasons can't be an impenetrable circle! Get to work and find a weak spot.'

*Vienna, 27 April 1787*

At a secret meeting chaired by Ignaz von Born, Wolfgang gave him a progress report on *Don Giovanni*. Afterwards, the Venerable wrote a few lines in the composer's album:

> *Fair Apollo! You who have bestowed on our Brother Mozart the gift of your methods and Numbers so that, with a sovereign lyre, he can repay you with sounds that hand and mind make high or low, fast or slow, harmonious or dissonant, loud or soft, and that blend with no offence to the ear, let the Number of each blessed day and the Harmony of a bountiful life accord with the elected music of his lyre!*

Bolstered by this vital encouragement, Mozart went to see Lorenzo Da Ponte, who had read Bertati's libretto and Dante's *Inferno*, by way of immersing himself in the atmosphere of his new work.

'In my opinion,' he told Mozart, 'the main character is not Don Giovanni, but the Commendatore. Tragedy is unleashed because of his death. And what a *coup de théâtre* when we bring him back from the beyond! But we mustn't neglect the play's humorous side. We can use Leporello to comic effect, and we'll call this show a *dramma giocoso* or "jocular drama"!'

Wolfgang made no objection but told Da Ponte everything he expected from him.

The librettist was delighted to receive virtually the entire plot and some useful repartee; the body of his work had been done for him, and now, all he had to do was polish it up.

'In the morning,' he declared, 'I shall read Petrarch to help me write Martini's next opera; in the evening, I shall read Tasso to help me write Salieri's; and at night, for you, I shall turn my attention to Don Giovanni.'

'Aren't you afraid you'll wear yourself out and fall ill?' asked Wolfgang, anxiously.

'Oh, I have my little secrets,' the abbé told him, confidentially. 'I sit down at my table at midnight with my bottle of Tokay to my right, a box full of Seville tobacco to my left . . . and a sixteen-year-old German girl who answers to my call whenever I ring for her! I tend to abuse the bell a bit when I feel my inspiration drying up or going cold. She is a young girl who brings me either a cup of coffee, or simply a beautiful face that is always gay and smiling; I find it the perfect remedy to soothe a tired mind and rekindle poetic inspiration.'

Wolfgang did not really approve of his official librettist's methods, but he went away reassured.

*Vienna, 16 May 1787*

As he pondered the gravity of the task he had set himself in composing *Don Giovanni* and revealing secret aspects of the degrees of Fellow Craft and Master Mason, Wolfgang felt confronted by his own Masonic duties. He wrote a quintet in G minor,* a work that plumbed the depths of desolation and reflected his renouncement of the illusions of life on earth, like Don Giovanni's lust for power, or the elation of success of a brilliant pianist named Mozart, or that same musician's desire to win people's hearts.

It was not without a pang that he achieved this release, and the private, almost painful intensity of the chamber piece echoed his emotion.

As he tackled *Don Giovanni* and dared to depict the assassination of the Master of Work and the initiation of the Fellow Craft, Wolfgang relived those fearful moments and the steps towards Enlightenment.

*Vienna, 26 May 1787*

While Lorenzo Da Ponte fine-tuned the libretto for Act I of *Don Giovanni*, Wolfgang relaxed by composing several *Lieder*,† songs that were alternately darkly humorous and quietly sorrowful.

*K516.
† K517, in B minor, K518, in F major, K519, in F minor.

In 'The Old Woman', an elderly, squeaky voice reflected sadly on the good old days and expressed disillusionment about the present. Haunting and repetitive, the melody had a certain elegance, as though it could consign to oblivion the cruelty of fate.

'The Vanishing' was a romp compared with 'The Separation', which, with the musician's characteristic grace, evoked the despair of the angels.

When he woke up that morning, in one of the bedrooms of the Jacquins' house where he had spent the night after a secret meeting with some of the Master Masons, Wolfgang wrote a brief romance, 'When Luise',* describing the end of a love affair and the attainment of inner peace, as a woman burnt the letters of a man who had loved her and been unfaithful.

At breakfast, Wolfgang gave the manuscript to his Brother Gottfried von Jacquin.

'Since this *Lied* was composed in your house, it belongs to you.'

Von Jacquin read through the score.

'I am touched, extremely touched . . . How is your grand opera coming along?'

'Don Giovanni is not an easy Fellow Craft. He is unfaithful, he kills, he won't listen to warnings from heaven . . . But I shall see this through!'

---

* K520, in C minor.

# 57

*Paris, 26 May 1787*

After twenty-nine meetings and two and a half months of fruitless discussions, the second Congress organized by the Philalethes Lodge ended in confusion and disgruntlement.

'A number of Brothers liked your suggestions,' the Marquis of Chefdebien admitted to Thamos. 'If people had paid more attention to you instead of worshipping that French mystic Willermoz, we might have begun to build a future.'

'Could you not preach an open society of all Freemasons and all rites, without the paraphernalia of honours and administration, in the interests of reviving initiation? We could reform the Order by creating a body of genuine Masons with a true calling to search for truth; surely that would be an ideal worth striving for.'

'I agree with you,' the Marquis of Chefdebien concurred, 'and our Venerable is prepared to take up some of your suggestions when the Congress is over. But I fear he is too late. Freemasonry is beset by such diverse trends of thought, some of them conflicting, that the edifice is cracking. Our efforts to restore it will most likely prove in vain, because the unrest threatening France at the moment will destroy the lodges.'


*Vienna, 1 June 1787*


Wolfgang was just about to dispatch two of his Lieder, duly corrected, to his Brother Gottfried, together with a fresh, joyful piano sonata for four hands,* when he received a letter from Salzburg.

Thinking it contained a message from his father sending news of his health, Wolfgang opened it with a shaking hand.

The letter was signed Yppold, a friend of Leopold Mozart.

The composer was unprepared for such a shock.

Of course, his father had been sixty-eight. Of course, he had had various ailments. But he could not be dead!

How could a real father die?

Papa comes just after God, the child Wolfgang had thought, as he dutifully followed Leopold about the roads of Europe, with love and trust.

*K521.

But God did not grow old, nor did he disappear.

His father, who had brought him up and been his teacher, his Brother . . . So, he would never again see him on this earth.

In the letter he wrote to Jacquin, Wolfgang added a post-script: *I must tell you that I received today the sad news of the death of my excellent father. You can imagine my feelings.*

When he told Constanze the dreadful news, she was almost sick with grief. Star was mute and Gaukerl crouched miserably under the table.

'I loved Leopold very much,' she murmured. 'How we shall miss him!'

Mozart suddenly had felt the full tragedy of the Commendatore's death at the hands of Don Giovanni.


*Vienna, 2 June 1787*


Little Karl Thomas was the only one who could lift the heavy atmosphere in the apartment after the bereavement. Even Gaukerl sensed his master's grief and dared not ask him to play.

That morning, Constanze felt too overcome to get up.

'I shall call Dr Barisani,' decided Wolfgang.

'Exner will do. I think I am just tired; the last days have been so emotional. What are the terms of the inheritance?'

'I have no intention of going back to Salzburg and I shall ask Nannerl to settle matters.'

'Do you really trust her?'

'I shall have to.'

At nine o'clock, Dr Exner bled Constanze while Wolfgang wrote to his sister to ask her to act as his legal representative.


*Vienna, 4 June 1787*


Gaukerl gave a series of pitiful little yaps.

'What's the matter?' Wolfgang asked, stroking his head.

The dog tugged him towards Star's cage.

The bird was dead, the starling who had inspired the opening bars of the Rondo of Mozart's Piano Concerto in g Major.[*] Since 27 May 1784, he had helped the composer work and been present at every event in the life of the household, greeting them with a display of his vocal accomplishments.

Wolfgang was deeply moved and solemnly buried his faithful friend, whose cheeriness and intelligence would leave a huge absence, and he wrote an epitaph so that he should not be forgotten:

*Here lies a foolish little fellow. He was in his prime*
*when he had to suffer the tragic adventure of death.*
*My heart bleeds, when I think of it. Oh, reader, you*

*K453.

*too, shed a tear for him. He was not bad, just a shade too alert. He could sometimes be a crafty little imp, but he was certainly not a rascal! I should lay a wager he is already in heaven, thanking me for this friendly service, he who died so suddenly, without having time to think of the one who writes these pretty lines for him.*

*Vienna, 8 June 1787*

While *The Abduction from the Seraglio* was playing at the Kärntnertor Theatre, a meeting at Truth Lodge, where the Entered Apprentice Josef Haydn had never attended, was taking place in a nasty atmosphere.

Some of the Brethren were thought to be infected by pestilential mysticism and found themselves at loggerheads with the rationalists, themselves distrusted by good Catholics who could not bear their assaults on their monks and priests. With the Archbishop of Vienna's spies determined to impose their point of view, Ignaz von Born's followers felt it was becoming difficult, if not impossible, to go on.

Newcomers were dwindling, Masons resigning in droves, and some dozen Servant Brothers, who were no longer needed, had had to be sent away. If the lodge did not get a grip on itself, what would become of it?

Venerable Johann Baptist von Puthon was increasingly sorry that he had accepted this high-risk duty, the

315

source of so much tension. He ordered the Secretary to make a note of the incidents in the official report and took the document to the police.

Von Puthon concluded the works, intending to suspend them as long as was necessary. Well, if Truth Lodge had to perish, he would be glad of it and could devote himself fulltime to his prime duties as head of the National Bank of Vienna. At least that way he could be sure of the esteem of the emperor and the nobility.

# 58

*Vienna, 9 June 1787*

'In view of so much dissension,' Gcytrand informed Josef Anton, 'our friend the banker von Puthon has taken the admirable stcp of closing the works of his lodge without fixing the date of the next meeting.'

'Serious conflicts or just lively discussions?'

'Serious conflicts. Hoffmann believes a deep rift is opening up between von Born's followers and opponents. Brothers who want to study initiation and symbolism have clashed with believers who just want to praise the emperor, advocate charitable action and organize sumptuous banquets where everyone tries not to think. Von Puthon is keen to encourage this tendency but can no longer keep order. He is at a loss and worried about his excellent banker's reputation suffering through association with the Masons. He prefers to see his lodge fade out without fuss.'

'An attractive plan,' nodded Josef Anton. 'What's Mozart's reaction?'

'He was very upset by the death of his father and Brother, Leopold, who never attended a lodge once he returned to Salzburg. You should congratulate yourself, my lord. Your repeated sallies are causing Viennese Freemasonry to wither away.'

'I am not so sure. Von Born has gone underground and the initiates of Prague are laughing behind our backs. Total victory has not yet been won, my good Geytrand.'

When he opened the works at New Crowned Hope Lodge, the Venerable Master became the third president to accomplish the union of the Sun in the north and the Moon at midday.

So it was that, as at every meeting celebrated according to tradition, the miracle of the first morning was reproduced. Creation blazed forth again in its original purity, men became Brothers, and their hearts were joined with the hearts of initiates who had passed to the Eternal Orient.

This first degree meeting affected Wolfgang with particular intensity. He thought about Leopold's wonderment inside the temple, before his father had realized that so much mental effort was more than he could give. At least he had known the brute stone – the primary matter of the universe – the cubical stone – the universe itself in harmony – and the cornerstone at the heart of the Great Mysteries.

He gazed at the lodge insignia depicting a spirit level, a set square and a seated woman wearing a crown as an emblem of hope, and he felt enormous gratitude towards Thamos and the Freemasons. Imperfect as the society was, it had brought him Enlightenment. Whatever the dangers, he would keep his oath and defend Freemasonry to his dying days. He did not belong to that race of traitors and cowards who took flight at the first hint of danger.

The Brothers described what had happened at Truth Lodge. Some dismissed them as random incidents and unimportant; others saw them as a disaster attributable to the incompetence of Venerable von Puthon and sabotage by the Archbishop of Vienna. A few even thought that Truth would never open its temple door again.

'What do you think, Brother Wolfgang?' asked Otto von Gemmingen.

'What do ordeals and threats matter, so long as we stick to the path of honesty and integrity? Initiation is our mother and our father, and we owe it total loyalty. We shall never give it as much as it has given us.'

*Vienna, 14 June 1787*

As he thought of the extraordinary brotherly relations he might have developed with his father, Wolfgang paid his first tribute to him. *A Musical Joke,** a divertimento

*K522.

for two horns and string quartet, was quickly notated and poked fun at composers with pretensions who were really ignorant and oafish, and whom Leopold, with his impeccable technique, had heartily detested. It was thanks to his teaching and rigour that his son had avoided such pitfalls.

But this ruined and ruinous music brought him no satisfaction.

His father deserved better.


*Vienna, 24 June 1787*


On Constanze's advice, Wolfgang had written to his sister, Nannerl, on the 16th, to say that his financial situation obliged him to claim his share of the inheritance. He would have infinitely preferred not to associate his father's death with the sordid question of money and leave everything to his sister. But in his current straitened circumstances, he could not afford to, and he begged Nannerl to do what she could.

At the start of that forlorn summer, Wolfgang composed a song in memory of his father, entitled 'Evening Feelings',* celebrating the silver light of the moon, that night-time sun, in a clear sky. Between light and dark, between two worlds, he paid an intimate farewell to the departed, whom he would meet again in

---

*K523.

the afterlife. In everyday language and with very little tune, it expressed the serene trust between two men and Brothers, who had shared so much pain and so much happiness.

Wolfgang also wrote a brief *Lied*, 'To Chloé, when love speaks in your clear blue eyes',* evoking both the ideal woman, whom his father had known, and hope for another life beyond death. Light and almost carefree, the song seemed to suggest that the cruel hand of fate could be softened if it were ignored.

A dinner washed down with plenty of wine in the company of his Brother Anton Stadler dispelled the mood of melancholy. Although well brought up, Gaukerl was allowed to lick the plates clean while the clarinettist reeled off a succession of funny stories, much to the amusement of little Karl Thomas.

'Our Brother Leopold believed in God and in his son,' he recalled. 'He was an austere man but not above a game of darts, and he liked decent wine and a saucy joke. Even his dear and wonderful wife, excellent Catholic though she was and always trim and elegant, used to burst out laughing when conversation about the human condition turned scatological!'

'Death will pass you by,' mused Wolfgang. 'How could it strike you down if you don't take it seriously?'

'Compared with music, most particularly the clarinet, death has not the least importance! By the bye, since

* K524.

321

they banned you from composing for the lodges, you've been neglecting the instrument.'

'*Don Giovanni* is using up all my energy. Act I is finished, and I'm ready to start Act II.'

'How do you manage to write such enormous pieces?' Stadler asked, in amazement.

'When I'm on form and in good health, when I'm bowling along in a carriage or taking a walk after a good meal, or at night when I can't sleep, that's when ideas come flooding to my mind. I keep the ones I like and hum them to myself. If I warm to them, I gradually see how to set about fleshing them out. My mind is fired up, especially if nobody disturbs me. I work the music out in my head and I can see the whole thing in the blink of an eye, like a painting or a statue. That's the best moment, when I can hear the whole piece like that. Talking of which, my Brother, I feel Act II of *Don Giovanni* coming to me.'

# 59

Don Giovanni, *Act II, Scenes i to iii*

'Embodied by Donna Anna, Don Ottavio and Donna Elvira, the Three Great Pillars, Wisdom, Strength and Beauty, have identified the assassin of the Master of Work,' recalled Thamos. 'However, the faithless, murderous Fellow Craft Don Giovanni refuses to ackowledge his crime and continues to fight, convinced his power will sweep away all the obstacles and that he will come out of this affair unscathed.'

'At the start of Act II,' Wolfgang put in, 'Leporello, First Overseer though he is, no longer wants to be with this unworthy Fellow Craft and would rather leave him to his fate. If this were not a ritual of initiation, the nobleman would let his manservant leave and take on another, more docile servant. But the Fellow Craft could not progress without his First Overseer. So, he asks Leporello to make peace with him and gives him four doubloons, or eight escudos, the number of perfect harmony.'

'Now comes the moment to make the association between initiator and disciple lasting,' Thamos advised. 'Don Giovanni will not give up any conquest or any aspect of multiplicity, and, although he's been balked, he insists on adding to his list by seducing Donna Elvira's chambermaid. If he turns up dressed as a nobleman, he might frighten her off, so he suggests he and Leporello exchange clothes.'

'Leporello agrees,' Wolfgang went on, amused at the idea, 'because he can manipulate the Fellow Craft to a good end. It's not Elvira's chambermaid that comes to the window, of course, but Elvira herself. Embodying Harmony, she agrees to forgive Don Giovanni – who is really Leporello with the same voice! And the Fellow Craft, thinking he has control of the situation, thinks that there's no talent as fertile as his.'

' "You have a heart of stone," the First Overseer tells him. We're a long way from the alchemist's gold, and Don Giovanni, intent on bringing off his plan, advises Leporello to find an excuse to lead Elvira away.'

' "What if she recognizes me?" the First Overseer pretends to worry.'

' "If you don't want her to," the Fellow Craft says, lucidly, "she won't recognize you." In fact, Elvira, who is "all fire", and Leporello, who is "all ash", run off after Don Giovanni, who dares to threaten his First Overseer with death!'

324

'So, the way is open to him,' Wolfgang affirmed, 'and he can sing his serenade, right under the lodge windows!'

'The lodge has three windows in accordance with the words of the Ancients and they let in the light of the hereafter. In your libretto, no woman will appear at the window and the Fellow Craft will speak not to a human being but to love and death.'

' "Please," he says, "come to your window, my beloved. Please, come and dry my tears. If you refuse to give me this comfort, I shall die before your eyes. You, whose mouth is sweeter than honey, you, whose heart is gentle deep down, do not be cruel with me. At least let me see you, my beautiful love!" '

'The Fellow Craft will see no one,' said Thamos. 'True love transcends passion and possession and he is unworthy of it.'

'His aria will mark a turning point in the opera,' Wolfgang decided. 'The Fellow Craft implores ritual death, because she alone will enable him to reach the true love, which his list, long as it is, cannot include.'

*Paris, 26 June 1787*

The new head of the Illuminati, Johann Joachim Christoph Bode, a doughty standard-bearer of the crusade against the Jesuits, arrived in the French capital in a state of extreme irritation, to issue a firm reminder to the Philalethes of his beliefs.

If Freemasonry was to be saved, all the bigots of every persuasion should be immediately expelled and progressive ideas should be adopted to stop the Church and its partisans anaesthetizing people's minds.

The Hospitaller of the Philalethes Lodge gave his German Brother a friendly reception.

'Pleased to welcome you to Paris. How can I help?'

'I want to take part in the Congress.'

'My Brother, it has been closed for a month.'

'Did you receive my *Treatise*, in which I reveal that the practice of secret sciences is a trap laid for Freemasonry by the Jesuits?'

'Well, I—'

'I have not come all this way for nothing!' Bode declared. 'Open the door of the principal Parisian lodges for me, and I shall teach them the truth.'

The head of the Illuminati spared no pains and spread the word with his usual aplomb.

The results were disappointing. Most of the French Freemasons were slaves to religiosity and ingrained respect for the Church and King, and they dared not look reality in the face.

Sensitive to Bode's speech, some of them nevertheless dragged themselves out of their conformism and asked the German how they should proceed. There was only one solution, he insisted: they should set up secret groups of Illuminati where progressive thinkers would support their ideas and work towards their propagation. In that way, the great intellectual movement from

Bavaria would finally come to fruition and raise a whole people against the current regime.

*Vienna, 13 July 1787*

Wolfgang went out for a long ride, as he did every summer morning, on the advice of Dr Barisani. He had adopted a fine horse, and Gaukerl ran delightedly along beside them.

Work on *Don Giovanni* demanded considerable energy, so the composer relished these moments of relaxation when he could breathe in lungfuls of fresh air, as though devouring space itself.

Although prone to bouts of fatigue, Constanze was enjoying a smooth pregnancy and proving a devoted mother to Karl Thomas, who could sometimes be fractious and wayward. His parents were trying to bring him up strictly and instil in him a sense of work, so that he would grow up into a responsible adult. Leopold had paved the way and his son intended to follow it. Love without severity made a child spineless, but severity without love made him heartless.

*The Marriage of Figaro* had vanished from the Viennese repertory, *The Abduction from the Seraglio* would be given twice in July, and the Masonic publisher, Artaria, was about to market the Piano Quartet in E flat major.*

* K493.

But Mozart's name was no longer shining in the firmament of the empire's capital, where the glory of Antonio Salieri's anodyne mediocrity now dominated.

Wolfgang had never known jealousy, he who had so often provoked it. The only thing that mattered to him was the creative impulse that could break the chains of stupidity and degradation. But would he manage to get Don Giovanni to the Secret Fire?

# 60

Don Giovanni, *Act II, Scenes iv to x*

'Since this is a *dramma giocoso*,' Wolfgang reminded
Thamos, 'we mustn't forget to show that our Fellow
Craft has an unfailing sense of humour, even in adversity. Still wearing Leporello's clothes, Don Giovanni
sees Masetto coming accompanied by a crowd of peas-
ants. Masetto is furious and has armed himself with a
crossbow and pistol. What do they want? To bump off
that confounded Don Giovanni! The pretend Leporello
keeps his sang-froid, takes Masetto aside, beats him up
and disappears. Zerlina, carrying a lantern, finds her
wretched fiancé and tends his wounds "with a certain
balm she carries within her". By making him touch her
heart, the symbol of Strength, Zerlina puts Masetto back
on his feet.'

'What about the couple formed of Donna Elvira and
Leporello in the guise of Don Giovanni?' asked Thamos.

'I shall take them into the lodge, the house of Wisdom, Donna Anna. Outside is a dark courtyard with three doors, recalling the courtyard in front of the temple, where the only light comes from the glimmer of torches. The First Overseer is hoping to slip away so he can continue to look after the Fellow Craft, because it is not yet time to draw things to a conclusion. But he can't find the right door. Elvira feels close to death, Donna Anna and Don Ottavio appear to be dressed in mourning.'

'So the scene presages a funerary meeting,' Thamos observed. 'The Three Great Pillars have joined forces to put the Fellow Craft to the ordeal of the Fire of initiation.'

'Then Masetto and Zerlina arrive. Together with Anna, Ottavio and Elvira, there are now Five of them, the number associated with the Fellow Craft. They all demand the traitor's death, though not, of course, the death of the First Overseer. He explains, obviously, that this retribution is not meant for him and that Don Giovanni has abused his power to ravish his innocence. This time, Leporello finds the right door. Like the god Hermes, "he has wings on his feet", as Masetto says.'

'The judgement is pronounced by the Pillar of Strength,' Thamos decided. ' "After such excesses," Ottavio declares, "there is no doubt: the Fellow Craft, Don Giovanni, really is the Commendatore's assassin." As duty, pity and affection demand, vengeance will now be wrought.'

*Vienna, 10 August 1787*

Wolfgang's relations with his sister, Nannerl, had not improved. Try as he might, he could not get hold of the scores he had left behind in Salzburg and which he would have liked to rework.

Realizing the seriousness of the situation but engrossed in his work on *Don Giovanni*, Wolfgang no longer knew how to solve the thorny problem of his inheritance.

'Make her an offer,' suggested Constanze. 'She can keep all the furniture and give us a thousand florins in the empire's currency, not local money. We shall make around five per cent and need have no more to do with this wretched girl who clearly despises you.'

Wolfgang would have liked to come to his sister's defence but he knew Constanze's proposal was lucid and he followed her strategy. When this sorry financial business was put to rest, he at last wrote a proper tribute to his father's memory, a Salzburg-style serenade* that showed how fully he had grasped the classical rules Leopold had loved so much. *A Little Night Music* for chamber orchestra sealed, beyond the grave and for ever, the reconciliation of father and son, Brother Leopold and Brother Wolfgang. The serene beauty of this timeless piece expressed the ability of true Fraternity to dispel the suffering of the ordeals.

* Serenade No. 13 in G major, K525.

*Vienna, 18 August 1787*

The Middle Chamber of New Crowned Hope studied the myth of Hiram, the Master of Work, and explored its relations to the legend of Osiris, which Ignaz von Born had researched so thoroughly.

Everyone knew that Mozart was his spiritual son, and many thought that he was still seeing him and benefiting from his instruction. The Archbishop of Vienna's emissaries protested at every attempt to return to a pagan tradition, while the rationalists were suspicious of Egypt as too mysterious and therefore better avoided.

Brother Thamos, whose natural authority and knowledge impressed even sceptics, advised the lodge not to neglect the source and tradition of initiation. Without Egypt, Freemasonry would be nothing but an empty shell.

Thamos went further and interpreted the myth of Osiris point by point, showing how it related to the myth of Hiram in the authentic, unabridged rituals.

It was at that moment that Wolfgang saw and heard the end of his opera.

Out of the depths, the Secret Fire appeared as a talking stone: the statue of the Commendatore returned from the afterlife to force the Fellow Craft to face himself and his crime.

*Vienna, 19 April 1787*

'Mozart's lodge held a meeting in the degree of Master Mason, last night,' Geytrand told Josef Anton. 'There were several visitors from Truth Lodge, where work has ceased. Venerable von Puthon is resisting pressure from some of his Brothers and is biding his time before he decides whether to reinstate works there.'

'That will become more difficult as time goes by. The head of the National Bank of Vienna would rather concentrate on his official functions than be the arbiter of endless Masonic squabbles that could ruin his reputation and lose him his job. If you ask me, he is one of our best allies. What a miracle, my dear Geytrand: a Lodge Master acting against his own Brothers! It would have been impossible to imagine such a scenario a few years ago, when Freemasonry was in its heyday and we began our crusade. All the same, we have Mozart and von Born to contend with, the first in broad daylight, the other one lurking in the shadows.'

'As instructed, my lord, I have stopped my informants spying on the mineralogist. So, I have no information on him.'

'I understand your bitterness, but we cannot afford to take risks, because von Born is still one of the emperor's favourites and a respected scientist. He does not have any real leverage, so he is using Mozart to disseminate his ideas.'

'Mozart has enemies even within his own lodge,' Geytrand mentioned.

'Curious for the Brotherhood . . .'

'Freemasons are just men, my lord, and the vast majority is not keen on Brothers being too original: the thinking of such men threatens their routine.'

# 61

Don Giovanni, *Act II, Graveyard Scene*

'Don Giovanni and Leporello come to a graveyard where there are several mounted statues, including the statue of the Commendatore,' Wolfgang went on. 'These riders are Kabbalists, and, all unawares, the Fellow Craft enters a temple where a meeting to the Eternal Orient is being celebrated. "What a fine night!" he exclaims. "It is lighter than day!" Heedless of the presence of the assassinated Master of Work, Don Giovanni provokes him further by his boisterous laughter and raised voice, and by telling Leporello that he has tried to seduce – in vain – one of his beauties.'

'Then,' said Thamos, 'the Commendatore's voice echoes with impressive gravity: "You will stop laughing before the dawn." "Who was that?" asks the Don, in alarm. "A soul from the other world who knows you intimately," says the First Overseer." '

335

'This time, Don Giovanni loses his cool, puts his hand on his sword and, ordering Leporello to keep quiet, calls out: "Who goes there?" '

' "Leave the dead in peace," demands the Master of Work.'

'Don Giovanni finally makes out the statue of the Commendatore. He tells Leporello to go and read the inscription. But he has never learnt to read by moonlight and cannot satisfy his master's wishes, because the revelation of the Mysteries only happens by the combined light of the sun and moon. But bullied by Don Giovanni, and because the ritual demands it, he does as he is told. Engraved on the plinth under the Commendatore's statue are the words, "I wait here for revenge on the impious man who caused my death." '

'Will the Fellow Craft finally bow before the presence of the hereafter?'

'Not a bit of it!' exclaimed Wolfgang. 'He laughs at the statue of the old man and orders Leporello to invite it to dinner that very night.'

'The First Overseer thinks this is madness, because the statue shows every sign of being alive.'

'The Fellow Craft insists! Either Leporello obeys or else he will kill him and bury him here.'

'This is another critical moment after the assassination of the Master of Work,' Thamos pointed out. 'The First Overseer makes it clear that it is in the name of the Fellow Craft and not his own that he invites "the most noble marble statue" to dinner. Then, the statue bows its head as a sign that it accepts, the way the Venerable greets his Brothers in certain circumstances.'

'Don Giovanni is not looking at the statue and refuses to believe Leporello. Instead, he addresses the Commendatore directly: "Speak, if you can. Are you coming to dine?" '

' "Yes!" thunders the statue. Will the voice from the underworld shatter the Fellow Craft's vanity and arrogance, finally?'

'Not yet,' replied Wolfgang. ' "Strange statue, indeed," acknowledges Don Giovanni. What else can he do but go and prepare a sumptuous banquet?'

*Vienna, 1 September 1787*

A first degree meeting on 23 August passed off peacefully, and afterwards, Wolfgang composed a rather spare sonata for violin and piano* with constant key changes and a gay final Rondo. He and the other Master Masons were eagerly waiting for works at Truth Lodge to start up again, this time on a better footing.

However, Venerable Johann Baptist von Puthon's assessment of his workshop's activities was pessimistic. Although he welcomed the restructuring of Freemasonry decreed by Joseph II, he deplored the irresponsible attitude of some of the Brothers, who did not seem equal

*K526.

to the opportunity. Far too many Masons were still dabbling in the occult sciences, researching the secrets of the Ancients, or simply making barbed comments about official religion.

Von Puthon had decided that he would never be able to establish lasting peace. In accord with official Masonic management and, by implication, the regime, he was therefore taking the radical step of formally suspending Truth Lodge. No meeting would be scheduled until further notice. If reason demanded and circumstances permitted, they might possibly look forward to a reopening of the works at a later date.

This decision could not be appealed and there was to be no discussion.

Thamos, Ignaz von Born and Mozart gathered at the Countess of Thun's palace.

'You are on the front line,' the Venerable told Wolfgang, 'because your lodge will be under strict surveillance.'

'Today,' Thamos announced, 'we are going to have to go underground. Since our meetings will have to be celebrated in secret, we must be sure of every Brother. In the event of treason, the consequences would be disastrous.'

'We cannot force anyone to follow such a perilous road,' von Born said.

'Of course not,' Wolfgang acknowledged, 'but history has taught us that brotherhoods of initiation have often been persecuted by tyrants who cannot bear any thinking other than their own. It is my belief that Freemasonry and its symbols are vital to the future of humankind, and we swore that we would remain loyal and come to its aid, even in adversity. I am therefore staying at New Crowned Hope and we shall continue to hold Master Mason degree meetings in secret with Jacquin, Stadler and a few others.'

'And I shall make frequent trips to Prague,' added von Born, 'where Truth and Union Lodge still enjoy a modicum of independence.'

'According to my observations,' said Thamos, 'you are not being spied on any more. But tell our Brothers in Prague to be on the qui vive, because the emperor's police are necessarily interested in them.'

*Vienna, 2 September 1787*

'Works at Truth Lodge have been officially suspended for the foreseeable future,' Geytrand told Josef Anton.

'How have the Freemasons reacted?'

'They haven't, my lord. Venerable von Puthon denied his Brothers the right to discuss the move.'

'Fool! They should be allowed to have their say so that Hoffman can pick out the protestors, number one among whom would be Mozart. As it is, some Brothers will go into hiding and organize secret meetings. Thanks to the documents von Puthon sent, we are keeping a watchful eye on Truth but also New Crowned Hope. That lodge will now be on its guard.'

'You have my word that I shall spring its traps, my lord.'

# 62

Don Giovanni, *Act II, Scene xii*

'The assassin of the Master of Work cannot go unpunished,' Wolfgang said to Thamos. 'Which is why Don Ottavio, embodying the Pillar of Strength and opposed to the individual power of Don Giovanni, comforts Wisdom, Donna Anna. "We shall soon see the great crimes of this wretch punished," he declares, "and we shall be avenged." Anna, representing Wisdom, can think of nothing but her dead father. The idea of union with Ottavio is inconceivable to her while the murderer, Don Giovanni, is still strutting his stuff.'

'Ottavio is sorry to see his marriage put off but he shares Wisdom's suffering and yields to her decision. His attitude proves that his Strength is genuine, neither violent nor aggressive. Posterity,' Thamos predicted, 'will probably never fully appreciate Ottavio's true character. He will be seen as weak and vacillating, whereas in fact he represents righteous action, not *re*action, in the face of Don Giovanni's hyperactivity, which the profane world will find so beguiling. This brings us to the last phase of the ritual, the sumptuous banquet to which the Fellow Craft has dared to invite his victim, the Master of Work he assassinated.'

*Vienna, 3 September 1787*

Although Constanze's pregnancy was progressing smoothly, Wolfgang wanted to consult Dr Barisani, a leading practitioner at the Vienna general hospital. On two occasions, the sound ministrations of that excellent doctor had saved his life.

Barisani's assistant blenched.

'The doctor has just died,' he stammered.

'At twenty-six?'

'His death was sudden and unexplained.'

Wolfgang was deeply moved and wrote in his souvenir book: *That is right for him, but for me, for us, for everyone who knew him, it will never be right again, not until we have the happiness of seeing him again in a better world never more to separate.*

*Vienna, 10 September 1787*

'The Illuminati affair has ended in disaster,' Thamos told Wolfgang. 'According to the esteemed writer Schiller, the name of the movement's founder, Adam Weishaupt, is now on everyone's lips. Most Freemasons condemn him out of hand and wish he would disappear from the civic scene. In other words, none of them will dare to subscribe to his ideology on the empire's territory any longer.'

'A number of Viennese intellectuals could be in serious trouble; not even our lodge is protected.'

'Ignaz von Born is suspected of being on friendly terms with the Illuminati,' Thamos reflected, 'and you have often had dealings with them yourself. The imperial police could use that against you. If we are accused of pursuing Weishaupt's work and challenging the underpinnings of the empire, the authorities will come down very heavily indeed.'

'Josef II knows he has nothing to fear from the Freemasons,' objected Wolfgang. 'They have always upheld his policies, and in any case, he has muzzled them. Why should he harden his attitude further?'

'I hope you are right.'

'Are you really worried?'

'Those I loved have been killed, my Brother, and the beauty of my life has been destroyed. Nothing remains of my oasis, my palm trees, my monastery or my community. You are all I have left. And you are the only initiate who can revive all these wonders and pass them on, Mozart, the Egyptian. That is why I must protect you.'

Don Giovanni, *Act II, Finale, Scenes xiii and xiv*

'Although Don Giovanni dominates this opera, he only sings three arias,' Wolfgang reminded Thamos. 'In the first, he extols the delights of earthly nourishment; in the second, he glorifies love and death, while the third is a strategy to abuse Masetto before he roughs him up. But demonstrations of power are not enough to master Five, the number of his degree, which he constantly has to contend with.* Now, he hurtles towards his death, the necessary passage to a new state of being.'

'The Fellow Craft's behaviour and the demands of the ritual,' Thamos observed, 'lead to the apparition of the Secret Fire. Will he be bold enough to face it?'

'The scene has changed to a banqueting hall with a table set for a feast. Convinced that the Commendatore's statue is stuck to his plinth and won't come, Don Giovanni has no thought other than to enjoy himself. Of course, he must listen to music! A small orchestra plays popular airs while he wolfs down food and drink with the insatiable appetite of an ogre.'

'Are you going to include a little Mozart?'

'Let's treat Prague audiences to Figaro's aria they so much admired! And Leporello remarks: "Aha, I know that one only too well!" '

---

* The number Five is embodied by the Fellow Craft's adversaries and initiators, Anna, Ottavio, Elvira, Masetto and Zerlina.

'Don Giovanni is given one last chance: Donna Elvira bursts in and offers him the proof of her love. In exchange for her loyalty and mercy, she asks for nothing by way of recompense and is prepared to forget the philanderer's inconstancy, provided he changes his ways. But how can the Pillar of Beauty, associated with the degree of Entered Apprentice, save the Fellow Craft, associated with Strength? "If he is not moved by her grief," Leporello declares, "Don Giovanni's heart is made of stone or else he does not have one at all." '

'I shall have Leporello, Elvira and Don Giovanni sing together,' Wolfgang decided. 'While the First Overseer sings of the "heart of stone", which the Fellow Craft needs to meet the stone guest at the ritual banquet, Elvira insists on the iniquity of Don Giovanni, who celebrates good wine and women as the sustenance and glory of humanity.'

' "Humanity," proclaims Don Giovanni; "Iniquity," corrects Elvira. In this way, the two words become synonymous!'

'Donna Elvira can do no more, and she leaves the banqueting hall. On her way out she comes face to face with the spectral guest arriving and screams in terror. Don Giovanni orders Leporello to go and see what is going on. Another cry of horror! The First Overseer announces the arrival of the stone guest, the white man whose steps echo on the flagstones. And now, he hammers on the door. "Open up!" Don Giovanni orders Leporello.'

'The First Overseer has fulfilled his function by leading the Fellow Craft to the final encounter,' says Thamos. 'Don Giovanni now has to let in the light himself and open the door in person, while Leporello hides under the table from where he can observe the ritual scene, knowing full well how awful it is. Do you feel ready, my Brother, to pass on the Secret Fire without giving away our Mysteries?'

'I am not allowed to be afraid,' Wolfgang answered promptly. 'But will I be able to make the invisible appear?'

# 63

Don Giovanni, *Act II: The Apparition of
the Commendatore and Judgement*

'Don Giovanni opens the door to the banqueting
hall,' said Thamos, 'and the statue of the assassinated
Commendatore crosses the threshold. "You invited me
to dine with you," he reminds him, "and I have come." '

' "I'd never have believed it," admits the Fellow
Craft, stunned, "but I shall do what I can." Controlling
his emotions, he holds the stone guest's gaze and
orders Leporello to set another place. And the First
Overseer exclaims, not without reason: "We are all
dead!" '

'The Commendatore cuts short social niceties,' said
Thamos, ' "He who lives off heavenly nourishment has
no need of mortal nourishment," he declares. "Other,
more serious concerns and other wishes have brought
me down here. You invited me to dine; now you will

346

know your duty. Answer me: would you now come and dine with me?" '

'The First Overseer makes a show of trying to protect the Fellow Companion and pretends he doesn't have time! But they both know that reciprocity is one of the major laws of initiation. The initiate who has called forth the invisible cannot escape. Leporello warns his charge to be cautious, but Don Giovanni has Strength on his side and boldly announces: "My heart is firm in my chest. I am not afraid: I shall come." '

'Statements of intention are not enough,' said Thamos. 'The moment has come to accomplish the ritual act that the opera has been heading towards. "Give me your hand in agreement," orders the Commendatore.'

'Usually, a handshake allows two Brothers to recognize their common allegiance,' remarked Wolfgang, 'but the Commendatore embodies the hereafter. So, when Don Giovanni brazenly complies, he feels an icy chill.'

' "Repent and change your life," demands the stone guest. "Your last moment has come." '

' "No, no, I don't repent," retorts Don Giovanni, "get away from me!" Three more times, making five refusals, the number of his degree, he provokes judgement. The earth trembles, flames leap up and a choir emerges from the depths to claim that this is a small thing compared to his sins and that a far worse evil exists.'

'Don Giovanni suffers real torture and his soul is ripped to shreds. He experiences anguish and terror, then he is dragged down and swallowed up by Mother-Earth.

What a difference from the forgiveness granted to his predecessor, the count, by the countess in *The Marriage of Figaro*! Now we come to the end of the Fellow Craft's trajectory, after his betrayal and the assassination of the Master of Work. There will be no pardon and the Fire of transmutation must accomplish its work.'

'The "far worse evil" referred to by the choir,' added Wolfgang, 'could be seen as the Fellow Craft's cowardice, because he cannot go all the way. In this case, his journey ends up in the abyss, and the Fire is destructive.'

'Nothing remains but to conclude the ritual and close the works. The number Five appears, and the First Overseer tells Anna, Ottavio, Elvira, Masetto and Zerlina that Don Giovanni has gone far away. The stone guest came to fetch him and a demon swallowed him up in one gulp. Nothing is left of the Fellow Craft. Either he was totally destroyed or else he has gone to another universe, the universe of the Secret Fire, which has purified him and opened the doors of Mastery.'

'There can be no question of marriage, because we still haven't touched on the highest degree,' said Wolfgang. 'Anna asks Ottavio to wait a year. Masetto and Zerlina are happy to go home and dine in good company, while Elvira will end her life in a convent. As for Leporello, he will continue to act as the First Overseer and he goes off to the inn to find a better Master, that is, another Fellow Craft worthy of gaining access to the next stage.'

'According to Masetto, Zerlina and Leporello, who is well informed, Don Giovanni is living with Proserpina, the goddess of the Great Mysteries of Eleusis, and Pluto, the beneficent god of the Underworld who dispenses all forms of wealth. So, the alchemical operation has succeeded, and the Secret Fire has created another Master Mason.'

'Five will end, however, with the old song,' declared Wolfgang. ' "This is the end of the evildoer. And the death of a sinner is always equal to his life." If transmutation failed, the evil would not succeed any more.'

'This is one of the most grandiose works ever to deal with ritual death,' Thamos considered. 'Few people will grasp its true meaning, but your magic music will be played down the centuries.'

'We still have considerable work to do and time is running out!'

*Vienna, 29 September 1787*

Leopold Mozart's possessions were auctioned in Salzburg between the 25th and the 28th. Nannerl had finally decided to send her brother the thousand florins he suggested and now had to find a way of hastily collecting the money, because Wolfgang and Constanze were leaving for Prague on 1 October.

'Let's give the money to my Brother Puchberg,' the composer suggested. 'He is an honest and able merchant. He can pay it out to us over time, according to our needs.'

'Are you quite sure of him?' asked Constanze, anxiously.

'Absolutely.'

'In that case, we shall be travelling together. Don't worry: our little boy will be well looked after.'

'But you're six months pregnant, darling. Shouldn't you stay at home?'

'I want to be at the opening night of *Don Giovanni*. Everything I've heard fascinates me. And I can help you manage the day-to-day problems, so you can finish your opera without external worries.'

Wolfgang hugged his wife to him tenderly.

'I shall be over the moon to have you with me. You don't know how much I need you.'

*Prague, 5 October 1787*

Together with Gaukerl, always delighted to join in a new adventure, the Mozarts stopped at the Three Gold Lions Inn, where they enjoyed a hearty meal.

At dusk, while Constanze was resting, Wolfgang took his dog for a walk. Thamos soon caught them up.

'Our worries were not unfounded: since we left Vienna, three carriages have followed us in relays. Make sure there are no Brothers to welcome you. The dignitaries at Truth and Union Lodge are probably now under surveillance. We shall have to be extremely cautious about organizing secret meetings, but we will find a way. From tonight, I shall put our Brothers on the alert. There is bound to be a spy at your inn, so no one must contact us there.'

'I can go and stay with my friends the Duscheks at their beautiful Villa Bertramka. They are expecting me to visit. They often put up artists who are passing through, and I won't have to worry about police presence there.'

'Excellent idea.'

'Also, I shall be totally undisturbed to finish off *Don Giovanni*. I should have liked to add two or three scenes, but there may not be time.'

'Are you happy with Da Ponte's work?'

'When he gets to Prague, I shall ask him to change a few details.'

Wolfgang was clearly on edge. The Egyptian had to shelter him from the threats hanging over him.

# 64

*Prague, 8 October 1787*

Da Ponte was on the verge of a nervous breakdown.

'I am overwhelmed by work,' he announced to Mozart. 'Leaving Vienna was like bringing off a stunt!'

'I'm afraid I can't let you relax. I want you to make some changes.'

The abbé did not protest. He knew the composer well enough to realize it would be pointless and that his best course of action was to hear him out and do as he suggested.

'Do you know that the illustrious Casanova is in Prague? He is here to settle a matter concerning the publication of his novel, *Icosameron*. He will be intrigued to find that an opera with the title *Don Giovanni* is playing and is bound to attend the first night. Of course, he will try to make out that his dissolute existence has influenced us: he is terribly arrogant.'

'You seem to know him.'

'At one time, we had dealings with one another. He is a truly dreadful writer but he had the nerve to criticize my poems in public. We never spoke to each other again. Anyway, I am going to settle in comfortably and take up my pen.'

Da Ponte would have as much wine and tobacco as he needed, though no young servant girl to answer to his call.


*Prague, 14 October 1787*

The day was a nightmare.

To begin with, Da Ponte was recalled to Vienna by Antonio Salieri and had to leave Prague in a hurry. Between the swaggering Salieri and the modest Mozart, there could be no hesitation. Wolfgang would have to see to the final changes to the libretto himself.

Then, the local diva was indisposed and the composer had to make do with a troop of dilatory singers whose vocal ability left a lot to be desired. Given the technical demands of the score, they were heading for disaster.

Their one hope was to defer the première of *Don Giovanni* and replace it with *The Marriage of Figaro*, still just as popular in Prague.

Wolfgang wrote to his Brother Gottfried von Jacquin to say that he was furious and that everything was being delayed. *I have to give too much time to other people*

353

*and too little to myself*, he confided, meaning that he could not afford to attend a meeting and work with his Prague Brothers, if he was to avoid the first night being a resounding failure.

It was lucky he had Constanze to cheer him up and soothe his irritation.

'I have spared no pains and no amount of toil to produce something excellent,' he told her wearily. 'People are wrong to say I have always found music easy. No one had as much trouble as I did in mastering the art of composition. And there have been so many unforeseen problems that I still haven't written the overture!'

'I'm sure it will all be fine.'

Gaukerl gave a cheerful bark of encouragement.


*Prague, 26 October 1787*


At last: a rehearsal that was almost satisfactory! By dint of persuasion and detailed indications, Wolfgang managed to shake the singers out of their torpor and interest them in the complex piece they were about to perform for an audience eager to hear Mozart's new opera.

Given the general standard of the players, Wolfgang would not achieve perfection, but he could not let everything pass. Above all, Zerlina could not bring out a convincing scream at the end of Act I, when Don Giovanni tried to lay hold of her. The pathetic gurgle the frail young woman produced would never have been enough to summon the three masked figures, who came to confront the Don with his crimes and warn him that he would be punished. Wolfgang patiently explained what was needed, but the result was just as feeble.

Finally, just as Zerlina was taking a breath, he sneaked up behind her and grabbed her round the waist.

In her surprise, she let out a piercing scream.

'That's it, you've got it at last!' the composer exclaimed, delightedly.


*Prague, 27 October 1787*


The day before the première of *Don Giovanni*, whose date could not be moved, Wolfgang gently took his wife's hands in his and looked deep into her eyes.

'I only have tonight to write the overture: the copyist is coming for the score at seven in the morning. I can't hear the different sections of the orchestra successively, they are all sounding together, and I'm sure I won't have time to notate the whole thing. I'll just have to remember it as I conduct. Make me some punch, my darling, and tell me funny stories to keep me awake while I write.'

Constanze used up her entire repertoire.

'I'm not making progress fast enough!' Wolfgang groaned, exhausted.

'Go and sleep for a bit,' his wife advised. 'I'll come and wake you in an hour.'

She gave him two, because she could see he was worn out.

At five in the morning, he sat back down to work and finished off a tumultuous overture where the Fellow Companion's Strength clashed with true power, the power of ritual death, the necessary passage to other Mysteries. Mutation, a change of state, the Secret Fire beyond the grave: Mozart represented the full ritual tragedy that Don Giovanni would suffer.

At seven o'clock, as arranged, the copyist came to take the manuscript.

'I shall make do with my conductor's score, incomplete though it is,' Wolfgang told his wife. 'And I owe you one last confidence, my helpmeet, who know how important my Masonic commitments are to me: I have written this opera for me and for my friends.'

*Prague, 29 October 1787*

*Don Giovanni* or *The Rake Punished*, a jocular drama in two acts, received its first performance that evening, under the baton of its composer.

A number of Brothers attended, and they all appreciated the Masonic dimension of this sung ritual.

It played to a full house and was a triumph for Mozart. Casanova himself applauded till his hands ached. For the citizens of Prague, the real subtitle of the opera was still *The Stone Banquet* because it celebrated the appearance of the hereafter on earth and its confrontation with human nature.

Thamos let Mozart's splendid music resonate within him throughout the evening. Not a weakness, not a note out of place, every situation pertinent, and every symbol transposed into a character so that everyone in the audience could interpret in his own way. Supremely controlled and endlessly expressive, Mozart's music was nothing short of a miracle.

Yet this was only the second stage on the journey that would lead him to reshape initiation for the future.

How many lodges would realize the true importance of the ritual devised by the Great Magician? How many Brothers would change their approach to the degree of Fellow Craft and accord it its true symbolic dimension?

None, perhaps, not yet, and the future would obscure the truth still more. But Mozart would continue to forge a way to the Light. Was he not crossing death and rekindling the Secret Fire?

As tradition said, it only takes one man to save the world.

# 65

*Prague, 3 November 1787*

Gaukerl adored Villa Bertramka, the Duscheks' country house where the Mozarts were staying. He went for long walks with his master while Constanze rested.

*Don Giovanni* was a success, in spite of some rather negative reviews criticizing the opera for its 'extreme difficulty'. On the day of the fourth performance, given for Wolfgang's benefit, he was surprised to find himself shut in his study.

'You can't come out!' sang Josefa Duschek.

'What is all this about?'

'I shall only release you on one condition: I want you to compose an aria on the tragic theme of a dying hero who bids farewell to the woman he loves and asks to be avenged. You have plenty of pens, enough ink and reams of manuscript paper. If you want your freedom back, you must do some work!'

'I refuse to be blackmailed like this,' Wolfgang laughed. 'I shall set my own terms: if you make one mistake when you sight-read the score, I shall tear it up.'

Josefa Duschek looked through the score in alarm.

'That passage is terrifying!'

'A pact is a pact. I shall accompany you on the piano.'

The singer sang heroically, and as she had an excellent technique, the bravura aria *'Bella mia fiamma'*\* escaped destruction.


*Prague, 4 November 1787*


Wolfgang's letter congratulated Brother Gottfried von Jacquin: at last, he had decided to lead a calmer, more settled life. Like Don Giovanni, Gottfried had had countless affairs and neglected his Masonic duties. *Surely, the pleasure of flighty and capricious love*, his Brother Wolfgang wrote, *will always be a long way from the true happiness that real, reasonable love can bring.*

Seducing women was not the same as loving them. Competing with other men and collecting conquests was vain and vacuous. Faithlessness amounted to breaking an oath. For Wolfgang, frivolity and unbridled passions were incompatible with balance and serenity, and he rejected them.

\* K528.

None of his female characters was vile or sordid, because he was too aware of their mystery and magic. From the first note of *Thamos, King of Egypt*, he had sensed that his career as a man and an initiate would lead him to celebrate the marriage of the king and queen, the true union of a couple without which initiation was meaningless.

'The news is not great,' Thamos told him, when he came to dine at the Villa. 'I have spotted several plain-clothes policemen and the lodge is under permanent surveillance. If you don't turn up, it will look suspicious. Our enemies would conclude that we are organizing secret meetings and step up their measures. The official meeting is on the 10th. Tomorrow evening, the Master Masons will get together out of the way of prying eyes and ears.'

*Prague, 5 November 1787*

From the most distinguished Brothers, like Count Canal, down to the most humble, all the Master Masons in Truth and Union Lodge were there. Venerable Ignaz von Born opened the works of this secret meeting, held in a secure apartment.

During the banquet, Count Canal congratulated Mozart on his stupendous research into the genuine power at the heart of the Secret Fire, with his *Don Giovanni*.

'*The Marriage of Figaro* and *Don Giovanni* are both

great successes, Brother Wolfgang. Prague has adopted you and wants to keep you. Vienna audiences are fickle and superficial; it will be hard to win their hearts. I doubt they will ever appreciate *Don Giovanni* because it shows up the mediocrity of Salieri and his emulates. In Prague, you could work in peace and we would do everything we could to help you settle in.'

'From the bottom of my heart,' Wolfgang answered, deeply moved, 'I thank you for your offer, and I am very touched by it. Since the success of *Figaro*, I have often dreamed of living in Prague. But Venerable Ignaz von Born has entrusted me with a mission and I have promised to see it through: come what may, I must maintain the ideal of initiation in Vienna. My Lodge, New Crowned Hope, is the only hope of accomplishing it. Current circumstances are not very favourable but the future may prove more encouraging. Whatever happens, I cannot abandon my Viennese Brothers and run away.'

The citizens of Prague admired the courage of this Master Mason who put his Masonic duty before his private and professional interests.


*Prague, 10 November 1787*

On the 6th, Wolfgang had composed two short *Lieder*,[*] one of which was 'The Dream Vision', which he sent to

* K529 and K530.

361

Jacquin, as if keen to preserve the precious moments he had spent in Prague.

The first-degree meeting at Truth and Union Lodge was announced and celebrated according to the traditions of local Freemasonry, and they drank to the health of Brother Mozart, their honoured visitor.

Participating in a properly conducted ritual was a tremendous energy boost. Internal squabbles ceased, anxieties faded, and the presence of the symbols erased the vagaries of the moment and human mediocrity.

The Three Great Pillars, which had been so important in *Don Giovanni*, were lit up and the lodge heavens appeared, revealing the rays of the initiates who had passed to the Eternal Orient.

Yet each Brother was haunted by doubt: had the emperor's police managed to corrupt a Brother who was spying in their midst? Since they could not be sure, they restricted themselves to banal commentary on the importance of charity and respect for social and religious standards, and they spent only a brief time studying the symbol, the Pillar of Harmony, also called Beauty, directly associated with the degree of Entered Apprentice. Mozart's music was an expression that enabled them to perceive the echoes of the Universe that the Great Architect had created.

In three days, Wolfgang would be leaving Prague and returning to Vienna, where he hoped to enjoy a better music season than the previous one. But who still believed in him, apart from a small circle of friends and a few Brothers wanting to experience initiation fully? He would help them do battle with adversity by conveying the encouragement from Prague.

He would never give up, nothing was yet lost.

# 66

*Vienna, 16 November 1787*

'Mozart has just returned home,' Geytrand told Joseph Anton. 'In Prague, his *Don Giovanni* was a distinct success, whatever the critics say. Here is the libretto, my lord.'

'Masonic activities?'

'Mozart attended the Entered Apprentice meeting at Truth and Union Lodge, on 10 November. I have it from a few careless words that nothing subversive was said.'

'Do we have a serious informant, at last?'

'Unfortunately not, but I have not given up looking for one. The citizens of Prague are not easy to approach, and the Brothers of that Lodge still less. One false move and they will clam up even more. All the same, I have set in place a network of observers. They are gradually gathering information.'

'Any results from shadowing Mozart?'

'Nothing exciting. He did a lot of work and spent the greater part of his time at the theatre or in his hotel room. We lost sight of him for a few days, when he went to stay in the country with his friends the Duscheks.'

'It all sounds most unpromising,' considered Anton. 'Prague is seething with Freemasons and they are giving us the slip and celebrating their meetings more assiduously than ever. Is Mozart trying to become their ambassador in Vienna?'

The Count of Pergen read the libretto of *Don Giovanni* attentively and his fears were confirmed. Mozart was no ordinary musician. He was passing on a vision of initiation through his operas and their magic touched even the most profane.

Fully versed in Masonic rituals, Joseph Anton marvelled at the composer's skill in putting Da Ponte's talent to such good effect. Mozart had not simply evoked the ceremonies, symbols and science of numbers, he was extending them. To adepts of the Royal Art, he offered a new approach that would embellish the rituals. From now on, it would be impossible to perceive the secrets of the degree of Fellow Craft without having heard *Don Giovanni*.

How far would Mozart go?


*Vienna, 1 December 1787*


In order to lighten the burden of the rent and despite the condition of Constanze, whose happy pregnancy would soon reach its term, the Mozarts moved to 27, Unter den Tuchlauben, in the centre of town, a narrow street near the famous Graben, where they were still visited just as often. In a good location but without much charm, it was the tenth apartment in Vienna the composer had occupied. Constanze and little Karl Thomas settled in happily and Gaukerl took possession of a comfortable chair.

Their first visitor was Baron Gottfried Van Swieten.

'I come with excellent news, Mozart, and . . . news that is not so good.'

'Let's have the excellent news first to give us heart to bear the less good.'

'Gluck, the composer of *Orpheus and Eurydice*, died on 15 November, and his position at the court was declared vacant. A number of dignitaries and I have asked the emperor not to scrap it but to offer it to an obviously accomplished musician of repute. We have persuaded His Majesty to appoint you musician of the imperial chamber.'

'And the less-good news?'

'The salary is far below what Gluck received. He was given 2,000 florins. Because of the political and economic situation, Josef II has cut all the budgets except the army's. You will be given 800 florins per year, and your work will only involve composing dance music.'

'I shall have to accept, even if it is too much for what I do and too little for what I can do.'

An official position at the Court of Vienna: Leopold's dream was coming true.

# The Brother of Fire

While his wife was giving birth, Wolfgang looked back over the events of this exhausting year.

Death had deprived him of his father, his Brother Hatzfeld, his doctor and Star. Death was the central theme of *Don Giovanni*, seen, not from the human point of view, but in ritualistic terms. Like his hero, he was reaching the peak of his powers by finding, in his innermost being, the music that would express his ordeal.

Since returning from Prague, he had composed nothing but a futile song* that played on the idea of time running out. *The Abduction from the Seraglio* continued to be put on but not *The Marriage of Figaro*. In other words, he should do nothing to upset anyone and content himself with amusing the Viennese public.

But he would persevere.

*Don Giovanni* had brought Wolfgang to an important stage that involved offering his own powers to the Fire of Initiation. He would stick tirelessly to the path he had been treading, day after day, since meeting Thamos, and he would travel to Egypt to the community of priests and priestesses of the sun.

His friend and Brother, Joseph Haydn, was fighting for him and had been quick to write to the President of the High Court of Prague: *I am indignant at the thought that a man so singular as Mozart is still not engaged*

* 'The Little Spinning Girl', K531.

*in an imperial and royal court.* Despite the composer's Masonic connections, Josef II had repaired this injustice, at least in part.

Prague ... What a wonderful temptation, what a welcoming city, what a gilt-edged treasure trove! But it was here, in Vienna, that he was conducting his struggle beside the Jacquins, Stadler, von Gemmingen and other Brothers who rejected the tyranny of materialism and tried to preserve initiation.

'You have a girl!' announced the midwife. 'She is splendid and her mama did not suffer too much.'

Wolfgang kissed the smiling Constanze and his heart was full as he looked down at their fourth child, Theresia, whose first screams suggested a lively appetite for life.

'What pretty hair,' remarked Constanze. 'She will turn into a very beautiful young woman.'

Karl Thomas felt a sense of awe and dared not approach the baby.

'Will she be nice to me?'

'Of course, she will,' answered his father.

'Then, I'll protect her!'

'That will be your duty as her older brother.'

Gaukerl observed the new family member with a melting expression. What fun and cuddles to look forward to!

'Let us baptize her immediately,' begged Constanze.

'Frau Trattner will carry Theresia to the font of St Peter's church,' Wolfgang decided. 'A little girl ... How lucky we are!'

# 67

*Vienna, 3 January 1788*

After Christmas, which Wolfgang spent celebrating with his family and dandling Theresia, who had quickly become the household idol, he composed the first two movements of a sonata:* an energetic Allegro that showed how fully he had assimilated Bach's art of fugue, and an Andante, whose opening serenity was broken by strife and painful questioning before tranquillity was restored. To make a whole piece, he added an unusually slow Rondo with bursts towards the light of the hereafter, composed in 1786, and he sent the sonata to his Brother, the publisher Hoffmeister, to pay off a small debt.

Then, he went to see Lorenzo Da Ponte, still up to his eyes in work.

* K533.

'*Don Giovanni* was a great success in Prague, was it not?'

'I am hoping you will help me to get it performed in Vienna,' said Wolfgang.

The abbé snorted, contemptuously. 'That will not be easy.'

'I have a position at court, now, and—'

'I know, Mozart, I know! But you are only required to produce dance music. Opera is the domain of Salieri and his friends. And in any case, with all these rumours of war, the Viennese will be in no mood to attend a tragedy like *Don Giovanni*. They want to laugh and have fun.'

'Didn't we write a *dramma giocoso*?'

'Very well . . . I promise I shall do everything I can, but I can't guarantee the outcome.'

*Vienna, 4 January 1788*

'If Da Ponte is dragging his feet,' Thamos told Wolfgang, 'I shall do my bit. The task will not be easy because those little people are jealous of your success in Prague. Also, the atmosphere is pretty dismal. This time, conflict with the Turks seems inevitable.'

'If we do nothing to stop them, they will destroy Europe, and all forms of art, starting with music, will be banned.'

'Josef II realizes that he must come to the defence of civilization. Although, unlike the Prussians, he has no taste for war, he will not retreat. All the same, the alliances need to co-ordinate their efforts and the Austrian Empire cannot afford to find itself paralysed or isolated.'

'The Freemasons and I myself in particular will openly support him.'

'Your attitude will pacify the secret service that is hounding us. To restore Freemasonry's good image, as we enter a period of upheaval, I suggest Crowned Hope Lodge* organizes a grand concert on 12 January, to mark the occasion of the wedding of Archduke Francis. You will be one of the musicians, together with profane ones who will sing and play side by side with initiates and confirm that the Freemasons are splendid subjects for the Emperor and not fearsome rebels.'

*Vienna, 13 January 1788*

'Touché!' exclaimed Josef Anton, perusing the press. 'Crowned Hope Lodge has reasserted its good name with a concert attended by a number of Freemasons and Viennese worthies. The Brothers are now decent men, tolerant, respectful of the State and Church, art lovers, amateur scientists . . . in short, virtuous little angels!'

'A random event of little importance,' said Geytrand, dismissively.

* The adjective 'New' was soon removed.

'Don't you believe it! Viennese nobility is bewitched and all sorts of prescriptions will disappear. And who do you think was the great conqueror of the evening? Mozart, of course! He engineered the whole thing to loosen the bands. What a crowning success.'

Anton rarely lost his sang-froid. His anger surprised Geytrand, who was suddenly stuck for soothing arguments.

'Mozart has declared war on us,' the Count of Pergen concluded. 'He doesn't know who we are but he senses our presence and can see the efficiency of our actions. This time, he is taking the initiative. But his triumph will be short-lived.'

*Vienna, 27 January 1788*

The carnival season was in full swing, and since its start on 6 January, from nine in the evening until five in the morning on Thursdays and Sundays, three thousand people crowded into the small and great ballrooms of La Redoute at the Hofburg Imperial Palace in Vienna. Everyone ate and drank and twirled in fancy dress to dances and contredanses by Mozart, like 'The Storm' and 'The Battle',* whose fighting spirit cheered the revellers.

On his birthday, Wolfgang presented the party-goers with six German dances for orchestra, and the company

---

* K534 and K535.

was enchanted. The emperor had not been wrong to engage so accomplished a musician, for he knew how to amuse a vast public and distract them from their troubles.

Light-hearted, carefree and gay, the dances recalled the character of *The Abduction from the Seraglio* that had been sadly absent from *The Marriage of Figaro*.

'You were right,' Wolfgang told Thamos. 'The world is ruled by stupidity.'

*Vienna, 28 January 1788*

Since sundown, Thamos had been surveying the environs. The success of the concert organized by Crowned Hope Lodge would have been certain to provoke the anger of the secret service charged with spying on the Freemasons.

Anyone who came prying was easily found out in midwinter: either they perished from the cold or they were obliged to take a few steps to keep warm. In principle, the countess was above suspicion of harbouring secret meetings, but the Egyptian was on his guard and preferred to make sure.

Ignaz von Born was the first to cross the threshold, followed by Stadler, Mozart and Jacquin. Otto von Gemmingen was the last to arrive.

Tonight, there would be no low spirits.

For Mozart, this meeting was a source of hope. The little group gathered in the temple organized by Countess

373

Thun and two of her Sisters, set about designing the initiation of the future. Thamos revealed passages from *The Book of Thoth* that not even the lodges knew about. These ritual texts came from the sanctuaries of Ancient Egypt and gave unsuspected depth to the degrees of Entered Apprentice, Fellow Craft and Master Mason, whose reformulation would take considerable time. And the initiation of women was alive again.

When the exultant evening was over, the countess turned to Mozart.

'May I ask you a favour?'

'I hope I can grant it.'

'Prince Karl von Lichnowsky, one of your Brothers of the defunct Charity Lodge, would like to become your pupil. I know you hate teaching, but would you accept this candidate?'

'Since it is you who ask, my Sister, how can I refuse?'

'To be honest, the prince seems very interested in one of my daughters and she appears not indifferent to him. My husband and I would not oppose the union. The prince can only improve through contact with you.'

'I am a very imperfect teacher!'

The countess smiled. 'You are Mozart.'

# 68

*Vienna, 4 February 1788*

Brother Josef von Bauernfeld, normally so jovial, was looking disconsolate.

'I should never have bought this theatre out in the suburbs,' he told Mozart. 'It's a dead loss – I'm throwing good money after bad!'

'Don't be so pessimistic. We'll put on some shows and you'll soon be back on an even financial keel.'

'Haven't you heard? Tonight is the last performance of your *Abduction from the Seraglio*!'

'Have people lost interest?'

'The Kärntnertor Theatre is closing until further notice, like most of the other theatres in Vienna. The German company has been disbanded.'

'Are we at war?'

'Yes, my Brother. The music season will be reduced to a strict minimum and cultural life to somnolence.

Forget philanthropy, eager audiences and dazzling concerts: Viennese nobility has been called up to fight the Turks.'


*Vienna, 9 February 1788*


To bring relief and assistance to its Russian ally, Austria declared war on the Ottoman Empire.

Emperor Josef II decreed massive mobilization and assembled an army of 315,000 men, which included the cream of the aristocracy and valuable craftsmen; hundreds of workshops were left empty.

The emperor passed several special fiscal decrees to finance the huge numbers of troops, and everyone hoped they would be enough to drive back the barbarians and save Western civilization.

Even Leopold, who did not like the liberal policies of his brother Josef II, came to his aid.

The Turkish army was fearsome. Its soldiers were waging a holy war to force their beliefs on the world. Since death took its heroes straight to a heaven peopled by virgins for their enjoyment, they had no reason to retreat before the enemy.

There were no further concerts, no viable publications, no Viennese première of *Don Giovanni*, and Wolfgang's taxes had risen. In spite of his handsome salary, he wondered how long he would be able to maintain his lifestyle.

'I am playing at a concert for Dolfin, the Venetian Ambassador,' he told Constanze. 'It should make a few florins.'

'Don't worry too much. If needs be, your Brother Puchberg will act as your banker. We must enjoy our happiness as we can. We love each other and we have two beautiful children and a mischievous little dog! Like you, I fully support the emperor's decision. Not fighting the Turks would be disastrous for Austria.'

*Vienna, 24 February 1788*

Undeterred by the bad weather, Anton Stadler organized a concert on the 20th that featured, for the first time, a bass clarinet manufactured by Brother Theodor Lotz, who worked for the imperial and royal court. This marvellous instrument played two notes lower than the standard clarinet and produced wonderfully new, rich tones.

The collaboration between the three Freemasons Mozart, Stadler and Lotz thus bore its first fruits, but composer and investor had bigger ideas for the basset clarinet's deep voice and would not stop there. Lotz had been truly inspired in using boxwood, as being more solid than maple; but new keys would have to be added and that would cost money. Mozart was excited by the project and determined to pursue it, regardless of his money troubles.

With his mind travelling back to Prague, where he hoped to perform again one day, Mozart finished a brilliant piano concerto.* The sublimely beautiful Allegro of the first movement expressed cloudless happiness, until the call to battle with adversity. Soloist and orchestra – initiate and brotherhood – were not in conflict and supported one another so effectively, in a joint meditation, that they achieved total weightlessness. Truth and Union: Truth in Union. The slow movement came as a detachment from the self, a release from one's own inner prison, and led to an aptly named Allegretto.

'Baron Gottfried Van Swieten wants to see you,' Constanze told him.

The head of censorship waved a score under his nose.

'This is a cantata† by Carl Philipp Emanuel Bach, a son of that outstanding genius we so much admire, you and I. I am giving you eighty-six instrumentalists, thirty choristers and three renowned soloists including Aloysia Lange and her husband. I have managed to persuade Count Esterházy, your Brother, to have the piece played at his palace in two days' time, on condition that you conduct. An excellent opportunity for your fame.'

---

* Concerto No. 26, in D major, K537, known as the 'Coronation' because it was played on 15 October 1790 in honour of Leopold II's coronation.
† *The Resurrection and Ascension of Jesus.*

# The Brother of Fire

At the Leopoldstadt Theatre, Friedrich Baumann sang Mozart's latest work, a war song with orchestral accompaniment entitled, 'I should like to be the Emperor,'* which put the musician firmly on the side of Josef II's valiant soldiers.

Aloysia Lange and her husband, Mozart's Brother, congratulated him.

'Sometimes, you surprise me,' she declared. 'I had no idea you could be so bellicose! All the same, I prefer the aria you have just given me'†

'You voice is still as radiant and you have lost none of your virtuosity.'

'Were you afraid I might have done?'

'So little, that I want you to sing Donna Anna in the Venice production of *Don Giovanni*.'

Aloysia gave a shiver of pleasure.

'In the current climate, do you think we shall manage to produce such a difficult opera?'

'Don't listen to the gossip. The Burgtheater is still open and I shall find some loyal friends to help me.'

'You can count on me, Wolfgang.'

---

*K539.
† '*Ah, se in ciel*', K538.

*Vienna, 10 March 1788*

Thanks to his connections with Venerable Otto von Gemmingen, the Professor of German Language and Literature, Leopold-Aloys Hoffmann was an important piece on Geytrand's chessboard. An ex-Illuminatus who went by the pseudonym of Sulpicius he had betrayed his Brothers and was continuing to do so at Crowned Hope. A born whistle-blower, he wrote anonymous texts savaging the Freemasons, gave away their rituals and sold information.

'The reputation of your lodge has improved considerably of late,' Geytrand remarked.

'That is Mozart's doing. Was there ever a better patriot? He makes even the Viennese aristocracy dance to his tunes.'

'Don't you think it might be a smoke screen?'

'Personally, I don't have much to do with him. But you may find you can exert a little leverage with one of his pupils, Brother Karl von Lichnowsky, a spineless, venal aristocrat who may be open to informing on the composer's doings. He is constantly in need of money and naturally grasping, so I am sure he will be sensitive to your propositions.'

'Has he really no morals?'

'The idea is completely foreign to him! Lichnowsky is using Freemasonry only to build his network and consort with the well-to-do.'

'Which Mozart patently isn't,' objected Geytrand.

'If Lichnowsky is having a go at music and wants to receive his illustrious Brother's instruction, that is because it is somehow in his interests. It is up to you to find out why.'

Intrigued, Geytrand wrote up a detailed report for his boss. An informant closer to Mozart would be difficult to imagine.

# 69

*Vienna, 19 March 1788*

What a ghastly morning! Wolfgang was vainly trying to drum a few basics about the piano into Karl von Lichnowsky, his least gifted pupil, who had just borrowed money off him. Invoking Masonic fraternity and a difficult moment, the prince had charmingly and convincingly wheedled the money out of Mozart, who need have no hope of seeing it again.

Although he was doing all he could, Da Ponte had failed to reach an agreement with the Burgtheater to put on *Don Giovanni*. There had been no definite refusal, but the administration and musicians had shown no enthusiasm, either. Vienna was at war and audiences wanted feel-good entertainment, nothing too heavy and nothing too light. Da Ponte protested that his 'jocular drama' answered precisely to this requirement, but he was going to have to win over opponents and waverers.

Faced with future uncertainty and the struggle to live by the Masonic ideal in a profane world, Wolfgang wrote a searing Adagio in B minor for piano,* a meditative piece of extraordinary intensity, full of deep silences and agonizing voids. It was useless to think otherwise: at the heart of ordeals and regardless of fraternal bonds, ultimately one was alone. Alone with the blackness of night, men's feet of clay and your own limits; but you should never give up and, in the depths of the abyss, continue the search for tomorrow's word.

*Vienna, 25 March 1788*

All Vienna was talking about it: Josef II was leading his troops out of the capital and into the country to fight the Turks.

Everyone applauded the monarch's courage and went about with superficial optimism. In fact, everyone feared the worst. If the war went against them, if the Ottomans got the upper hand, invasion and massacres would follow.

Wolfgang went to cheer himself up with Anton Stadler, who, having just had another child, was out of pocket and low on enthusiasm.

'Josef II is cautious and calculating. He wouldn't have

* K540.

383

rushed into this perilous adventure if he hadn't been sure of victory.'

'The Turks are the fiercest warriors imaginable,' countered Stadler. 'Vienna's noblemen are spoilt and overfed. They won't stand a chance against the barbarous horde.'

'Don't underestimate our professional soldiers. They have experience and courage on their side.'

'You're right: let us trust in our future! Here's to your *Don Giovanni*!'

'Negotiations are slow-moving, but Da Ponte will get there. At the moment, I can't arrange concerts, so I am launching a subscription for three quintets. The copies will be sent to our Brother Puchberg, and clients can get hold of them from July. I am hoping for good sales.'


*Vienna, 24 April 1788*


'We have been given the all-clear,' Da Ponte announced. 'Our *Don Giovanni* will be put on, on 7 May. There are just a few minor details to settle.'

'What are they?' Wolfgang asked, anxiously.

'The tenor is having a lot of trouble with Don Ottavio's aria and wants you to compose an easier alternative.'

Wolfgang produced a heroic and solemn aria in which Ottavio proclaimed his veneration for Anna and his determination to avenge her: 'My peace depends on hers,' he sang, 'I live from what pleases her and die from her sorrows. If she sighs, I sigh, too. Her anger is mine, her tears are mine, and I have no happiness if she has none'.*

'We'll replace Don Ottavio's old aria,' Da Ponte suggested, 'with the kind of comic scene the Viennese adore: a row between Zerlina armed with a knife and the wretched Leporello. She grabs his hair and takes him prisoner, determined to tear out his heart, then she ties him to a chair with a rope attached to a window, hoping, through him, to win Don Giovanni's heart. Leporello prays to Hermes and manages to free himself. The episode will cause a laugh and relax the tension.'

Wolfgang was unenthusiastic, but he agreed to the insertion.

'Maybe, for dramatic effect, we ought to drop the last part of the finale and finish with Don Giovanni's death?' the abbé went on.

'Certainly not!' Mozart protested, careful not to explain to the librettist the true meaning of the death. 'Leporello and the five protagonists have to reappear, declare Don Giovanni dead and announce their intentions. I don't mind shortening the finale a bit for the first Viennese production, but I want it played in full in future performances. And I'm going to add an aria.† In Act II, just before Leporello leads Don Giovanni to the graveyard where he meets the Commendatore's statue, Donna Elvira sings of the philanderer's excesses and wicked-

---

* K540z, No. 11 in the score.
† K540c, recitative and aria, '*Mi Tradì*', one of the peaks of Mozart's music.

ness. Heaven's wrath will soon strike him down, the mortal gulf will yawn. Cheated and abandoned, she still feels pity. Revenge is certainly necessary, but her heart beats when she thinks of the risk Don Giovanni is taking by confronting invisible forces.'

As the embodiment of the Pillar of Harmony, Elvira questions the difficult transmutation of the Fellow Craft, associated with Strength, whose access to Wisdom is so tenuous.

*Vienna, 30 April 1788*

'We have had confirmation that *Don Giovanni* will have its first performance in Vienna on 7 May,' Thamos told Wolfgang. 'Da Ponte has batted valiantly, and a few influential friends finally convinced the more reticent ones. As you know, you are not short on enemies at court and in musical circles.'

'All they want is another *Abduction from the Seraglio*, where they can laugh without thinking! *The Marriage of Figaro* unsettled reactionary minds, and they won't get much comfort from *Don Giovanni*!'

'You are opening people's hearts to essential truths with your libretti and music and giving new voice to the rituals of initiation. That is why *Don Giovanni* must be reborn and flourish in Vienna.'

Thamos's encouragement was decisive. He never flattered his Brother and never hid his thoughts from him.

His teaching ceaselessly opened up new horizons. With him, Wolfgang enjoyed true fraternity worthy of the temples of Ancient Egypt and the brotherhood of the priests of the sun.

# 70

*Vienna, 30 May 1788*

On the appointed day, 7 May, *Don Giovanni* was finally put on in Vienna, in the absence of Josef II. Aloysia Lange sang Donna Anna and, as intended, the Commendatore and Masetto were sung by the same bass. The opera was performed again on the 9th, 12th, 16th, 23rd and the 30th.

Mozart earned 225 florins, but the opera's reception was cool. The only review in the *Wiener Zeitung*, on 10 May, commented: 'The music is by Herr Wolfgang Mozart, Kapellmeister at the imperial court.' In other words: nothing to hear and nothing to see. Rosenberg, the Director of Shows, was laconic: 'Mozard's (*sic*) music is far too difficult to sing.'

Antonio Salieri and his friends gloated over the general indifference. It was obvious that *Don Giovanni* would run to no more than fifteen performances before being withdrawn from the repertory and forgotten about altogether. No one denied Mozart's accomplishments, but he did not understand Viennese tastes and wrote difficult music. If he had stuck to the gallant style and the pretty fantasy of *The Abduction from the Seraglio*, the public would have stayed loyal to him.

The Archbishop of Vienna and his counsellors were similarly disparaging of an opera where a spectre took the place of God to chastise a profligate. The living statue of the Commendatore looked too much like the devil and did not conform to Church doctrine. What more could one expect from a Freemason with subversive ideas?

*Vienna, 1 June 1788*

'*Don Giovanni* is a total flop. You should be pleased,' Geytrand told Josef Anton. 'The general consensus is that the opera will not last long. Mozart should have stayed in Prague.'

'He may be struggling, but he has not given up trying to get Freemasonry a foothold in Vienna. And this *Don Giovanni* is a true masterpiece and proves it.'

'You . . . you surely didn't like it, my lord?'

'I can see exactly what Mozart is doing. He is working to a detailed plan and doggedly sticking to his objectives, regardless of the circumstances. Every day, he grows more daring and more dangerous, and this setback will not stop him. But we have other things to worry about. The situation in France is deteriorating. The parliaments have been dissolved and there is unrest in Paris and the provinces. The King is going to have to call the Estates General to quell the uprisings.'

'How are the Freemasons behaving?'

'According to my informants, who include Angelo Soliman, an ex-Freemason, the situation is extremely complex. Some of them want to follow the Federal Constitution of the United States, inspired by the Masons. However, there is another more radical group influenced by Mirabeau, an Illuminatus, who is critical of the Prussian monarchy and thinks, like Bode, that Freemasonry has been infiltrated by Jesuits. They have learnt from Jean-Paul Marat, a proponent of violent political revolution. Many of the nobility, wealthy or not, are leaving the lodges because there is too much talk of equality. Brothers from the middle classes who believe in liberalism are afraid that extremist ideologies will result in disorder. A hard core is refusing to hold old-fashioned rituals and has become politicized and wants to overthrow society. Brethren who oppose the royal family and the Church have set up Para-Masonic societies, calling them "philanthropic societies", and they talk of economy, progress, industry and the abolition of privileges.'

'Why doesn't the regime stamp out these subversive movements?'

'Only tyrants like Louis XIV can govern France. And Louis XVI is not the same. He misguidedly believes people will respect his position. When the leader is wrong, the people similarly fall into error. Then, all it takes is a handful of skilful manipulators to make wild animals of them.'

'Aren't you being a bit pessimistic?'

'Only realistic. And it could be the Freemasons who cause this wave to break over Austria.'


*Vienna, 1 June 1788*


The failure of *Don Giovanni* did not cool Mozart's ardour to pursue the plan of action that would lead to the end of his Quest.

'How shall we get to the next stage after the Fellow Craft?' he asked Thamos. 'How can we describe the Great Mysteries without giving them away? Maybe the high degrees will help me.'

'I am afraid not,' said the Egyptian. 'Their main obsession is to catch and punish the three guilty Fellow Crafts who assassinated Hiram. In the ritual, the lodge is hung with the murderers' skeletons and the candidate for promotion stabs a blade into a model's heart, causing blood to spurt from a lamb's heart concealed under branches, then he brandishes a head made of card.'

'What a silly parody!' exclaimed Wolfgang.

'Which is why the "high degree" systems collapsed. The traditional system from Ancient Egypt of Entered Apprentice, Fellow Craft and Master Mason provides a sound enough basis, provided it is studied and experienced with intensity.'

'Then, I shall write a series of three symphonies that lead from the Temple door to a vision of the Light from the Orient.'

'If you do that,' Thamos assured him, 'you will find an original design for your third ritual opera about the degree of Master Mason.'

# 71

*Vienna, 2 June 1788*

While an opera by Alfonsi, with an aria for bass writ-
ten by Mozart,* was playing at the Burgtheater, the
Count of Pergen was dining with Prince Karl von
Lichnowsky.

'You are one of Mozart's pupils, I understand?'

'I may not be very good but I do like making music.'

'Happy with your teacher?'

'He is like no one else! When he loses patience with
my mistakes, he shoos me away from the piano and sits
down to improvise for my delight alone.'

'He is a talented composer, but I gather he is beset by
unfortunate money troubles.'

'Oh, I didn't know.'

---

* K541, involving a cynical Frenchman trying to wise up a naïve lover
– a character sketch for Don Alfonso in *Cosí fan Tutte*.

'I must ask you not to repeat any of this, Prince von Lichnowsky.'

The prince looked surprised. 'Why not?'

'Because I know everything about you.'

'Everything . . . I don't understand.'

'Your allegiance to the Freemasons, your mistresses and peccadilloes . . . Everything. However, I am prepared to overlook them and not ruin your reputation if you agree to help me in silence.'

'Help you . . . to do what?'

'I want you to tell me what you find out about Mozart and then to spread certain rumours about him.'

'What sort of rumours?'

'The emperor is a thrifty administrator and hates prodigality. He would not like to find that Mozart is steeped in debt and squandering his resources.'

'But that's not true!'

'So what?'

'All the same, he is—'

'Your Lodge Brother? You have always acted for yourself and yourself alone, Prince von Lichnowsky, and you will continue to do so.'

'But why should we damage Mozart's reputation?'

The Count of Pergen's face darkened.

'Don't ask questions, just do as I say! You will help me to dishonour and impoverish him. He will incur heavy tax bills, then legal proceedings will force him to pay off an enormous debt.'

'But he is an honest man!'

Josef Anton smiled.

'That makes him all the more vulnerable.'

*Vienna, 3 June 1788*

Wolfgang was exhausted.

His three subscription quintets were unsuccessful and earned him scarcely anything. The current economic and political situation meant that Vienna was no longer interested in pieces that might deter amateur musicians by their technical demands. Van Swieten, one of the composer's few supporters, advised him not to give up. In the *Wiener Zeitung*, he posted the following notice: *Given the very low number of subscriptions, I am constrained to postpone publishing my three new quintets until early January. Subscriptions may still be bought from Herr Puchberg for the sum of four ducats or eighteen florins.*

No concert, no sale of sheet music, *Don Giovanni* a flop: the Mozarts' material future was darkening. He had to pay two master tailors, Constanze's and his own, the doctors, the pharmacist, the shoemaker, the vintner and several other merchants.

As a matter of urgency, he appealed to Puchberg, who acted as the Mozart family banker, to ask him for a hundred florins.

'Don't worry,' Constanze told him. 'It is just a difficult time. If we have to draw in our horns, we will still be happy.'

'There is no question of us lowering our standard of living! You must continue to wear pretty dresses and neither you nor our children will want for anything.'

Wolfgang was loath to discuss his material worries with either Thamos or von Born, feeling that they should not have to share his burden. It was up to him to shoulder the ordeal.

As he had not yet found the central theme of his third ritual opera, he made a start on the first of the three symphonies intended for the Masonic enterprise. No one had commissioned them and maybe no one would ever play them in Vienna, but it did not matter. They sprang from an inner drive and reflected Mozart's experience on the road to knowledge.

The first in the trilogy* evoked both the degree of Entered Apprentice and the necessary qualities needed to fulfil the function properly in the lodge.

The majestic edifice opened, unusually, with a solemn Adagio that formed the porchway into the three symphonies. Then came the first Allegro, reflecting the discovery of the way and the urge to speak the language of the symbols and commune with them. The movement represented an essential discovery: only an unshakable will, proved by Perseverance in the Chamber of Reflection, allowed one to continue on towards Enlightenment.

The Andante con moto described how Perseverance was nourished by overcoming impatience and any

---

*Symphony No. 39 in E flat major, K543.

instinct to hurry. Of course, there would always be the anxiety: am I capable of going all the way to the end of the Quest for initiation?

Short movements followed that enjoined the Entered Apprentice not to be idle and introspective but to take the initiative and develop his own power by continuing, come what may, spurred on by enthusiasm, a divine virtue that transformed a man into a Brother. God rejected half-hearted candidates; the desire for initiation was neither destructive nor oppressive, but liberating.

# 72

*Vienna, 10 June 1788*

Various issues with their landlord had prompted Wolfgang and Constanze to leave their home and move to an apartment called The Three Stars, at 135 Währingerstrasse, where the most pleasing feature was a garden. Gaukerl was allowed to run around in it and little Theresia could play in it with her brother.

'You aren't too sorry to be living in the suburbs?' Constanze asked anxiously.

'You know, I don't really have that much to do in town. If needs be, I can take a carriage. And will you be happy here?'

'Infinitely!'

Gaukerl wriggled in between his master and mistress: if they wanted to kiss one another, they would have to stroke him first.

Wolfgang's mind was on his grand symphonic plans

and he was grateful for this peaceful environment where he could work uninterrupted.

*Vienna, 16 June 1788*

The storm broke, just as Mozart was giving a repeat performance of *Don Giovanni*.

It was inconceivable: the tax office and an obscure public body were accusing him of running up vast debts, even suggesting embezzlement, and were taking legal action that threatened to ruin him and plunge his family into penury. He was warned that his salary could be seized and his possessions sequestered, meaning the end of his career, for the emperor, with his high regard for parsimony and good management, would banish him from court.

The theatres and concert halls would all be closed to him for ever and he would have no more publisher, not even a Brother, to bring out his compositions.

It was grossly unfair. Surely there was some mistake, some dreadful misunderstanding? No, they wanted to destroy him and get rid of him for good! Was it Salieri and his clique or an enemy of Freemasonry? Whoever it was had a long arm and could make the wheels of the public authorities turn.

The blow looked fatal, but Wolfgang could not give up creating. His vocation and his mission were what counted most and he refused to bow to circumstance and give in. The composer of *Don Giovanni* did not lack courage and power. They might think they had broken his spirit, but he would make a stronger comeback after this shattering ordeal.

But first he had to put out the flames and stop the legal action, by paying the sums demanded of him without unbalancing his budget. The only solution was to borrow money that he could repay over time, once fortune began to smile on him again.

As he did not want to worry Constanze, he said nothing about it to her but wrote instead to Puchberg, the only person he consulted on the matter:

*Very honorable Brother!*

*Very dear and excellent friend! The certainty that you are my true friend and that you know me to be an honorable man encourages me to open my heart to you and send you the following request. With my deepest sincerity, I shall come straight to the point with no fine sentences.*

*If you would have the goodness and friendship to come to my aid for 1 or 2 years with 1 or 2 thousand florins, against appropriate interest, you would be helping me to hoe my row! You will surely feel yourself that it is sure and true that one can only eke out a poor existence or that it is even impossible to live if a man has to wait for intermittent payments of money! Without the necessary minimum reserves, it is impossible to keep one's affairs in order. If one has nothing, one obtains nothing . . . I have now opened my whole heart to you on a matter of the utmost importance to me, and I have treated you as a true Brother, with whom I can be totally frank. And now I look forward eagerly to a favourable reply. Consider my letter as the true proof of my wholehearted trust in you and remain for ever my friend and Brother, as I shall be until death.*

*PS: When shall we get together for a little music? I have written another trio!*

Would Puchberg realize that Mozart was dependent on his help if he was to work with an easy mind and a light heart?

*Vienna, 17 June 1788*

Johann Michael Puchberg, a textile merchant, wore his forty-seven years lightly. Remarried the previous year, he prided himself on selling the finest silks in Vienna and stocking luxurious velvets, as well as splendid collections of ribbons, gloves, handkerchiefs and other items prized by high society.

He took great pride in his elegant shop on the Hohermarkt, as he did in his nearby apartment in a magnificent building that belonged to Count Franz-Xaver Walsegg-Stuppach, an enthusiastic collector of sheet music, which he bought from more-or-less famous composers and then signed with his name.

A Freemason since 1773, Puchberg had 'travelled' around several lodges in Vienna and met Mozart in Charity Lodge shortly after his initiation. He was genuinely fond of the passionate, talented young composer and he liked his works, even if some of them were difficult. Wolfgang was an excellent Brother and was developing ideas that few people understood, but their importance deserved respect. Puchberg had no misgivings about acting as his banker and helping him out; however, this letter took him aback. Why did Mozart suddenly need so much money?

It must be a moment's panic due to the conflict with the Turks. Business was slow, the aristocracy thought of nothing but the war, and without their interest in concerts Viennese cultural life was down to a minimum. Mozart must be feeling the pinch.

Puchberg decided to lend him two hundred florins.

*Vienna, 22 June 1788*

Momentarily saved by his Brother, Wolfgang had stalled the legal proceedings, but they were not over yet. They went on for months, for years, yet he was in no doubt that the outcome would be in his favour. Not having anything to blame himself for, why should he be held to account?

He knew Puchberg enjoyed chamber music and, by way of thanks, sent him the manuscript of a trio for piano, violin and cello.* Written in E major, a key Wolfgang rarely used, the piece was strange and rather severe. Not even the finale, with its central section in C major, offered any real gaiety.

The piano sonata,† on the other hand, was written as he looked out over the garden of his new apartment, and suggested peace and clarity.

Thamos, with Gaukerl settled on his knee, had the privilege of hearing this small masterpiece. How, he wondered, had Mozart achieved such perfection, untouched by human mediocrity?

'Our Brother Karl Leonhard Reinhold has published an interesting work under the pseudonym Decius, called *The Hebrew Mysteries* or *Ancient Religious Freemasonry*. He demonstrates that Moses, whose hieroglyphic name means "he who is born", was initiated in Egypt.'

'Reinhold has paid attention to your teaching and can expect the Church to come down on him like a ton of bricks!'

'Truth will out, some time or other, even if these troubled times are not the best moment.'

---

*K542.
†K545, often called 'little sonata for beginners', but which only concert pianists can render without massacring it.

*Vienna, 26 June 1788*

Three days after a repeat performance of *Don Giovanni*, Wolfgang wrote in his album the symphony he had just dedicated to the degree of Entered Apprentice, as well as a short March in D major, his last sonata, and an Adagio and Fugue for Strings,* in which he communed with the spirit of Johann Sebastian Bach and transcribed all the hardships of the ordeal he had just undergone. The severity and almost violent poignancy of the development, without ornamentation, reflected his readiness to confront his fate.

---

* Symphony No. 39, K543, K544, a lost work, given to a friend, K545 and K546 in C minor.

# 73

*Vienna, 27 June 1788*

The fire was still smouldering, and the legal and tax battles rumbled on, delaying payment and provoking further discussion. Wolfgang was thus forced to write to Puchberg again:

*Venerable Brother, Very dear and excellent friend!*
*I was hoping to come to town in the next few days to thank you in person for the friendship you have shown me. I do not now have the heart to show my face, because I must frankly admit that it is impossible for me to repay you so soon for the money you lent me, and I am forced to ask for your patience on that score! My position is such that I am obliged to borrow money immediately, but Dear God, whom can I confide in? There is only you, dear friend! And the lender has, it seems to me, enough guarantees*

*of my good character and reimbursements. Which is why I should like to have a rather larger amount for a rather longer period, so that I can avoid this happening again. My dear Brother, if you do not help me in this matter, I shall lose my honour and my credit, which are the only two things I wish to preserve. But I am wholly reliant on your friendship and fraternal love and I am confident that you will come to my aid with your advice and actions. If my wishes are answered, I can breathe again, because I shall then be able to put my affairs in order and keep them that way. Please come and visit me at my place; I am always at home. For the ten days I have been here, I have done more work than in two months in my previous accommodation. And if so many gloomy thoughts did not occur to me so often (which I have violently to repel), things would be better still, because my apartment is pleasant, practical and cheap. I do not want to detain you any longer with my chatter, and shall just be silent, now, and wait.*

*Vienna, 29 June 1788*

'We must call a doctor, quickly,' said Constanze, in obvious distress. 'Theresia is not well. Her head is burning and she is shivering.'

Wolfgang leapt into a carriage to go and fetch one of the hospital's best practitioners, who only made home visits at a price. Thanks to Puchberg's help, the composer was hoping to contain the breaking wave that threatened to engulf them and he would spend his last florin on saving his little girl.

Constanze fell weeping into her husband's arms. A second doctor achieved no better results than his colleague. Aged only six months, Theresia died of an unknown illness and was buried in the Währing cemetery.

*Vienna, 2 July 1788*

Grief-stricken though he was, Wolfgang had no time to give way. He had to comfort his wife and little boy, and even the dog Gaukerl, and attend to an urgent matter. Puchberg had not sent the money in time, and he had no choice but to take items of value to the pawnbroker's to cover expenses that were stopping the lawsuit from being resolved.

Then he wrote again to his Brother, begging him to react promptly:

> *I have now organized my affairs, painfully and anxiously, so that it will be enough to lend me a little money. I beg you, in the name of our friendship, do me this favour, but please do it immediately. I am sorry to insist: you know my situation. Oh, why did you not do as I asked! Do it now, and everything will go as I hoped.*

*Vienna, 11 July 1788*

'Mozart looks like a broken man,' considered Geytrand. 'Your subtle blow to his finances, my lord, has produced a remarkable effect. He has been reduced to pawning his belongings.'

'All the same, he has not given up yet.'

'In his naivety, he believes he can win his lawsuit! He will lose a small fortune in a pointless battle and end up totally bankrupt. His daughter has died, he has no more concerts and his subscriptions have failed. Mozart is finished!'

'But there was a repeat performance of *Don Giovanni* on the 5th and the opera is on again tonight.'

'A swan song,' said Geytrand, unimpressed. 'The piece has not been successful and will disappear from the repertory. The Viennese have clearly lost interest in Mozart. He should have settled for being a good pianist and given up composing: that is what enlightened critics are saying.'

'Any news from Prague?'

'We are homing in on the main leaders and observing them discreetly.'

'No false moves, Geytrand!'

Joseph Anton was worried about the war. News of recent developments was not great. The emperor was struggling and the outcome of the conflict remained unclear.

*Vienna, 16 July 1788*

The Mozart family faced the cruelty of fate with dignity. Little Karl Thomas had gone back to playing with Gaukerl and was enjoying the warm summer sunshine. With the insouciance and egoism of childhood, he had already forgotten his sister's shadow.

This third death strengthened the firm bonds that already existed between Wolfgang and Constanze. They lived through their joys and pains together, crossing the same hurdles and offering each other mutual support to surmount them and build a future.

Far from complaining, Constanze continued to run the household in an exemplary manner.

Wolfgang, meanwhile, was faltering. He composed a pretty, limpid sonata for violin and piano* and gave Puchberg a Piano Trio† containing a few Masonic allusions in the thirds and tied notes, and an aria for two sopranos and bass‡ with a view to a future opera. 'Out of a thousand lovers,' the text ran, 'you cannot even find two fine constant souls, yet everyone talks of fidelity! And these bad habits will spread, as long as the honest lover's constancy is now called naivety.' Nothing essential, nothing really satisfying: just a question of continuing to survive.

As always, Thamos the Egyptian was at his side. He asked no questions and offered no vacuous comfort but

* K547, the last he composed for these two instruments.
† K548.
‡ K549.

he shared Mozart's suffering as a brother. Once more, it was he who gave him the courage to go on.

'Don't you think it is time to compose your symphony dedicated to the degree of Fellow Craft?'

Wolfgang worked tirelessly, his mind feverish with the intensity of the piece.* As dramatic as *Don Giovanni*, the symphony opened with the Fellow Craft's long, relentless struggle with the invisible in the lead-up to the terrifying assassination of the Master. The slow movement captured the enormity of the crime and the perpetrator's realization of the gravity of what he had done. Would he ever find peace and Enlightenment? Fast-paced and tumultuous, the last two movements brought him the ritual answer: since the Fellow Craft had killed a man, he would receive death himself. He was therefore borne away to a hereafter and endured the flames of hell without knowing if he would ever get out.

The symphony ended with a question already expressed in *Don Giovanni*: would the Fellow Craft find the Master Mason's secrets, would the Fire destroy him or would he be reborn in its flames?

*Vienna, 21 July 1788*

On this fine summer's day, Josepha Weber, Constanze's older sister, who, as Stadler delicately put it, had at last

---

* Symphony No. 40 in G minor, K550.

found a shoe for her foot, was married to the court musician, Franz de Paula Hofer in St Stephen's Cathedral in Vienna.

'Tonight,' he reminded his Brother, 'your *Don Giovanni* is playing. Hofer should rise to the occasion and go and listen. His own list of conquests is not very long, they say. Marriage: what an ordeal! To talk of more interesting things, I need a little money to finance our research into that wonderful bass clarinet our Brother Lotz is working on. He is the best instrument-maker in the world and I'm sure he'll come up with one some time soon.'

Wolfgang was eager to further the project, and he produced the necessary florins.

# 74

*Vienna, 2 August 1788*

According to relatives in Salzburg, Nannerl used a short stay in Vienna to distil a new poison and put about the story that her brother, Wolfgang, had given up his official job, stopped writing to her since their father's death and was frittering his money away, shirking his parental duties and lolling in idleness encouraged by his wife, herself the subject of considerable speculation.

Keen to avoid a definitive split, Wolfgang wrote a letter to try to re-establish the truth:

*Dearest sister! You are right to be cross with me! And will you be even crosser when the coach brings my last piano compositions? Oh, no! That, I hope will put things back in place.*

*I am sure you know in your heart that, every day,*

412

*I wish all sorts of pleasant things for you, so you will forgive me being a bit late sending my greetings for your name day. My dearest sister, I ardently wish you, with all my heart, everything you think would be best for you, period.*

*My dear sister! You cannot doubt that I have a lot to do and you know very well that I am a bit of a dilatory letter-writer.*

*As for my position, the emperor has officially engaged my services in the imperial chamber but for the time being for only 800 florins. But no one else in the chamber receives that much.*

Wolfgang also told Nannerl about the revival of *Don Giovanni* and begged her to send him the scores of several religious works by Michael Haydn, which he wanted to study. At Constanze's request, however, he said nothing about the harsh blow fate had just dealt them.

*Vienna, 10 August 1788*

The assembly of Master Masons in the Middle Chamber judged the Fellow Craft by separating the pure from the impure, and the mind, which could be initiated, from the mortal individual. The survivor of the Fire lived a new life: he was no longer Don Giovanni but a new Master Mason reborn out of fearful combat.

So began the last symphony* in Mozart's trilogy about initiation. The slow movement described the construction, radiant and serene, of the new Master Mason. He had risen from death and was welcomed into the Middle Chamber where he could contemplate the Great Mysteries.

From the Orient, he received the strength of the Wise, expressed in the third movement. The final Allegro conveyed the almost supernatural joy that accompanied this extraordinary event.

It is doubtful whether the Viennese ever heard these three symphonies written with such creative vigour in response to an inner drive.

When he read through the scores, Thamos could hear the music echoing well beyond the Austrian borders, which at that time were so under threat that Mozart hastened to re-emphasise his support by writing a patriotic song for children, 'Going Off to War, Faithful to the Emperor's Call!'†

*Vienna, 24 August 1788*

At four o'clock, three young Danish actors, drawn by Mozart's reputation, knocked at his door. Constanze was sharpening quills for the copyist responsible for

---

* Symphony No. 41 in C major, called the 'Jupiter', K551. There are only two crossings-out on the manuscript of this masterpiece!
† K552, song for voices with piano accompaniment.

disseminating the sheet music, and a pupil was toiling over a composition. To the great delight of his visitors, Wolfgang sat down at the piano and improvised at length.

When the recital was over, they turned to the garden where they heard a boy's voice singing recitatives.

'That's my son, Karl Thomas,' Wolfgang told them, proudly.

'Aren't those passages from your splendid *Abduction from the Seraglio*?' asked one of the Danes.

'*The Abduction*? That was just tinkering!'

The copyist came for the quill pens, Wolfgang corrected the first bars of his pupil's clumsy attempt at a sonata, Gaukerl hopefully wagged his tail for biscuits, Karl Thomas came in to ask for his tea, and the visitors, marvelling at what they had heard, went back to Denmark.

*Vienna, 27 September 1788*

Worn out by the creative fever that had gripped him as he worked on his three symphonies, Wolfgang devoted the rest of the summer to his family and lodge works. Since the emperor had left to go and fight the Turks, the lodge was enjoying a period of calm. The Brothers studied the basic symbols, such as the rule, the set square and the compass: the Three Great Lights of Freemasonry.

Wolfgang paid frequent visits to Venerable Ignaz von Born, whose sciatica had made him something of an invalid. He still kept up his research into alchemy and Egyptology, using documents brought to him by Thamos, and he continued to work on improving the rituals. Since Viennese Freemasons had not become mired in systems of higher degrees, the current Brothers studied those of Entered Apprentice, Fellow Craft and Master Mason.

On 2 September, Wolfgang wrote nine canons for voice* in his album, two on religious themes, two about love and five of a bawdy nature sung by Stadler and other Brothers who liked their drink and a saucy joke.

Meanwhile, his money troubles had abated and the publisher Artaria was selling his Trio for clarinet, viola and piano,† while Wolfgang wrote another,‡ which he gave to his Brother Puchberg. As he composed, he took stock of how he envisaged his art: it had solemnity and tension but also joy and boundless energy, after so many ordeals that might have destroyed him. And what pleasure it gave him to refer to Johann Sebastian Bach as he created his own music!

In the battle between light and dark, it was the light that won; song united with the rigour of counterpoint, and peace triumphed over anguish. Puchberg would be charmed by the joyous final Rondo with its popular theme.

---

* K553 to 562.
† K498.
‡ K563, for violin, viola and cello.

# The Brother of Fire

*Lyons, 10 October 1788*

The scandal was enormous, but the Knights Beneficient of the Holy City, under orders from their Grand Profess, Jean-Baptiste Willermoz, agreed that it should be kept secret within their little circle, which many Freemasons regarded with hope.

Many acknowledged that they should have listened to the warnings of Thamos, the Egyptian, who advised them not to stray into the mystical systems of higher degrees dreamed up by Willermoz.

Contrary to the predictions of the Unknown Agent, with whom only Willermoz had the privilege of intimate contact, the Prophet had still not appeared to his disciples.

And the Agent was no longer unknown.

He was, in fact, a flesh-and-blood female, Madame de La Vallière, Abbess of the Convent of Remiremont. A highly accomplished noblewoman and numerology enthusiast, she had been initiated by her Brother Willermoz into the benefits of magnetism and went into trances at which he was present and took notes.

If his prophecies had come to pass, the Knights Beneficient of the Holy City would have helped build New Jerusalem. But Lyons was still Lyons, France was rocked by violence, and the Church was becoming the target of fanatical ideologies that suggested the worst.

The dreams of the Profess were shattered and the sorry truth remained. Perhaps it would have been better to join Strict Templar Observance for real,

417

rather than duping its credulous leaders. Did French Freemasonry, torn between defending the Old Regime and supporting the new intellectual movements, really have a future?

# 75

*Vienna, 30 October 1788*

On the 24th, a repeat performance of *Don Giovanni* met with indifference. Having given his Brother Puchberg a piano trio,\* a delicate, tranquil piece that delighted the merchant, Wolfgang turned to his official duties and composed two contredanses† for the society balls in a city eager to block out its anxieties. No one was sure of a happy outcome to the war and there were rumours that the emperor's health was deteriorating. For how long would Vienna dance in the ballrooms of La Redoute? If Islam triumphed, singing, dancing and laughter would be forbidden.

'Mozart!' exclaimed Emmanuel Schikaneder, whom the composer, lost in thought, was about to pass without

\* K564, Mozart's last trio.
† K565.

noticing. 'Come and have a beer. My shout.' With his twinkling eyes and cleft chin framed by thick, curly dark hair, the corpulent Freemason and impresario exuded good humour.

'Not bad, your *Don Giovanni*, but not entertaining enough. The good people of Vienna don't want to think, just have fun. My wife, Eleonore, has her own travelling company and in a month's time they'll be at the theatre Auf der Wieden. With a bit of advice from myself, I think she'll make a go of it. Not easy, at the moment, with this wretched war. So many wealthy noblemen have been killed in battle and there's no money for the theatre and music. But we'll find a way, believe me! Our emperor won't be floored by those barbarians. We must get together and set something up. I have projects coming out of my ears! As soon as the situation improves, we'll step up the pace.'

*Vienna, 3 November 1788*

In spite of further performances of *Don Giovanni*, Mozart had to put up with being slated by the critics. 'A marked taste for the supernatural and for complexity,' considered Cramer's *Magazin der Muzik*. And the great specialist, Alois Schreiber, took a swipe in Frankfurt's *Dramaturgische Blätter*, an intellectual paper that saw its opinions as indisputable: 'Yet another opera that bludgeons our audiences! A lot of noise and pomp, all to impress the crowds. Cultivated persons will find it bland and insipid.'

'Impress the crowds . . .' The idea could not have been further from the musician's mind! Wounded by such sniping and stupidity, he nevertheless continued to believe in his opera about initiation. Having had both success and failure, he knew not to be beguiled by one or the other. The main thing was to follow the path he was treading, day after day, towards the temple, towards Enlightenment. Like the old Masters of Work, he was not content to dream but built with the material he had mastered: music.

*Vienna, 5 November 1788*

'The emperor is back!' Anton Stadler announced to Mozart, who was composing six German dances.[*]

'Is there talk of victory?'

'Unfortunately not . . . But not defeat, either. Our troops are holding out and are still in good spirits. They know they are the last bastion between us and barbarism. At least we know one thing, now: we will not recoil before fanaticism. Isn't that one of our duties as Freemasons?'

'Why has Josef II left the front?'

'He contracted a serious illness.'

[*]K567.

'You mean, the predators are approaching his throne.'

'A favourite, his brother Leopold II, Archduke of Tuscany, where he ended the Inquisition. Quite a good sign, don't you think?'

'Josef II is a strange and tormented man,' said Wolfgang, thoughtfully. 'Without banning Freemasonry, he has shackled it considerably. He preaches liberal policies but criticizes himself. Although he declares himself an enemy of the Pope and Catholic intransigency, he lets the Archbishop of Vienna contest his reforms. From our point of view, the picture doesn't look good.'

'We are still alive and we still celebrate our rites! What more can we ask?'

'True liberty.'

'You are always so excessive!'

*Vienna, 12 November 1788*

Although Mozart still did not know who the obdurate enemy was that was bringing a case against him, his financial situation had improved. With the money his Brother Puchberg lent him, he had managed to stall proceedings. Sooner or later, he would prove his innocence and escape from this hornet's nest.

The publication of three piano trios by his Brother Artaria brought him some money and, above all, Baron Gottfried Van Swieten had not deserted him. As a great admirer himself of Johann Sebastian Bach, he deplored the neglect such a genius suffered and was consequently sensitive to Mozart's distress, now that he had fallen out of favour in Vienna.

So Van Swieten suggested he write a modern arrangement of *Acis and Galathea*, a 'pastoral entertainment' by Handel, another composer he admired, and conduct it for his own benefit in the Jahn Hall. The income was modest and the work humble, but Wolfgang welcomed the opportunity.

*Vienna, 15 November 1788*

At the performance of *Don Giovanni*, Josef II's seat remained empty.

The audience was thin on the ground and its reception frosty.

Lorenzo Da Ponte came up to Mozart.

'The emperor is ill but still reigning. He, and he alone, takes the major decisions. I had the privilege of talking to him and I begged him to support the cultural life that is so important to the Viennese.'

'What does he think of *Don Giovanni*?'

'He thinks the opera is divine, but it is not to the taste of his Viennese audience.'

'Give them time to chew on it!'

'Time, dear Mozart, is what we do not have.'

'What do you mean?'

'Given the opera's reception, tonight will be the last performance. *Don Giovanni* has been removed from the repertory for good,' Da Ponte said, with regret. Then he walked away.

There was nothing Mozart could do but write a dozen minuets* for dances at La Redoute and confine himself to his obscure role as court musician.

'You've not given up, I hope?' Thamos the Egyptian, asked, laying a hand on his shoulder.

'Adversity seems too powerful.'

'Whatever the hardships, you should accomplish your number, the number of the man who will enlighten the priests and priestesses of the sun.'

Wolfgang would live off that aspiration and try to make it real.

'I shall not give up,' he promised.

*K568.